ACCLAIM FOR KATHLEEN FULLER

"Fuller's inspirational tale portrays complex characters facing real-world problems and finding love where they least expected or wanted it to be."

—BOOKLIST, STARRED REVIEW, ON *A RELUCTANT BRIDE*

"Fuller has an amazing capacity for creating damaged characters and giving insights into their brokenness. One of the better voices in the Amish fiction genre."

—CBA RETAILERS + RESOURCES ON *A RELUCTANT BRIDE*

"This promising series debut from Fuller is edgier than most Amish novels, dealing with difficult and dark issues and featuring well-drawn characters who are tougher than the usual gentle souls found in this genre. Recommended for Amish fiction fans who might like a different flavor."

—LIBRARY JOURNAL ON *A RELUCTANT BRIDE*

"Sadie and Aden's love is both sweet and hard-won, and Aden's patience is touching as he wrestles not only with Sadie's dilemma, but his own abusive past. Birch Creek is weighed down by the Troyer family's dark secrets, and readers will be interested to see how secondary characters' lives unfold as the series continues."

—RT BOOK REVIEWS, 4 STARS, ON *A RELUCTANT BRIDE*

"Kathleen Fuller's *A Reluctant Bride* tells the story of two Amish families whose lives have collided through tragedy. Sadie Schrock's stoic resolve will touch and inspire Fuller's fans, as will the story's concluding triumph of redemption."

—SUZANNE WOODS FISHER, BESTSELLING
AUTHOR OF *ANNA'S CROSSING*

"Kathleen Fuller's *A Reluctant Bride* is a beautiful story of faith, hope, and second chances. Her characters and descriptions are captivating, bringing the story to life with the turn of every page."

—AMY CLIPSTON, BESTSELLING AUTHOR OF *A SIMPLE
PRAYER* AND THE KAUFFMAN AMISH BAKERY SERIES

FAITHFUL TO
Laura

ALSO BY KATHLEEN FULLER

THE AMISH OF BIRCH CREEK

A Reluctant Bride
An Unbroken Heart
A Love Made New (available September 2016)

THE MIDDLEFIELD AMISH NOVELS

A Faith of Her Own

THE MIDDLEFIELD FAMILY NOVELS

Treasuring Emma
Faithful to Laura
Letters to Katie

THE HEARTS OF MIDDLEFIELD NOVELS

A Man of His Word
An Honest Love
A Hand to Hold

NOVELLAS INCLUDED IN

An Amish Christmas—A Miracle for Miriam
An Amish Gathering—A Place of His Own
An Amish Love—What the Heart Sees
An Amish Wedding—A Perfect Match
An Amish Garden—Flowers for Rachael
An Amish Second Christmas—A Gift for Anne Marie
An Amish Cradle—A Heart Full of Love
An Amish Market—A Bid for Love
An Amish Harvest—A Quiet Love (available August 2016)

THE MYSTERIES OF MIDDLEFIELD SERIES FOR YOUNG READERS

A Summer Secret
The Secrets Beneath
Hide and Secret

FAITHFUL TO
Laura

A
MIDDLEFIELD
FAMILY
NOVEL

KATHLEEN FULLER

THOMAS NELSON
Since 1798

Published in Nashville, Tennessee, by Thomas Nelson. Thomas Nelson is a registered trademark of HarperCollins Christian Publishing, Inc.

Thomas Nelson titles may be purchased in bulk for educational, business, fund-raising, or sales promotional use. For information, please e-mail SpecialMarkets@ThomasNelson.com.

Scripture quotations taken from the King James Version of the Bible. All rights reserved.

Publisher's Note: This novel is a work of fiction. Names, characters, places, and incidents are either products of the author's imagination or used fictitiously. All characters are fictional, and any similarity to people living or dead is purely coincidental.

ISBN: 978-0-7180-8277-2 (RPK)

Library of Congress Cataloging-in-Publication Data

Fuller, Kathleen.
  Faithful to Laura / Kathleen Fuller.
    p. cm. -- (A Middlefield family novel)
  ISBN 978-1-59554-776-7 (pbk.)
  1. Amish--Fiction. 2. Middlefield (Ohio)--Fiction. I. Title.
  PS3606.U553F35 2012
  813'.6--dc23

                          2012014077
              Printed in the United States of America

            16 17 18 19 20 21 RRD 6 5 4 3 2 1

GLOSSARY

appeditlich: delicious

bann: shunned, excommunicated from the church

bu: boy

buwe: boys

daed: dad, father

danki: thank you

Dietsch: Pennsylvania Dutch, the language spoken by the Amish

dumm: dumb

Englisch: non-Amish

familye: family

fraa: wife, woman

geh: go

grossdochter: granddaughter

grosskinn: grandchild

grossmammi, grossmudder: grandmother

grosssohn: grandson

grossvadder: grandfather

gut mariye: good morning

guten nacht: good night

haus: house

kaffee: coffee

kapp: prayer cap

kinn: child

kinner: children

lieb: love, sweetheart

maedel: girl

mammi, mamm: mom, mother

mann: man

mei: my

mudder: mother

nix: nothing

onkel: uncle

Ordnung: the unwritten Amish rule of life

perfekt: perfect

rumspringa: the period between ages sixteen and twenty-four, loosely translated as "running around time." For Amish young adults, *rumspringa* ends when they join the church.

schwester: sister

sohn: son

schee: pretty, beautiful

schwoger: brother-in-law

vadder: father

wie gehts: how are you?

ya: yes

yung: young

CHAPTER 1

"Laura . . . you're so beautiful."

Laura Stutzman held her breath, her skin tingling as Mark King touched her smooth cheek. She'd known him for such a short time; less than three months ago he had arrived in Tennessee and found his way to Etheridge, to their little community . . . and to her.

He wasn't like the other Amish men she had known all her life. His handsome smile, the all-consuming way he looked at her, as if she were his treasure. He always seemed to know what to do to make her happy. What to say to make her feel cherished.

"I love you, Laura."

Then he began to laugh. His voice seemed to come from above her, and she looked up. High in the dim recesses of the barn, he braced himself against the rafters, clutching a small steel box to his chest. A box she recognized immediately—the one that held her parents' life savings.

"Mark?"

The image of his face blurred as a haze of smoke drifted between them. Her breath came in gasps, and the smoke stung her eyes. She turned, panicked, trying to find a way out.

But out of where? The barn was shrinking to a fraction of its size, smaller and smaller. The rafters vanished, and Mark with them.

She started to run, stumbled, and tripped. A body lay unconscious at her feet.

Adam Otto.

How did Adam get here? Where was she? She caught a glimpse of a door, ran to it, and yanked on the doorknob. Locked.

The scent of gasoline made her stomach lurch. She rushed to the window and put her hand on the latch. But before she could open it and call out for help, Mark's face appeared at the windowpane. His lips twisted in a sneer that chilled her heart.

"You're a fool, Laura. A stupid, gullible fool."

He held something in his hand. Flames shot from the top of it. He took a step back, raised his arm, and threw.

"Mark!" she cried out. "Nee!"

Laura tried to shield her face, but it was too late. Shards of glass tore into her skin. Cutting. Burning. Smoke choked her throat.

When she pulled her hands away from her face, her fingers were covered with blood.

"Laura!"

Hands gripped her shoulders. The smoke cleared; the searing pain in her face subsided.

"Mark?"

"Laura, it's Adam."

She blinked and came to with a sharp October breeze slicing through her thin nightgown. It was nearly dawn. The pale gray light revealed a pile of ashes where Emma's grandfather's workshop used to be.

"Are you okay? I was in Emma's barn feeding the horses, and I heard you scream—"

Exposed and vulnerable in her nightdress, Laura pulled away and crossed her arms over her chest. "I'm fine."

"You're shivering." Adam took off his coat and put it around her shoulders.

Embarrassment heated her face. Being caught outside in her nightgown was bad enough. Even worse was the lingering fear the nightmare left behind. The terrifying dreams were coming every night, and now she had sleepwalked to the place where the attack had happened. Memories slammed into her, taking her back to that horrible day, making it seem as if it were happening all over again.

She touched her hand to her cheek, felt the fine ridges of the now-healing scars. It was *real*.

"It's not a *gut* idea for you to be out here."

Laura looked at Adam Otto, the Shetlers' next-door neighbor. Saw the understanding in his eyes. Mark had attacked him too. But he was healing. His hair was growing out, and he could hide his scar with his hat. He had the ability to move past the damage Mark King had caused him and the Shetler family.

She looked at the ash heap again.

Mark was gone, but his lies and sneers and jeering laughter

remained, burrowing deep into her subconscious, coming to the surface in her dreams.

What a fool she had been!

Shame wrapped around her heart, a razor-sharp strand of barbed wire, and despite the fact that the scars were healing and the ashes had grown cold, she doubted that she'd ever be free or whole again.

"Are you sure you don't want to come?"

Laura fought the urge to cringe as Leona Shetler's clear, pale eyes questioned her. Leona was a kind soul who had welcomed Laura into the home she shared with her granddaughter Emma.

The old woman was wearing her Sunday clothes, complete with black bonnet, leaning on her ever-present cane. Emma was downstairs, also dressed in her best, and ready to go. But they weren't going to church today. Instead, they were attending a wedding.

Laura's hand went to her face. A wedding was the last place she wanted to be.

"If you're fretting about an official invite, don't give it a second thought. The Mullets will be happy to have you."

Leona smiled, and the lines deepened at the corners of her eyes. Lines earned through seventy-five years of living.

The scarred lines on Laura's face were Mark King's parting gift.

"Maybe next time."

Laura faced the bedroom window and looked outside. Adam was hitching his horse to a fine-looking buggy. Like Emma and Leona, he was also well dressed, with a black felt hat, slim black pants, black vest, and a crisp, white long-sleeved shirt.

Leona put her hand on Laura's shoulder. "You can join us for this Sunday's service, then."

Her encouraging smile didn't alter Laura's mood. She wouldn't be any more willing to attend church on Sunday than the wedding today. "*Ya,*" she replied, "Sunday service."

"Ready to *geh?*" Emma called from downstairs.

"*Ya.*" Despite her years, Leona's voice rang strong. She peered over Laura's shoulder and looked out the window as Adam climbed into the buggy. "I see Emma's *yung mann* is ready too."

Laura tried to summon a smile at Leona's pleased tone. Although she hadn't known the Shetlers long, they had instantly treated her like family. Emma and Adam were in love. Anyone could tell.

At least they're happy.

"I'd better hurry. Don't want to keep them waiting." Leona's version of hurrying amounted to shuffling her feet across the wide plank floor while she balanced with her cane. Laura started to ask if she needed help, but she knew Leona would refuse. Laura understood about the need for independence.

She remained at the window after Leona left, watching as the two women walked to Adam's buggy. He helped Leona into the backseat. Once they were all settled inside, they drove off, leaving Laura to wrestle with her thoughts.

She sat on the bed and looked around the room. It was a little larger, but quite similar to her simple, sparse bedroom at home in Tennessee.

Home, she thought. Family. A job. A life. All she'd left behind. But she couldn't go back to any of that. Not when she'd failed those who trusted her most.

Her nerves were taut as a bowstring. She got up and paced across the room, then back again.

Maybe a bath would help settle her down. In the bathroom she leaned over and drew the water, watching it fill the tub as she tried to push ugly thoughts away. She undressed, turned off the tap, then halted when she caught a glimpse of her face in the mirror over the sink.

Spidery red scars crisscrossed her cheeks and forehead. A thicker one slashed across her chin. Her eyes weren't damaged. The doctors called that lucky.

But she wasn't lucky. Or blessed, as Leona and Emma would say. They insisted that the daily applications of vitamin E oil were helping the scars fade. But there were deeper scars, invisible ones.

No cosmetic treatments could heal a soul.

Laura slid into the warm water, letting it rise up to her chin, then pulled her head underneath. She could stay under. Breathe in the water, let it fill her lungs and drain her life. Then there would be no more scars. No more pain. No more hate growing like a thorny vine around her heart.

Her head pounded as she held her breath. Her lungs felt on fire. The instinct for survival thrummed its message in her pulse. *Breathe in! Breathe in!*

Close to bursting, she sprang from the water, gasping for air. She put her hand on her chest and felt her heart racing beneath the wet skin. Salty tears mingled with the tepid bathwater.

She couldn't do it. Couldn't take her own life.

There would be no escape for her. No freedom, no sweet oblivion. The past would hold her in its clutches—and never let her go.

CHAPTER 2

"I'll admit I thought you and Mary Beth might end up together."

Sawyer Thompson looked at Johnny Mullet in surprise. The wedding had ended a couple hours ago, and after helping with the outside cleanup, the two friends had remained in the backyard. "Why would you think that?"

Johnny shrugged and looked out onto the pasture in front of them. The Mullets' three cows munched on the last remnants of fall grass. Soon it would all be brown stubble. "Just thought it would be nice to have you as a brother-in-law."

Sawyer clapped Johnny on the shoulder. "In my mind, we're already brothers." He nodded toward the house, where Mary Beth and Christopher Shetler were still inside, along with other family members and friends from the community. "Besides, even if I thought of Mary Beth as more than a sister, I don't think I would be much competition."

"*Ya*. She's been writing about Christopher in her diary for years."

Sawyer's brow lifted. "You knew that?"

Johnny faced him, grinning. "You didn't think you were the only one who read her diary?" He laughed and faced the field again. "Although I just did it to get under her skin. Worked too. She didn't talk to me for days. It was great. Finally, a break from all that chattering."

Sawyer chuckled. For all his teasing, Johnny couldn't fool him. He knew that Johnny loved his twin sister; the three of them had been inseparable since the first day they met five years ago.

At fourteen, Sawyer had run away from foster care and hidden out in an old run-down barn near the Mullets' property. A lifetime ago, it seemed. He had found Mary Beth's diary, and ultimately the friendship of the Mullet family.

"Don't get me wrong," Johnny said. "I like Christopher. He's a *gut mann*." He tilted his black hat a few inches off his forehead, revealing a shock of dark brown hair. "But it would have been great to have you as an official part of the *familye*."

Sawyer gripped the fence and leaned back, smiling. It was nice to be wanted. To be a part of something. After his parents had died, he hadn't thought that would ever happen again.

"Me and Mary Beth?" Sawyer said. "Nah. I always thought of her as a sister. And she's had her sights set on Shetler for a long time."

"True."

"Speaking of someone who has her sights set . . ." Sawyer grinned and tilted his head toward Katherine Yoder as she approached. "Your girl is coming."

Johnny stepped away from the fence. "She's not my *maedel*."

"She'd sure like to be."

Practically all of Middlefield knew that Katherine Yoder had a crush on Johnny Mullet. Sawyer teased Johnny about it mercilessly.

"*Nee*. I'll see you later." Johnny poised to make a break for it. Sawyer grabbed his arm. "Chicken."

"Yep, that's me." His panicked eyes flitted in Katherine's direction. He pulled away from Sawyer, made a clucking sound, and scurried away.

Sawyer started to follow him, but Katherine had arrived.

"Where did Johnny go?"

He shrugged. It would be a lot easier if Johnny would just take care of Katherine himself. Why did he keep avoiding her? Whenever Katherine came around, Johnny bolted like a goat on a barbed wire fence. "You know how he is. Here one minute, gone the next. Guess he went inside."

"I'm sure it's because he saw me coming."

Sawyer didn't respond. They both knew the truth. If Mary Beth had been foolish for Christopher for the past five years, Katherine had loved Johnny twice as long.

"Oh well." Her tone was light, but her blue eyes reflected disappointment. "I guess I'll talk to him later." She walked away, the white ribbons of her *kapp* fluttering against her navy jacket.

Sawyer shook his head and stuck his hands in the pockets of the black Sunday pants his adopted mother, Anna Byler, had made for him. What was wrong with Johnny? The guy had everything—a great family, a steady job working at a machine repair shop, and a pretty girl who thought the sun rose and set with him. Most of all, his friend had a secure sense of himself. He'd joined the church at seventeen without hesitation. So had Mary Beth, Christopher, and Katherine. None of them had a second thought about making a lifetime commitment to the Amish faith.

Sawyer, on the other hand, was filled with second thoughts. And thirds. And fourths.

He couldn't seem to make up his mind. He enjoyed working with his adopted father, Lukas, in the family carpentry business, yet wondered if he shouldn't go on to college. He'd had the chance to date Yankee girls in high school, but he never did. He ignored any attention from the Amish girls too. They were all nice. Friendly. Available. But he wouldn't string them along. Not when he didn't know what the future held.

"She's gone?"

Sawyer turned to see Johnny behind him. "Yeah, she's gone. Where did you disappear to?"

"Other side of the barn."

"Look, man," Sawyer said, "you need to do something about Katherine. You're nineteen years old, not twelve. If you don't like her, tell her so she can move on."

"It's not that simple."

"Sure it is."

"*Nee*. It's not." Johnny's brown eyes grew solemn. "Maybe you should consider taking your own advice."

"What?"

"I'm not the only one who needs to deal with something. Unless you're planning to spend the rest of your life seesawing between the Amish and Yankee worlds."

Sawyer grimaced. "It's not that—"

"Simple?" Suddenly Johnny grinned, as if the quick moment of seriousness never happened. "It's *mei schwester's* wedding. We should be inside celebrating. Or commiserating with the groom."

"They make such a nice couple," Emma said.

Adam moved closer and touched Emma's back, letting his palm linger against her waist. "I know who else makes a *gut* couple."

His touch sent her nerves spiking. But she stepped away from him.

His grin faded. "What's wrong?"

Emma glanced around the room, filled with people from their district, celebrating Mary Beth Mullet and Emma's cousin Christopher's wedding. She couldn't talk about anything personal, not when anyone might overhear the conversation. Adam should know that. Just as he should have known not to touch her in such an intimate way in public. But Adam wasn't a typical Amishman.

As if he had read her thoughts, Adam jerked his head toward the door. "I'll get your coat."

"I'm not ready to leave."

"Don't worry. We'll come back."

She followed. What was he thinking? He'd given her the space and time she'd asked for. Yet now he seemed different.

He handed over her black coat and she slipped it on. They left the house, Adam striding to the row of buggies parked on the side of the Mullets' yard. He stopped in front of one of them. Then he suddenly took her hand and pulled her behind it. "Don't you want to get married?"

His blunt question threw her off. She cast her gaze to the ground. "Adam, you promised we would take this slow."

He sighed and stepped away. "I know. It's just that seeing Christopher and Mary Beth . . . Emma, you know how I feel about you."

Heat suffused her cheeks, ran through her body until she didn't feel the nip of the winter air. The pain of the past still gnawed at her. She had trusted him once, and he had betrayed her.

"You're afraid," he said.

"And you're a mind reader."

"I don't have to read your mind. Your feelings are written all over your face." He lowered his voice. "Your beautiful face."

When he looked at her like that, his hazel eyes filled with such love and promise, Emma couldn't think. And in the past, not thinking had torn her heart in two.

"I'm sorry. I'm pushing you and I said I wouldn't."

She nodded. "I can't give you what you want, Adam. At least not now."

"I know." He stepped away. A cool breeze kicked up,

rocking the bare branches on the trees surrounding the Mullets' property. "It's just that I'm ready to begin my life again."

"But you have. You've joined the church. You've reconciled with your family . . . and with God."

"I have," he said. A ghost of a smile flitted across his face. "And I've decided that I want to join my *daed* and help him run the farm."

"But I thought you didn't like farming."

"Things change. I've changed. Coming back home, surviving the accident, knowing that I belong here." He lifted his hand toward her face, then pulled it back without touching her. "It's hard for me to wait."

Emma finally smiled. He'd never been a patient man. "I need more time, Adam. I need to be sure about us, about—"

"Me." He nodded. "We better get back before we're missed."

"*Ya.* I don't want *Grossmammi* to be upset that we're alone together."

Adam grinned. "I have a feeling she won't be."

After the wedding, Adam took Emma and Leona home. Once they were inside, he went next door, put his horse up in the barn and his buggy underneath the covered shelter, and headed for the house. His parents had left the wedding early, right after the ceremony. It was unlike them to pass up an opportunity for fellowship with the community.

But then, things hadn't been the same with his parents since he'd returned to Middlefield two months ago.

He'd tried to puzzle out what was wrong, especially with his mother. Was she sick? Still mired in grief over Mary Shetler's death? They had been best friends, so that made sense. But even Emma and Leona had started to move past the pain of their mother and daughter-in-law's passing. Why couldn't his *mamm* do the same?

He trudged to the pasture, certain to find his father there. It was past time he and his *daed* had a talk.

His father was in his favorite spot, leaning against the split rail fence, staring out at the acres of pasture in front of him. For a moment Adam had the chance to study his *daed* objectively. Norman Otto, the consummate Amishman. Deacon of the church. Helper of those in need. Strong. Stubborn. Unyielding.

His father turned and saw him. "Need something?"

"Just thought I'd join you." During the spring and summer months, their herd of cows had eaten down the grass until there was little left but stubble. "They'll be needing hay soon, *ya?*"

His father nodded. "And feed. I've been buying it from the store, keeping it in the silo. Had to stop growing *mei* own feed corn when—"

Adam's mind finished the sentence: *When you left.*

He swallowed down a lump of guilt. It was cheaper to grow feed than to purchase it. But he hadn't been here to help.

He tilted back his black hat, the felt fabric rubbing against his short, rough hair. The doctors had shaved his head in order to stitch the long gash in his scalp. He could have died in that fire. No thanks to Mark King, he had survived, gotten off easy. Easier, at least, than poor Laura Stutzman.

"Why are you really here?" his father asked.

"Just wondering why you and *Mamm* left so early."

"Maybe I should be asking you why you stayed so late."

Adam frowned at the subtle accusation. He was tired of fighting his father, and yet he steeled himself for another argument. *Old habits die hard.*

"I'm twenty-two. And it was a wedding. Everyone's expected to stay afterward. How much trouble can someone get into at an Amish wedding, anyway?"

"When it comes to you, plenty."

Adam bristled. Had their relationship come down to this? He thought once he rejoined the church and was accepted back into the community, his father would give him a break.

Norman sighed and stared down at the fence rail. "Sorry. Didn't mean that."

Adam shoved his hands into the pockets of his dress pants. "Is *Mamm* all right?"

Daed straightened. He put both palms on the fence rail and curled his fingers around it. "She seems normal to me. If you'd been here these past two years, you would know your mother better."

"You've said that before."

"Maybe you need to hear it again."

Adam forced himself not to shake his head. Time to change the subject. "So I was thinking about helping you plant feed corn next year. It would save on buying the winter grain."

"I thought farming wasn't *gut* enough for you."

He gripped the top rail of the fence. The hard wood bit into the skin of his palm. "I was wrong. I've missed it."

His father scratched his chin through his beard, still looking at the pasture in front of him. "You missed the hard work? The early hours, the sick cows, the unpredictable weather?"

"*Ya.*" Wasn't it enough to tell him he wanted to work for him again?

"You've been spending a lot of time with Emma." His father didn't look at him. "Does that have something to do with it?"

"This isn't about Emma and me. It's about us. Working together again."

"Because we were so successful at it the first time."

Adam pulled off his hat and gripped the brim tightly. "*Daed*, please. I'm really trying."

There was a long silence, then his father said, "I can't promise anything right now."

Anything involving me. The unspoken words floated between them, souring the conversation. Again. Adam was done. "I'm going inside. To check on *Mamm.*"

"You do that."

Adam left. He had so much to prove to everyone—Emma, his father, his mother. Especially God. He wasn't sure he could do it. But he had made the commitment, and he would see it through.

It would take time for those he loved to trust him again. But he was willing to work at it.

He was willing to wait.

CHAPTER 3

"You've been quiet lately, *sohn*. Something on your mind?"

Sawyer blew the sawdust off the top of the coffee table. Particles danced in the sunlight that beamed through the window of Byler and Sons.

"No," he said. He moved his palm against the wood, feeling the rough texture. He gripped the sanding block and ran it over the surface. The scratching sound filled the silence between him and his father.

"Nothing you want to talk about, I take it."

"There's nothing to talk about." He moved the sanding block faster, waiting for his father to go. It wasn't like him to stop work in the middle of the day to chat. Lukas Byler ran the family business with precision, the same way he made his furniture, and the store had flourished since his father had retired several years ago.

Finally Sawyer stopped sanding and looked at his father. "Is there something *you* want to talk about?"

His dad looked at the ground, crossing his thick arms across his chest. "I've been trying to find the right time to say this. Guess there really isn't a right time."

Sawyer dropped the block on the table. He glanced around the shop. His uncle Tobias, Lukas's older brother and business partner, was in the back office. He steeled himself against a sudden rush of dread flowing over him like an icy waterfall. "What is it?"

"Your mother and I wondered if you've come to any conclusion about the future." He stroked his beard and looked up at Sawyer, who was several inches taller.

He leaned against the work table. "I haven't given it much thought." It wasn't the truth, of course. Lately his future—or lack of it—had been the only thing on his mind.

"We don't want to push you into making a decision. We never wanted you to be someone you're not. If you want to quit the business and *geh* to college, we'll support that."

"I know. And thanks—*danki*." His adopted parents had never required him to live by the strict Amish *Ordnung*, only asked that he be respectful of their faith and, more importantly, respectful of the Lord. "I owe you both so much."

Lukas shook his head, his straw hat slipping a bit. He pressed on the crown, securing it in place. "You don't owe us anything, Sawyer. You're our *sohn*. You were from the day you started living with us, before we adopted you." He smiled, his dark eyes shiny.

Sawyer's eyes burned. It wasn't like his father to show emotion. "I wish I could tell you I want to join the church. Or that

I want to go to college." He sighed. "Some decision, any decision. But I just don't know what I want to do. Isn't that stupid?"

"*Nee*. It's not *dumm*. Not after what you've been through,
losing your parents, living with us as a teenager, away from
your friends. Many young people struggle with this choice even
when they've lived all their lives as Amish. This decision, it's
not to be taken lightly. I'm glad you're giving it a lot of thought
and prayer."

Thought, yes. Prayer, not so much.

A bell rang in the front of the shop, preventing Sawyer
from saying anything else. Lukas nodded at him and headed
to handle the customer. Sawyer turned, facing the rough table.
By the time he finished it, the surface would be smooth as satin,
without a single splinter or notch. But it would take time to get
the wood to that point, where it would be a beautiful piece of
furniture.

Time, and lots of work.

The aroma of roasted coffee beans filled the Shetler kitchen as
Emma sliced the still-warm cherry pie. She handed a piece to
Grossmammi, then one to her sister Clara. She met her sister's
eyes as she handed her the dessert. Clara smiled. She sat close to
her husband, Peter. The tension between them, once so palpable
to everyone, had eased.

Grossmammi straightened her curved back as much as she
could. "Emma, sit down so we can get started." She met each of

FAITHFUL TO LAURA 21

their gazes, resting on Emma's last. "We haven't had a *familye* meeting since the fire."

Peter turned pale. "I'm so sorry for what *mei* cousin did."

"You can't take responsibility for Mark's troubles." *Grossmammi* touched her coffee cup but didn't pick it up. "Or his actions. Mark's decisions are between him and God."

Emma thought about Laura, who had gone upstairs to her room right after supper. She was glad Laura couldn't hear any of this. "Have you heard from him, Peter?"

"*Nee.* I did write his parents and told them what happened." Peter twirled the fork in his hand. "They didn't seem surprised. I don't want to say this, but it appears they've all but turned their backs on him."

"He's in the *bann?*" Emma asked.

"Not officially, since he hasn't been home for months. But when—or if—he returns, he will be disciplined by the church."

"And by the law," Clara added.

"We don't know that yet." Peter laid his hand on her slender arm. "But remember what the police said. He committed arson. And he attempted to kill Adam and Laura. They will press charges if Mark ever comes back to Middlefield."

"And we would condemn him as well?" *Grossmammi* asked.

"For what he did?" Clara gripped the edge of the table. "I think he should get the justice he deserves."

Leona took a sip of her *kaffee*. "God will dispense that justice."

"And until that time, we have to forgive him." Clara's mouth twisted into a frown of disgust.

"*Ya.*" *Grossmammi* peered over the top of her wire-rimmed glasses. "We do."

Emma sighed. "Do we have to talk about Mark anymore?"

Her grandmother shook her head. "*Nee*, he's not our concern, other than praying he finds his way back onto God's path. In the meantime we need to decide what to do about the workshop. Are we going to rebuild the fabric store?"

They all looked at Clara. "We don't have to. Peter has a *gut* job now, and I've started taking in sewing. I already have three orders for winter coats." She looked at Emma. "Do you still want your shelter?"

Emma's mouth dropped open. At one time she'd wanted to convert the workshop and equip it to take in stray animals. But she had given in to Clara's demand for a fabric store. "Are you sure?"

Clara nodded. "I am."

"Then it's settled." *Grossmammi* smiled. "I think your *grossvadder* would be happy with the decision."

"I just wish we hadn't sold all of his tools," Clara said.

"We didn't," Peter said.

"What?"

"I saved a few things." He glanced at Clara. "There were some items I didn't want to part with. I thought we could hand them down to the *buwe*."

"You didn't tell me," Clara murmured.

"I didn't want to upset you. You were so set on raising money to build the fabric store. I didn't want you to think I wasn't helping."

She pressed her lips together before she spoke, her voice soft. "I'm glad Junior and Melvin will have something from him."

A short while later, Clara and Peter prepared to leave. Emma stepped out on the porch with Clara while Peter went to the buggy. "What made you change your mind?" Emma asked her sister.

Clara shivered. Her thin legs were covered with black stockings, but they seemed to offer her little protection from the evening chill. "I realized that I was only thinking about money. Not about what you really wanted."

"But I know you were worried about me and *Grossmammi* surviving after *Mammi's* death. I understood."

Clara snuggled deeper into her jacket. "It wasn't just that. I was mad at Peter for not having a job. I worried too much about paying the bills. But we always had enough. God never let us *geh* without." She swallowed. "Peter didn't deserve the way I treated him."

"He loves you, Clara."

"I am lucky to have him." The horse whinnied. "I don't want to keep him waiting."

"All right. See you at church, then."

"*Ya.* We'll be there."

Emma watched them drive away. She smiled. After years of strife, she and her sister were finally on solid ground.

Reluctantly, Laura put on her Sunday dress and adjusted her prayer *kapp*. She had finally agreed to go to church, not because she longed to worship, but to get the public humiliation out of the way. She couldn't hide forever. Might as well get it over with. Yet how could she face these people with her skin marked by scars?

She rode with Adam, Emma, and Leona. The three of them talked almost continuously. Laura kept her mouth shut. With each roll of the buggy's wheels, the knot in her stomach hardened. Her skin itched. She longed to scratch the scar on her chin. Instead, she pulled the sides of her black bonnet forward, obscuring her face as much as she could.

"Everything all right?"

She turned and looked at Leona. Nodded. *"Ya."*

"Gut." Leona smiled but didn't say anything else. Laura was gaining an appreciation for the old woman, who seemed to know exactly what and how much to say.

They arrived at the home of Aaron and Elisabeth Detweiler. Instead of having church in the barn, the way they usually did at home, Emma led Laura to the Detweilers' spacious basement. She pointed out a few people, explaining who was related to whom.

"I'm sure you won't remember all this," Emma said as they sat down on a wooden bench. "But eventually you'll learn who everyone is."

Laura remained silent. She didn't plan to be here that long.

During the three-hour service, her thoughts ran rampant. She clenched her teeth so hard that pain sliced her jaw, and tension squeezed her shoulders like a vise. The preacher spoke about forgiveness. The word burned her ears.

When the service was over, the entire group of worshippers made their way upstairs for fellowship and the communal meal. Laura stood apart from the rest of the crowd as they milled about in the large living room and spilled over into the kitchen and dining areas. A long table filled with food stood against the wall. Cold cut platters, bowls of potato and macaroni salad, pickles, cookies, and plenty of fresh sliced bread and homemade butter. People were already lining up to eat.

Laura stayed put, her desire for fellowship as nonexistent as her appetite. Several kids walked past her. By the girls' black *kapps* she knew they were under twelve years old. She couldn't blame them for their curiosity, or their revulsion. Still, she squirmed beneath their attempts to get a look at her scars without staring at her.

"I'm glad to see you at church today."

Laura turned to see a red-haired woman close to her own age. "Have we met?"

"*Nee.* Not yet, anyway. But we're meeting now."

Laura frowned. The woman had a sweet voice and lovely blue eyes. But what she said made little sense.

She giggled as if she'd read Laura's uncharitable thoughts but wasn't bothered by them. "I'm Katherine Yoder." She held out her hand. "I was hoping I would see you today."

Laura paused before giving Katherine's hand a quick shake. "Laura Stutzman."

"I know. You have a pretty accent. I've never heard anyone talk so slowly before."

"I didn't realize I was."

"I have something for you," Katherine said, holding up one finger. "Can you wait a minute? It's in *mei* buggy. I'll *geh* get it."

She disappeared.

Confused, Laura remained in the corner of the room and watched as people around her talked, laughed, and ate. Everyone seemed relaxed and friendly.

Middlefield was different from her small district back home. Everything in Etheridge was stricter. Outsiders weren't particularly welcomed, as Mark had discovered when he first arrived. Still, it hadn't taken long for his charm and lies to win everyone over, including her parents. Now the district would be even more closed than before.

She caught a glimpse of Adam and Emma on the opposite side of the room. He stood close to Emma, claiming her as his, deep in conversation. Laura had known that heady feeling of love, even if it was illusory and short-lived. But after her experience with Mark, she doubted she would ever trust any man enough to fall in love again.

Katherine reappeared at her side. "Here it is."

She held out a folded quilt. The colors were stunning: teals, golds, rusty oranges, arranged in long rectangles. It reminded Laura of fall. Of warmth. "Is this for me?"

"*Ya*. It's a prayer quilt. When I heard what happened to you and Adam, I started this quilt. With each stitch, I said a prayer."

Laura ran her hand across the fabric. She swallowed. "But why would you do such a thing? You don't know me."

"You needed prayer, *ya*? That's reason enough. I hope you like it."

"I do. It's beautiful."

"It's only a lap quilt. I wanted to get it to you before you went back to Tennessee."

"I don't plan on leaving y'all just yet."

Katherine let out a little giggle. "*Lea-vin' ya'll just yet.* See? That's so cute." Her smile widened, revealing two dimpled cheeks. "It's *gut* you're not going right away. Then we can get to know each other better."

Laura shrank from the offer. She couldn't afford friendships. Yet she wouldn't be rude either. "*Danki.*"

Katherine nodded. "I hope the prayers are working."

She was saved from answering by Emma's arrival. "Adam has to get back home." Her gaze went to the quilt. "Katherine, did you make this?"

"*Ya.*"

"It's so *schee*. You have such a talent."

Katherine's cheeks turned pink. "It's something I like to do."

Emma smiled, then turned to Laura. "Are you ready to *geh?*"

Laura nodded. She looked at Katherine. "Thank you. This is a wonderful gift."

"Enjoy it."

As she climbed into the back of the buggy with Leona, Laura clung to the quilt. She marveled at Katherine's generosity, to make something so lovely for a person she didn't even know.

So many stitches.

So many prayers . . .

Not that they would make any difference. All the prayers in the world couldn't change what had happened.

She fingered the quilt, and her mind drifted back to the service. All the preacher's fine words about God's plan concerning forgiveness.

Forgiveness was the Amish way, no matter what the offense. She was expected to forgive. Required to forgive.

But how could she ever forgive Mark King? He had taken everything from her—her trust, her heart, her parents' life savings. The life she had known. All gone.

And he got away with it.

"God's justice is not our own," the preacher had said.

That was clear enough. God was nowhere to be found when Mark King robbed her. When he permanently scarred her. Where was the justice in that? God allowed it to happen and let Mark get away unscathed.

And she was supposed to accept and forgive?

When they arrived home, she went upstairs to her bedroom. She laid the quilt on the bed, running her hand over the soft fabric again. But if the prayers Katherine said while she stitched the quilt were supposed to calm her, they didn't. She felt more agitated than ever.

She walked to the window and looked outside. She couldn't spend her life like this, isolating herself from everyone. Yet she couldn't go back to Tennessee. Not yet.

What she needed was money, and God wouldn't drop dollars out of the sky. She had to get a job. Working was the only way she could earn back the money Mark stole.

She ran her hand over her chin and felt the scar. Who would hire her looking like this?

Laura turned and looked at the quilt again. "I have to finish what I came here to do," she whispered. She wouldn't let her scars hinder her. She would find work. And once she had enough to pay back everyone she owed—her parents, Leona, and Emma—then she would search for Mark. And she would have her revenge.

Because revenge was all she had left.

CHAPTER 4

"Did you enjoy your supper, Señora Easely?"

"Yes, Manuela. Thank you." Cora dabbed at the corner of her lips with a fine linen napkin. She had ordered cordon bleu from her favorite restaurant, a five-star establishment with a waiting list months long. Cora had the chef's personal cell number on her speed dial.

But she had little appetite. Manuela cleared Cora's full plate and left the dining room.

Cora took a sip of her wine and looked at the nine empty chairs around the glossy, rectangular dining room table. She'd purchased the antique set years ago, anticipating family dinners and parties and holiday feasts. Little did she know that she would be the only one to use it.

She picked up her glass of white wine and went to the living room. Six months of this new décor, and she was already sick of it. It looked like a cross between *Out of Africa* and a Moroccan market-place. She made a mental note to hire another designer next week.

Her kitten-heeled slippers sank into the rust-colored carpet as she stood at the huge window overlooking New York City. She'd lived her entire life here. From the penthouse view she could see the tops of apartment buildings, the maze of alley-ways and streets that ran vertically and horizontally between the buildings, the masses of people who seemed little bigger than ants scurrying to their destinations. During the day, the noise and activity energized and inspired her.

But at night the loneliness returned.

She perched on the edge of the zebra-striped club chair and clicked on the fireplace remote. Flames appeared behind the clear glass. Her diamond bracelet jiggled on her thin wrist, the stones sparkling in the firelight. Normally she was mesmerized by the refracting colors. Tonight she was too restless to care.

Manuela appeared in the doorway. "Do you need anything else, Señora Easely?"

Cora looked up at her live-in maid. "Would you like to play a game of cards?"

Manuela's eyes widened. Cora had never asked her to play cards or to interact on any personal level. She firmly believed in professional distance between an employer and the help. Yet tonight the lonely ache spurred her to cross that line.

"I—I would like to, señora. But you said I could have tonight off." Manuela folded her hands against the crisp white apron of her uniform. "*Mi nieto*—my grandson. His school play is tonight."

"Oh yes. I remember." Cora waved her hand. "Of course you may go. Have a good evening."

"*Gracias.*" Manuela hurried away.

Cora stared at the fireplace and took another sip of wine. She thought about inviting someone over. But as she mentally went through her contact list, she realized anyone worth spending the evening with already had plans. Some were attending the theater. One had a gala she was sponsoring. Cora had been invited but wasn't interested in going. Maybe she should have. But it would be in poor taste to show up after she'd sent in her RSVP.

"I'm leaving, señora," Manuela called from the foyer. "Do you need anything before I go?"

"I said I didn't." Her tone was sharper than she'd intended. She didn't apologize.

Cora drank the last gulp of wine as the latch on the front door closed. She looked at her empty glass. She hated drinking alone. Tonight, however, she didn't seem to have much of a choice.

Her emerald ring clinked against the crystal glass. On her way to the kitchen, she passed by the maid's room. Manuela had left the door open.

Cora stopped. She rarely gave a second thought to Manuela's living quarters, but tonight curiosity—and boredom—drew her inside.

The room was neat and sparse. Just as Cora expected—and demanded. She couldn't abide untidiness. A crucifix hung on one wall. A colorful wool blanket lay at the end of the bed. But those weren't the two items that captured her attention. Cora stepped toward Manuela's small dresser. The top of it was covered with framed pictures.

Manuela and her late husband, Juan. A cheap studio portrait

of the couple and their four kids, taken more than a decade ago. Photos of young children—Manuela's granddaughters and grandsons. All smiling. All happy.

Next to one of the picture frames lay a crayon drawing, a bright rainbow arched over the childishly lettered words: *Happy Birthday, Abuela.* She opened the crude card.

I love you, Grandma.

Cora closed the card and replaced it on the dresser, careful not to disturb anything.

Maybe she'd have that drink after all.

Cora poured another glass of wine and went back into the living room. Thousands of dollars worth of expensive furniture, knick-knacks, and original paintings filled the vast space. But not a single family photo. No child's artwork to post on her state-of-the-art refrigerator. No handmade cards tucked away in a scrapbook.

She went back to the kitchen and dumped the glass of wine down the sink. The bottle of Valium in her medicine cabinet beckoned. One pill and she wouldn't be lonely. She wouldn't remember the past, what it had felt like years ago, when she had a family of her own.

Two days later, Cora sat in her living room, staring at the news clipping in her hand. She looked up at the private investigator and crossed one slender leg over the other, ignoring the sharp twinge of arthritis in her hip.

"Are you sure this is authentic, and not another ruse?"

Detective Peters nodded. "I'm sorry, Mrs. Easley. The obituary is valid."

Cora's hand shook. She placed it on top of her leg and clutched her kneecap. The expensive linen pants wrinkled beneath her grip. "Thank you for your diligence." She glanced at the antique silver tea service Manuela had brought out. The burly detective had refused his cup. She didn't dare touch hers. "My accountant will send you a check. With a bonus."

He cleared his throat. "That won't be necessary, ma'am. Just doing my job." He paused. "I'm sorry for your loss."

"I expected it, after not hearing from her for all these years." The lie twisted inside her. When the detective arrived a few minutes ago, she'd hoped he'd have some good news. Instead, he brought a new nightmare, one printed on smeared, gray newspaper.

She looked at the obituary again. Her only daughter, and the man Cora had never approved of. Both dead. And she couldn't do anything about it.

Cora Easley, one of the richest women in the country, a woman who held the elite of New York society in the palm of her hand, was at this moment completely powerless. For the first time in over two decades, all her wealth, authority, and influence could do nothing to alter her circumstances.

The pain of loss drove its spike into her. Then she gathered herself and did what she'd always done when emotions threatened to consume her: she ignored them, lifted her chin, and stood. She looked at the detective, and when she spoke, her tone was cool as the autumn wind. "I'll have Manuela show you out."

But the detective made no move to leave. "Ma'am that's not all the news I have for you."

"And what else might there be?"

He fingered his mustache. "There was a child. A son."

Cora held in a gasp. Kerry had a son? She had a *grandson*? "Are you sure?"

"Yes, ma'am. Once I found out where your daughter lived, I did a little more digging."

"Where is he? What's his name?" She turned away. "I have to bring him back home as soon as possible."

"That might be difficult, ma'am. When no relative came forward, he was placed in foster care in Ohio."

She spun around. "How could I come forward when I didn't even know he existed?" Anger rose inside her, but she tamped it down. "I'm coming forward now. I will claim my grandson and bring him back here. Where he should have been all along."

The detective tilted his head. The look of sympathy he gave her felt like a slap in her face. "Like I said, that could be difficult. He's not a child. He's twenty-one years old, and from all accounts well settled in Ohio."

He would be more settled in New York. She would see to it. Cora Easley always got her way. "Where in Ohio?"

He pulled a small notepad from the pocket of his jacket. "Middlefield."

"Never heard of it."

"It's a small town southeast of Cleveland." He flipped his notepad shut. "Amish territory, from all I can tell."

Amish? What did Amish people have to do with her grandson? She waved her hand. "I must go to Middlefield as soon as possible. He has a right to know his family."

And she had the right to know her grandson. He was the only heir to a vast fortune that over the years meant less and less to her. But now that she had someone she could groom to take over the family business and secure his place in New York society, that money suddenly became the upmost of importance. She would use whatever resources necessary to bring this young man back home. "What did you say his name was?"

"Sawyer." The detective put his notebook away. "Sawyer Thompson."

The detective left, and Cora went straight to her bedroom. "Manuela," she called. "Pack my bags. I'm going to Ohio."

Manuela appeared in the doorway. "Should you be traveling, Señora Easely? You have a doctor's appointment tomorrow."

Cora spun around and glared at her. "Why are you questioning me? Besides, that quack doesn't know anything. I'm getting a second opinion." She stared unseeing at the walk-in closet, nearly the size of the bedroom itself. "Pack only the essentials. No more than three bags. I don't plan to be gone long."

"*Sí.*" Manuela went inside the closet and pulled down a large suitcase.

As her maid packed, Cora called her travel agent to book a flight. An hour later she sat on the edge of the bed, her travel arrangements made, her suitcases packed and ready for her driver to load into the car first thing in the morning.

She glanced at her watch. Nine o'clock. She'd just missed the last flight to Cleveland, the closest airport to Middlefield. It figured that some small-town Amish backwater wouldn't have an airport.

She stood and paced the length of her bed, trying not to think about Kerry. About how she died. About all the lost years. Instead, she focused on her grandson. The detective said it might be difficult for her to convince him to come back to New York.

But Cora had no choice.

Sawyer Thompson had to leave Ohio with her. He had to come home. His future—and what was left of hers—depended on it.

CHAPTER 5

"Looks like we're gonna need another office assistant."

Sawyer set the rocking horse Tobias had made on top of the worktable and looked at his father, who was working at the opposite end of the table. "What happened to Hannah?"

"Getting married in a couple of weeks." Lukas adjusted the lathe and began sculpting a spindle for the back of an oak rocking chair. "I'm starting to think I need to hire a Yankee *maedel* if I want to keep help around here. We're so busy right now, with the Christmas season coming up, I can't wait much longer to hire someone." Lukas looked at Sawyer. "Do you know of anyone? Maybe someone you went to school with?"

"Do you definitely want a Yankee?" Sawyer tried to think about some of the girls he knew from high school. But he hadn't kept up with his friends after graduation.

Lukas stroked his beard. "At this point it doesn't matter, Yankee or Amish. I'll put an ad in the paper if I have to."

"I'll try to come up with someone." Sawyer knew his father

liked to hire within the community if possible. He really must be getting desperate if he was thinking about paying for a want ad. The man was pretty tight with a dollar. But that was one reason the family business was so successful.

Sawyer went back to work fine-tuning and smoothing out the head of the rocking horse. Later he would varnish and paint the child's toy. They only sold these around Christmas time, and they were one of the most popular items in the shop. Sawyer did all the detail work, while his father and uncle constructed the basic horse shape and added the rockers at the bottom.

For the next several minutes he focused on his task, but in the back of his mind he was thinking about single women who would be good for the job. "Emma," he said at last. He looked at Lukas. "Emma Shetler."

Lukas tilted back his straw hat. Flecks of sawdust speckled his dark brown beard. "Isn't she the one who had that fire at her *haus*?"

"*Ya*. Her grandfather's workshop burned to the ground."

"And so soon after her *mudder* died." He shook his head. "That *familye* has been through a lot the past few years."

"What *familye*?" Tobias joined them.

"The Shetlers." Sawyer moved toward the brothers.

Tobias's usual jovial expression turned grim. "*Ya*. That they have."

"I think Emma might be interested in the job. As far as I know, she's not working anywhere. I could stop by her house after work and ask."

"It can't hurt."

After work Sawyer got in his pickup and drove to the Shetlers' house. He had bought the truck from Adam Otto before Adam joined the church. It was in good shape and handled well. Best of all, he could get around fast. Ten minutes and he was at the Shetlers' front door. It would have taken him three times as long in a horse and buggy.

He parked the vehicle on the gravel driveway. When he stepped outside, the overpowering smell of cattle reached him. He heard the lowing of a cow coming from the Ottos' pasture, where the herd grazed in the fading sunlight.

The early November air was cool and crisp as a ripe apple. Sawyer knocked, and as he waited for someone to answer, he surveyed the empty space next to the house where the shop used to be, now nothing but ashes and soot.

He remembered the day he heard about the fire. Although he didn't know the Shetlers well, when tragedy affected the community, it affected everyone.

A cat rubbed against his right leg. He gave it a gentle nudge with his foot. "Scat." He didn't care much for cats. Dogs were a different story—one dog in particular, Roscoe. The mutt had kept him company when he was on the run and living in the abandoned barn. Roscoe was getting old, and now lived with Mary Beth and Christopher. Yet the unspoken rule was that he belonged to everyone.

The door opened. "Hello, Sawyer." Emma stepped forward and pulled the door wider. *"Wie gehts?"*

"Doing fine, thanks."

"What brings you by?"

"I wanted to talk to you about a job. If that's okay." He shoved his hand in the pocket of his jeans. "I know it's near suppertime, but I thought I'd see if you had a few minutes."

"You're welcome anytime. Come inside."

As Sawyer crossed the threshold, the yeasty scent of freshly baked bread reached him. Now he wished he'd waited until tomorrow to come. "I didn't mean to interrupt your dinner."

"We're just getting started. Why don't you join us?"

His stomach growled. They both heard it.

Emma chuckled. "You're definitely staying." Sawyer followed her to the kitchen. Emma's grandmother, Leona, sat at the end of the table nearest the door, and at the opposite end, a young woman Sawyer had never met. She held her head down, keeping her face shielded by blond hair parted down the middle and tightly tucked into her *kapp*.

"Hi," he said. He reached out his hand. "Sawyer Thompson."

Finally she lifted her head, and he caught sight of thin red scars across her face like a spiderweb. Instantly he recognized her: the young woman who had been injured in the fire along with Adam.

The old scar on his forearm tingled underneath his long-sleeved shirt, as if in sympathy for the scars she bore. A tough brown circle, courtesy of a cigarette butt smashed into his skin by one of his former foster brother's friends. At least he could hide the scar with long-sleeved shirts, jackets, and sweatshirts. In the summer he didn't bother, since no one really cared about it anyway.

But how could she hide her face?

She glanced away for a moment, then lifted her face to look directly at him. Her eyes were so blue and clear they looked like shards of glass. "Laura Stutzman."

Sawyer hesitated at the sound of her soft, drawling voice. The scars seemed to disappear, and he could envision what she looked like before the attack. *Beautiful.*

"Come, sit," Leona said. She gestured with her hand at the seat between her and Laura. "I'm glad you can join us, Sawyer."

With considerable effort he forced his gaze from Laura's and sat down. Emma had already placed a dish, fork, and knife in front of him.

He tried to focus on the food—a simple dinner of pot roast, mashed potatoes, cooked carrots, navy beans, and fresh bread. Despite his hunger, even Emma's delicious cooking couldn't command his attention. One look at Laura and he couldn't think straight.

Emma sat down. They all bowed their heads for prayer. He lost his will and glanced in Laura's direction, expecting her eyes to be closed.

Instead, their gazes met. But there was no reaction in her blue eyes. He wished he could say the same for himself.

She kept her hands folded in her lap and inclined her head in prayer. He followed suit and prayed silently according to Amish tradition.

When they were finished, Emma looked at him. "So you wanted to talk to me about a job?"

"Yep." He took a sizable helping of cooked carrots and passed the bowl to Leona. "It would involve some bookkeeping, taking orders, scheduling deliveries. Stuff like that. The woman doing it now is getting married soon, so we have to hire somebody else."

Emma exchanged a glance with Leona.

Sawyer put down his fork. "Let me guess. You already have a job."

Emma shook her head. "I don't. But I don't think I can accept the job. We're building an animal shelter to take the place of *Grossvadder's* workshop. I'll be busy with that for the next few months."

"Oh." Sawyer picked up his fork again. "That's too bad. I mean, it's great that you're building the shelter. But I'd hoped you could take the job."

Laura kept her head down, pretending to focus on her meal. But excitement sparked within her. She gripped her fork. Sawyer Thompson didn't know it yet, but he was offering her the opportunity she'd been hoping for. If she went to work for him, she wouldn't have to go out into the community and interview for jobs. Wouldn't have to see the look of shock and disgust on the face of some prospective employer, or watch them trying to judge whether her appearance would repel customers. She wouldn't have to suffer the indignity of being turned down.

While Sawyer was talking, she ventured a glance at him. He had on a homespun Amish-style shirt, but made out of plaid fabric. He wore baggy blue jeans, not the peg-legged pants other

Amish men wore. His hair was cut short, yet when he walked into the house he had worn an Amish hat. There was a little scruff on his chin, as if he hadn't shaved in a couple of days.

Maybe he was engaged? Or maybe he had been English for a while and then decided to join the church? If that was the case, why did he continue to wear baggy jeans and drive a pickup?

"Laura?"

She jerked to attention and looked across the table at Leona. The old woman had caught her staring, and the realization made her flush. Fortunately Sawyer didn't seem to notice. *"Ya?"*

"Supper not to your liking? You're not eating much."

She might say the same thing about Leona. The woman ate less than a sparrow. But in her short time here, Laura had learned that Leona's outward frailty hid an iron inner strength. Her family adored her, and Adam treated her almost reverently.

But it wasn't just strength and kindness that radiated from Leona Shetler. There was something else—bright, comforting, intangible—that drew people to her.

Laura suddenly felt Sawyer's gaze on her. Maybe he had noticed her paying attention to him. Or maybe, like Leona, he'd realized she wasn't eating. She shoved a huge helping of mashed potatoes in her mouth and swallowed. It should have been delicious, all hot and buttery, but like most food since the fire, it didn't appeal. *"Appeditlich,"* she said.

Emma grinned and served herself a large portion of pot roast. *"Mei mudder* taught me. She was a *gut* cook. One of the best."

Leona took a small bite of food and set down her fork. "That

FAITHFUL TO LAURA 45

she was. I remember *mei sohn* saying that shortly after they were married. And I told him, '*Gut* thing, since you love to eat.'"

Emma chuckled. Even Sawyer smiled. But Laura lost interest in the conversation and returned to thinking about Sawyer's job offer. She should have spoken up as soon as he mentioned it. Why the hesitation? She couldn't let fear guide her anymore, or hold her back. But that was exactly what she was doing, letting trepidation eat away at her like termites on wood.

"Maybe you should pray about it."

Her mother's voice. That was her solution to everything: pray, pray, pray. Well, Laura had prayed for a husband. God had answered her petition.

With Mark.

The last thing Laura needed was more prayer. What she really needed was courage. And that would only come from within.

Sawyer wiped his mouth with his napkin. "Thanks for supper." He patted his flat stomach. "I'm stuffed."

"So no dessert?" Emma asked.

He shook his head. "Not unless I want to explode." He started to push away from the table.

Laura clenched her hands in her lap. If he walked away, he would take the job offer to someone else. She couldn't let that happen. "What about me?" she blurted out. "The job, I mean. I could do it."

Everyone turned in her direction. Sawyer was gaping at her. She took a breath and tried to put their curious stares out of her mind. So what if her scars were ugly? This wasn't about what other people thought about her appearance. This was about earning money, any way she could.

"Are you sure?" Leona asked

Laura lifted her chin and looked directly at Sawyer, ignoring the tiny flip in her stomach when their eyes met. She'd been drawn in by a handsome man before. He'd brought her nothing but ruin. She wouldn't be fooled again. "Is the job difficult?"

Sawyer lifted his brow. "I've never done it, but I don't think so. No one ever seemed to have much trouble getting the work done."

"Any special qualifications?" Her tone remained business-like, despite her nerves tingling. The scar across her chin began to itch. She resisted the urge to scratch it.

"Hmm." Sawyer drummed his fingers on the table. "You need to be organized. Taking orders, scheduling." He stared at her intently. "You'll be dealing with a lot of people, Amish and Yankee alike."

Was that a challenge? Did he want to see if she'd cower, believe herself to be less qualified because she was disfigured? She'd done office work before, for her family business. But he wasn't wondering about that, she was sure of it. They were both thinking the same thing.

Can I handle people staring at mei *face?*

Laura swallowed. Forced a smile.

"When do I start?"

CHAPTER 6

Laura tried to steady her hands as she clipped metal barrettes to the sides of her *kapp*. Her first day working for Byler and Sons. *It's just a job*, she told herself. *Just a job*.

But it wasn't just a job. Working brought her closer to her goal. She avoided looking in the mirror, unwilling to let her scars break her fragile confidence. A knock sounded on the bathroom door.

"Laura?" Emma said. "Sawyer's here."

Sawyer? Her stomach dropped. Had he changed his mind? If he did, what would she do? She opened the door. Seeing Emma smiling confused her even more. "What's he doing here?"

"He's taking you to work." Emma kept grinning.

Good, he hadn't changed his mind after all. But she didn't have to accept a ride from him. "I was planning to walk."

"It's a pretty far walk. You're not going to turn him down, are you?"

Laura paused. She was already beholden to him for the job. She owed so many people so much. She didn't want to add Sawyer Thompson to the list.

"Laura," Emma said, "you shouldn't keep him waiting."

She had no choice. "Please tell him I'll be down in a minute."

"I will." Emma smiled again and moved to leave.

A thought occurred to Laura. "Emma? Did you ask him to pick me up?"

Emma shook her head. "*Nee,* I never said a word. I gather it was his own idea."

Laura went back into the bathroom. She paused and couldn't help but glance in the mirror, despite not wanting to. If this were her house, she would have smashed every single mirror to pieces. She took a deep breath and hardened her resolve. When she went downstairs, she saw Sawyer standing at the doorway. Today his entire outfit was Amish, from his straw hat to the pegged jeans and dusty, worn work boots. The only trace of English she saw was his short haircut. A flicker of curiosity passed through her. Just how Amish was he? Then again, why did it matter?

"Ready to go?" he asked.

She nodded, pulling her coat over her navy blue dress. "You didn't have to pick me up."

"I know." He smiled at her, a crooked, boyish grin. "I figured you'd need a ride."

She wasn't about to be sucked in by his charm. Or his kindness. "Next time I'll walk," she said, and strode past him and out the door.

Sawyer blinked and looked at Emma. "Was it something I said?"

Emma shrugged, frowning. "I don't see how. That was kind of rude, though."

"It's okay." He'd been rude when he first came to Middlefield too. Rude and bitter. Considering what Laura had been through, he couldn't hold her attitude against her.

"I'm sure she's nervous about the job," Emma said.

"Could be." But he thought there was more to it than just nerves. "See you later, Emma. I'll bring Laura back this afternoon." He paused. "If she'll let me."

"I'm sure she will. *Danki* for giving her the job, Sawyer. She's barely left the house since the accident."

"It wasn't my doing. Lukas approved of it."

"You came along at just the right time." Emma looked at him. "God's timing."

Sawyer wasn't so sure of that, but he nodded anyway. He hadn't grown up attending church, and it had taken time for him to understand that this community attributed everything in their lives to the Lord. Their belief that God guided everything confused him. How could that be possible? That theory left so many things unexplained. Like his parents' death.

He walked toward the truck. Laura waited by the passenger door. He left it unlocked. Why hadn't she gotten inside?

Maybe she was waiting for him. When he opened the door, she lifted her brow but got in without a word.

The chance of her letting him take her home seemed

increasingly remote. Didn't matter. He'd try anyway. He jumped in the truck and turned the ignition on. His foot slipped and he revved the engine. "Sorry."

She nodded and kept looking straight ahead.

He yanked the truck into reverse. This was going to be a long ride.

Laura was surprised that Sawyer opened the truck door for her. And what were he and Emma talking about? She wanted to ask but forced herself not to.

"Fine morning, don'tcha think?"

"*Ya.*" He didn't speak with the long Southern drawl she was used to. More nasally. But pleasant. Appealing.

Laura shifted in her seat. She folded her hands in her lap and turned her face toward the window. Big tall trees dotted the yards along the road. The last of autumn's leaves hung from spindly branches. The landscape resembled winter in the south more than fall. It was colder here too.

"So what's Tennessee like?" Sawyer asked.

She flinched, his voice jerking her out of her thoughts. "Cold. Wait, no, it isn't. I was just thinking that it's cold here. *Colder* here, I mean." She bit her bottom lip. *Stop rambling.*

"Oh." He turned left. "Different from Ohio, then?"

"*Ya.*"

"What's different other than the weather?"

"Is it all right if we don't talk right now?" She cringed at her own impoliteness. She never used to be curt. Now she had to work at not being downright rude.

"I'm sorry," he said. "I shouldn't pry. I know what it's like to be homesick."

"I'm not homesick." But she didn't sound convincing, even to herself.

"I like living here," he continued, "but when I first came, it took a long time to get used to a new place." He pulled into a driveway next to a large white house with a simply landscaped lawn. The sign on the side of the building read Byler and Sons.

"We're here."

"Already?" Emma was wrong. It wouldn't have been that far of a walk from the Shetlers'. The ride was unnecessary. Emma must have known that. Surely Sawyer did too.

As soon as he turned off the ignition, she scrambled out of the truck and waited by the front door of the shop. He was close at her heels and opened the door.

The chemical scent of varnish hit her first, followed by strong undertones of different kinds of wood and sawdust. Her family ran a bakery, but her cousins worked construction, so the smell was familiar.

She glanced around the room. Two Amish men were hard at work. One on the stocky side, with dark brown hair and a long beard. The other man was tall and wiry. Curly sandy-blond hair poked out beneath his straw hat. His light brown beard was shorter, only a couple inches past his chin.

Sawyer motioned for Laura to follow him farther into the shop. They stopped near a table in the middle of the spacious workroom. He gestured to the shorter man. "My father, Lukas. And that's his brother, Tobias."

They were brothers? They didn't look anything alike.

"*Gut mariye.*" Lukas came toward her, his hand extended. She shook it, feeling the calluses on his palm against her skin. "Glad to have you here."

"*Ya,* "Tobias said from the back of the shop. "Lukas's head would have exploded if he had to do any more office work."

Lukas shot his brother an annoyed look. "Don't listen to him."

Despite herself, Laura almost laughed. They might not look like brothers, but they sure acted like them. Seeing the family bond caused an ache inside. And she'd just told Sawyer she wasn't homesick.

"Can you get her started? Tobias and I are finishing up that hutch. Got a customer from Cleveland coming out day after tomorrow."

Sawyer nodded before glancing at Laura. "Let me show you the office."

She trailed him to the back of the woodshop and into a small room that had a door with a window in the upper half so you could see through to the shop. Sawyer held the door open and stood aside to let her pass.

One quick scan of the room and she could see the office was already organized. Lukas might not have liked doing paperwork, but from what she could tell he had kept on top of it.

"Everything you need is in the desk. Pens, pencils, paper. Order forms, invoices, all that stuff. There's a solar calculator in the top right drawer."

He walked to a three-drawer filing cabinet next to the desk. "Files are in here. You can hang your jacket or coat on one of the pegs." He gestured behind him to the row of wooden pegs nailed to the wall. Then he opened the middle top drawer and pulled out a spiral-bound notebook. "Everything you need to know is in that book. My Aunt Ruth put it together a few years ago. Still, if you have any questions, just ask any of us."

She nodded, flipping through the book and taking in the neat handwriting. "Looks like organization runs in your *familye*."

"I might agree, except that you haven't met my Aunt Elisabeth. Organization is not her thing." He chuckled. "I'm sure you'll meet everyone soon. They all drop by here from time to time. We're pretty close."

She heard the touch of satisfaction in his voice and buried her gaze in the notebook. She didn't want to know about his family, only about the job.

"I'll let you get to it." He stopped in the doorway and looked over his shoulder. "Let me know if you need anything."

Laura nodded but didn't look at him. She pulled out the chair, pretending to be consumed by the contents of the notebook.

The door shut with a click. She breathed out and rubbed her fingers across her forehead. The job would be easy. Ignoring the homesickness wouldn't. The same held true for Sawyer and his *daed* and *onkel*. All three seemed genuine. Kind. She hadn't thought there were any kind men left in the world.

"Think she's going to work out?" Lukas asked as Sawyer walked back into the workroom.

Sawyer nodded. "She seems sharp. Eager to do the job." She also seemed eager for him to leave. That socked his ego a bit.

Lukas ran a brush thick with clear lacquer along the side of the hutch. "I wonder how long she's going to stay."

"What do you mean?"

"Has she moved in with the Shetlers permanently?"

Sawyer shrugged. "I'm not sure. I didn't ask her." He probably should have, before he hired her. But she'd seemed so eager to have the job he didn't want to tell her no.

"If she has plans to *geh* back home, we should find out." He paused. "Then again, as long as God sees fit for her to stay here, we'll appreciate her work. *If* she does a good job."

Sawyer shot a glance toward the office door. Through the glass he could see Laura already at work. "I think she will."

CHAPTER 7

Laura glanced at the clock on the desk. Like everything else in the office, it was plain and unadorned. Nearly five. The day had passed quickly. She rose from the chair and stretched. Straightened the ribbons of her *kapp*. Picked her dark blue coat off the peg and slipped it over her shoulders. When she opened the door, she nearly slammed into Sawyer.

"I'm sorry." She glanced up. She hadn't been this close to him before, hadn't noticed he was almost a head taller than she was. Her gaze flicked away. "You startled me."

"Sorry. I didn't mean to." Sawyer took a step backward. "Ready to head home?"

"I was just fixing to go." She tried to move past him, but he blocked the doorway.

"I'll go with you to the truck."

She held up her hand. "I can walk."

"It's getting dark outside. Not to mention cold."

"I've got a coat. And a flashlight."

Sawyer stayed in place. "It's no problem to take you home."

"I've been sitting in this chair all day. I need the exercise."

Sawyer grinned. "Sounds like an excuse to me."

"Call it what you want." She looked at him straight on. "Can you let me by?"

"You'd rather walk half an hour in the dark and cold than for me to give you a ride?"

He sounded petulant. Had he never been turned down before? Maybe his nice-boy act was just that, an act. Like Mark's had been. She nodded, not letting her gaze drift from his.

He stepped to one side. "By all means. Walk home."

She recognized that tone. Irritation? Maybe some hurt pride? She took another look at him before she walked away. Wait, that wasn't it. She knew when a man was irritated. She'd experienced enough of that when Mark didn't get what he wanted. Sawyer wasn't irritated. He didn't even seem upset.

He seemed disappointed.

It didn't make sense. Why should he care if she walked home or not?

Outside, darkness was falling, and the wind pierced through her thin coat. The air was cold, much colder than it had been that morning. Maybe near freezing

Laura flicked on her flashlight and looked up and down the dark road. Had Sawyer turned right or left into the Bylers' driveway? Why hadn't she paid more attention?

She rubbed her forehead with the tips of her cold fingers and turned right, hoping she'd made the right choice.

Sawyer shook his head. He noticed her rubbing her forehead again. She seemed to do that a lot. Maybe it was her way of getting her brain in gear. It didn't work; she took the wrong turn out of the driveway.

He strode to his truck and opened the door. Let her get down the road a little ways. Maybe she'd figure out she'd turned wrong. Next time when he offered her a ride, she'd take it.

He felt a twinge of guilt. He should have given her directions. Then again, she hadn't asked for any. She hadn't asked him for anything, except this job.

He turned on the ignition and waited for the truck to warm up. It was a cold night. Clear sky, but no moon. He had never paid much attention to moonlight until he'd run away. Then it was the only light he had at night, and he counted on it. Without it, he was in complete darkness.

Except for that one time, when out of desperation he stole Mary Beth's flashlight. Guilt had plagued him right after, and he'd returned it.

He shook his head, forcing the memories away. Thinking about that time brought his birth parents alive in his mind. And despite years of being content with the Bylers, the pain would sometimes return, sharp as a saw blade.

He shifted the truck into reverse and backed out of the driveway. He could see Laura's flashlight bobbing along as she continued to walk the wrong way home. He rolled down the passenger window and slowed, letting the truck propel itself along.

"Sure you don't want a ride?" he asked.

Her body jerked. She turned to him. He could barely see her face in the darkness. "Positive."

No mistaking her tone. Curt. Decisive. Yet not harsh enough to stop him. "You know you're going the wrong way, *ya?*"

She took a step. Stopped. He thought he heard her sigh. She spun around and headed in the opposite direction.

He quickly pulled the truck over and put it in park. He left it running as he jumped out and hurried to her. "You don't know your way home."

"I reckon I'll figure it out."

"Figure it out in the daylight. Not now." He stepped in front of her, losing patience with the silly game she insisted on playing. "Get into the truck."

She froze at his words. Raised her flashlight until the light hit his eyes. *"Nee."*

The force of that one word took him aback, almost more than the piercing flash of light. Spots danced before his eyes, and he blinked. By the time his eyes adjusted, she had walked away.

Fine. If she wanted to spend the night wandering around Middlefield, that was her business. He followed her, keeping his distance.

"Laura, this is stupid."

"I agree," she called out, not turning around. "You followin' me is stupid. 'Specially since your truck is still runnin'."

Despite his exasperation, Sawyer smiled in the darkness at the sound of her soft Southern accent. "Why are you being so stubborn?"

"Why won't you leave me alone?"

Answering a question with a question. He couldn't stand that. "You're fired."

That stopped her. She whirled around and flashed the light at him. This time he was ready. He put his hand up and shielded his eyes.

"What did you say?"

"You're fired?" He had her attention, but caught it in an underhanded way. He had no intention of firing her. He didn't think he even had the authority.

"You're firin' me because I won't ride home with you?" She stomped toward him. "That's coercion."

Nice vocabulary. His Aunt Ruth would be impressed. A former schoolteacher, she was always throwing around big words that sometimes made her husband, Zach, scratch his head. But Sawyer knew exactly what Laura meant. And she was right.

"Okay, I'm sorry. You're not fired. "

"I don't appreciate being manipulated."

"I understand." He took a step toward her. "How about if I ask nicely?"

The flashlight lowered a few inches.

"Please let me take you home. I promise I'll pick you up in the morning and show you the way to the shop—in the daylight." He paused. "Then if you don't want to ride with me again, you don't have to."

After a moment she spoke. "All right."

He waited for her to reach him. Then they both walked back to the truck. She got in. As he slid into his seat, he could sense her body shaking. She turned off the flashlight as he shut the door.

"Here." He turned a knob on the dashboard. Hot air blew through the vents. "Better?"

"*Ya. Danki.*"

"You're welcome."

He eased the truck onto the road. "Sorry about what happened back there."

Silence. "It's okay. I—" She sighed. "I should have taken you up on the offer in the first place. I would have gotten lost."

Sawyer stopped himself from nodding. No need to throw salt on a bit of wounded pride. He'd learned that the Amish try to ignore pride. Humility was stressed almost above all else. But everyone had it, no matter how hard they tried to keep it in check.

He suddenly thought about the conversation with Lukas earlier that day. "How long are you planning to stay in Middlefield?"

She didn't respond right away. "I'm not sure."

"Can you give me an estimate?"

"Why do you need to know?"

The bite was back in her voice. Touchy. He reminded himself about the fire. The wounds she'd sustained. Considering that, she was doing very well. He'd have to draw on his patience. Or learn to grow some.

"Lukas was asking. We've had a revolving door when it comes to that job. He wants someone who will be around for a while."

"I will." A pause. "You can count on that."

A few moments later he pulled into her driveway. "I'll be here in the morning."

She opened the door. The interior light of the truck switched on. In the dim light her scars were still noticeable. Yet they didn't detract from her delicate features.

"I'll be ready."

He watched until she went inside, the headlights of his truck illuminating her in the darkness. Petite. Pretty. That quivery feeling in his belly appeared again. No wonder Mark King had pursued her. Who wouldn't?

But obviously the jerk had underestimated Laura Stutzman. Beneath that slight exterior lay an unyielding strength. One that King couldn't break. Even though it was obvious he had tried, and not just by harming her physically.

Sawyer gritted his teeth as he drove away. Laura didn't deserve what had happened to her. No one did. But for some reason the accident and her injuries dug deep at Sawyer.

It was a good thing Mark King had left town. Sawyer didn't know what he'd do if they ever crossed paths.

Whatever it might be, his family and the Amish community wouldn't approve. Of that he was absolutely sure.

CHAPTER 8

Emma pulled two loaves of steaming meatloaf out of the oven. They nearly fell out of her unsteady hands. "Great," she muttered. The last thing she needed was to ruin the main part of tonight's supper.

"Relax, *lieb*." Leona shuffled up behind her. "It's just the Ottos coming for supper."

Exactly. Her grandmother didn't know how important—and nerve wracking—tonight was. Not only did she want the food to be perfect, she wanted to break the ice that had formed around the families' relationship. Carol remained distant, and Norman almost never came over anymore to check on her and Leona, even though it was his duty as a deacon. Maybe the problem wasn't just between Carol and Norman. Emma had yet to voice those suspicions to Adam, however. He was keyed up enough about his parents.

Emma heard the sound of the front door opening and closing. Surely they hadn't arrived already? She looked up to see Laura standing in the kitchen doorway.

Laura. Emma had forgotten all about her. She looked at the table. The five place settings. Quickly she went to the cabinet and pulled out another plate.

"Are you expecting company?" Laura asked.

"*Ya.*" Emma whirled around. "Adam and his parents."

"I see." Laura stared at the table again.

Emma hurried to place the plate on the table. "Sorry, I miscounted."

Laura picked up the plate and handed it to her. "That's okay. I'm not hungry anyway."

Laura's stomach let out a loud rumbling. Emma moved to put the plate back on the table, but Laura put her hand on Emma's arm.

"I really don't want to eat tonight."

Emma met her gaze and understood. She took the plate and piled it with meatloaf, mashed potatoes, gravy, and green beans. She handed it to Laura. "In case you change your mind. You can eat in your room, if you prefer."

Laura took the plate, nodded, and left the kitchen.

Emma leaned against the counter and sighed. The last thing she wanted was to make Laura feel separate from the family, and she'd done exactly that by forgetting about her for supper. Still, Laura seemed determined to separate herself from everyone who would reach out to her. Emma couldn't do anything about that.

A knock sounded on the back door. Three taps. A pause. Two more. Adam's secret knock from when they were kids. She hadn't heard it in years. For some reason that bolstered her mood. Maybe they could get through this meal tonight. She went and opened the door. Just seeing Adam made her smile.

"*Mamm* and *Daed* are on their way," he said, his voice low. "Are you ready?"

She nodded. "As ready as I'll ever be."

Leona dabbed at the corner of her mouth with her napkin. The meatloaf nearly melted in the mouth. Mounds of fluffy mashed potatoes, beaten to a smooth, creamy texture, didn't have a single lump. Same with the rich, savory gravy. The buttered green beans were cooked to a firm yet slightly tender texture.

Not a single person at the table had eaten more than a few bites.

She let her gaze pass over Adam and Emma. They sat on one side of the table, Carol and Norman sat opposite. Norman pushed his potatoes around on his plate. Adam fiddled with a green bean on his fork but didn't bring it to his mouth. Carol had her hands in her lap, while Emma, who normally wasn't shy about eating, continued to cut her meat into tiny pieces.

Leona cleared her throat. She had to get some conversation going. "*Gut* supper, Emma."

"*Ya,*" Adam said, giving Emma a smile. She returned it, cheeks flushed.

"*Appeditlich.*" Norman shoved his fork into the potatoes.

"Very," Carol added.

More silence. Leona stifled a sigh. The tension in the room was thicker than the butter Adam slathered on his bread. She thought about the last time they'd all been together like this.

Mary had been with them.

How she missed her chatty, boisterous daughter-in-law! Emma and Clara were more reticent, taking after Leona's son, James. If Mary were here, she and Carol would be talking non-stop about everything from Mary's grandchildren to who was hosting the next frolic and what food dishes the two of them would bring. She would have set everyone at ease.

Maybe.

The lack of Mary's presence wasn't the only thing causing friction at the table. Friction Leona couldn't put her finger on. Emma and Adam kept exchanging concerned glances. Norman and Carol barely looked at each other.

Leona tried to engage the couples again. "In for a cold winter, *ya*, Norman?"

He shrugged. "Not sure. Mild fall, so maybe. Never know about these things. Weather is in God's hands."

"As is everything else." She looked at Carol, who tore off a corner of bread crust and shoved it into her mouth.

Emma put her fork down. It clanged against the hardwood table. She blew out a long breath. "All right, everyone. This isn't getting us anywhere. We can sit here and pretend everything is fine—"

"Emma—" Adam's voice held a note of warning.

She held up her hand and looked at his parents. "Adam and I are worried about you." Her eyes grew wide, as if stunned by her own candor. She looked at Adam. He nodded, giving her hand a reassuring touch.

"As I told *mei sohn*," Norman said, narrowing his eyes at Adam, "there's *nix* to worry about."

"*Ya.*" Carol's voice sounded strained. "*Nix.*"

"I—we—don't think so." Adam leaned forward and looked at his mother. "Something is wrong. You don't seem like yourself."

"I'm fine." Carol lifted her gaze, her eyes hard as brown river stones. "I don't know how many times I need to tell all of you that. And I don't understand why none of you will believe me."

Leona frowned. Norman's gaze dropped to his lap. She suspected Carol wasn't just speaking to Adam and Emma.

"Then why aren't you eating?" Adam asked. "Emma prepared an *appeditlich* meal, and you've barely taken a bite."

"Neither have you."

Adam flinched.

Carol put the heel of her hand against her forehead. She pushed the plate away. "I'm sorry," she said, her voice nearly a whisper. "I have a headache. I need to *geh.*"

Norman shoved his chair back so fast it sounded like rusty nails against a tin can. "I'll walk with you."

"*Nee.*" She stood, not looking at him. "You stay."

He hesitated. Sat back down. Stared at his plate, his shoulders bent.

And Leona suddenly knew what was wrong. A cold dread filled her, and she clutched the napkin in her hand.

She thought she was the only one who knew. A secret

revealed to her in confidence, in desperation. One she had promised to take to the grave.

But she wasn't the only one who knew. And that changed everything.

Lord, help us all.

"Well, *that* was successful." Emma grimaced as she poured water from a bucket into Dill's water trough. In the next stall, Elijah whinnied. She and the new horse were still getting used to each other. When Adam sold his truck to Sawyer, he used the money to buy her Elijah. Although Adam seemed to get along better with the horse than she did.

"Just a minute, you impatient thing," she said. "You'll get your water and feed soon enough. *Fraas* first."

Adam walked to the other stall. "I'll take care of him."

"All right." She couldn't keep the disappointment out of her voice. Tonight had been a disaster. They were further than ever from finding out what was going on with Adam's parents.

"Emma. Don't worry about what happened tonight." He opened the stall door and stepped inside. "I guess you were right. Whatever is going on with my parents isn't anyone's business but theirs. They made that pretty clear." The stall door banged shut behind him.

Emma nodded. "I'm sorry. I wanted to be more helpful." She spread Dill's feed and looked at Adam over the mare's back. "I just don't think there's anything we can do."

He finished feeding Elijah and stepped outside the stall. "There might be."

She rubbed Dill's nose and left her old horse to enjoy supper. Too bad she and Adam and their families hadn't enjoyed theirs. "What are you planning?"

Adam grinned and tugged on one of the ribbons of her *kapp*. "You already know."

Her stomach fluttered again, a mix of anticipation and anxiousness. "Adam—"

He tugged harder on her *kapp*, coaxing her toward him. She couldn't resist. He cupped the side of her face with his hand. "A wedding would give *mei mudder* something else to focus on." He pressed his mouth against her ear. "Marry me, Emma."

His warm breath sent shivers through her body.

"And don't tell me *nee* this time." He pulled back, but not before he placed a gentle kiss on the outer shell of her ear.

"I—I never said *nee*." His nearness muddled her mind. She suspected he was doing it on purpose.

"You never said *ya*."

Since he'd brought up the subject of marriage, Emma had put him off. Asked for time to think and pray. Still, she never rejected him outright.

Not like he had rejected her.

She pulled away.

But he grasped her shoulders, not letting go. "Emma, please. Stop running from me."

"I'm not running."

"*Ya*, you are. I know you've asked for time. But there's

nothing keeping us from being together for the rest of our lives. Nothing except you."

"I think I have a *gut* reason to be concerned. Don't you?"

He released her shoulders and stepped back. The lone light of the lantern hanging on its peg cast his face in flickering shadow. "Emma, do you love me?"

She couldn't lie. "You know I do."

"Is it the past that's keeping you from facing the future? Or is it something else?" He paused. "Someone else?"

The pain in his voice propelled her toward him. "Adam, there has never been anyone else."

"Then how long do we wait? A month? A year?" He held out his hands. "The next ten? Tell me, Emma, because I need to know how long I have to pay for my past sins and put my life on hold."

She turned from him. "That's not fair."

Emma heard him move. When she faced him, she saw he had his back to her. His shoulders were slumped, much like his father's had been at supper. "Sorry," he said. "I said I wouldn't be impatient. And that's exactly what I'm doing."

"You're always impatient. And impulsive." Qualities she'd always found attractive. While she measured almost every decision, he plowed forward. She admired his ability to throw out caution. But she also knew it had caused him trouble and her heartache.

Slowly she walked toward him. With all her nerves dancing on edge, she put a hand on his shoulder and felt the muscles of his back tense beneath his shirt. A sigh escaped him. Her heart fluttered.

How long was she going to keep him dangling? Her indecision was hurting them both.

Maybe, subconsciously, that's what she wanted. Maybe she knew deep down that the more she put him off, the more he felt the need to do penance for breaking her heart two years ago. He was in pain, and it was because of her.

Now who was being selfish?

"*Ya,*" she whispered.

He froze. "What did you say?"

"I'll marry you, Adam." She laughed, her heart suddenly light, the words easier to say than she'd imagined.

He didn't move, didn't say anything for a moment. Then he suddenly grabbed her in his arms and kissed her. "I love you," he said against her ear.

She held him tight, savoring the words. Every reason she had given herself for not agreeing to his proposal flew out of her mind. This was where she longed to be. Where she belonged. In his arms. A permanent part of his life. How stupid she'd been to deny them both.

Adam let her go and took a few steps back. His breath quickened, and even in the dim light of the lantern she could see his hazel eyes had darkened. The way he gazed at her stirred a desire and deepening love she'd never felt before.

She wanted to feel that way for the rest of her life.

CHAPTER 9

"I thought you should be the first to know, *Mamm*."

"I see."

He'd run all the way from Emma's, unable to contain his excitement that she'd finally agreed to marry him. But when he told his mother, she reacted with two words and a frown.

"That's it?" he asked.

Suddenly her face changed, as if an invisible voice had spoken in her ear. She took Adam's hand. "I'm sorry, *lieb*. Congratulations."

Adam shifted in his chair. Her eyes still held a faraway look. As if she was here with him, yet wasn't. "But?"

She looked away.

"*Mamm*." He squeezed her hand. "Tell me what's going on?"

"*Nix*. Only . . ." She once again met his gaze. "I hope you're sure she is the one for you."

"She is. She always has been. I've been too hardheaded to realize it until I came back home." He grinned, wanting her to share in his happiness.

She pulled her hand away. "Just make sure you want to spend the rest of your life with her. Through *gut* times . . . and bad." Before he could respond, she finally smiled. "Have you set a date yet?"

"In the next few weeks. Probably in January, after Christmas."

"A winter wedding?"

"*Ya.*" He studied her for a moment. "Is that all right?"

"Your *daed* and I . . . we married in January too."

Why did she mention something Adam already knew? "We can change the date."

She shook her head. "*Nee.* You should marry when you want. Does Leona know?"

"By now, probably. I imagine Emma's already told her. Other than her sister, we're not telling anyone else."

"Even your *daed*?"

Adam rubbed his palms against his thighs. "I don't know. Should I?" When it came to wedding planning, usually the women took over that part. There wasn't a real need for his father to know about the engagement right now. Adam knew of couples who revealed their engagement to their families only at the last minute.

"Telling your *daed* is your decision. Not mine." She rose and went to the sink.

"*Mamm* . . ." The words died on his tongue as he saw her wiping her cheeks with her hands. "You're crying."

Her shoulders dipped. Even her *kapp*, which normally looked crisp and starched, seemed to droop. "I'm sorry," she whispered. She fled from the room.

Adam leaned against the counter, dumbfounded. Whatever was wrong with his mother, it was getting worse.

Carol ran upstairs with tears streaming down her face. She had tried to be strong, to put on a brave front while she was crumbling inside. But her emotions were taking over. She couldn't keep up the façade anymore.

She had lied to her son. Over and over. Something she'd never done before, with anyone, much less her only child.

She sat on the bed and closed her eyes, and the memories came flooding back. The afternoon she had gone to see Mary Shetler, just a few days before she died. She had paused unseen in the doorway, waiting for Mary to finish talking to Leona. Her heart broke at the sight of her best friend's pain. The way Mary reached for Leona. Clung to her hand.

And confessed what had happened between her and Norman.

Carol rubbed the sore place at the base of her neck. Mary's words had been almost incoherent, but she'd caught a few of them. Enough. *Guilt. Betrayal. Kiss.*

She fled before either woman knew she was there.

In that instant, her heart turned numb.

But she couldn't lay all the blame at her husband's feet. She had to bear some of the burden for his loneliness. They had grown apart, especially beneath the strain of Adam and Norman's broken relationship.

She tried to be loyal to her son while loving his father. But so often she had failed. She had withdrawn into herself. Norman, too, had pulled away and sought solace elsewhere—in the arms of her best friend.

Was Mary's cancer a punishment for that? Carol didn't want to believe that God could be so harsh, and yet she couldn't fathom God's judgment. No one could.

Mary had died not knowing that Carol had discovered her secret.

Discovered the secret, and kept it.

And that secret scraped away at Carol's soul, one agonizing layer at a time.

All she wanted was to forget. But nothing gave her release. The knowledge festered inside her, eating away at her like cancer, killing her soul as surely as Mary's cancer had destroyed her body. Carol tended the pain, groomed it with the attention of a master gardener.

Carol knew she had to forgive both Norman and Mary. It was the Amish way. It was God's way. But she hadn't been able to bring herself to that point, not deep inside, where it mattered.

She couldn't bear to confront Norman about his failure as a husband. If she did, she would have to confront her own failure as a wife.

Adam left the house and headed for the barn. How could his father be so oblivious to his mother's pain? This time he would make his father listen and pay attention. Not just about his upcoming wedding, but about the problems with *Mamm*.

Inside the barn, the gas lamps cast everything in a sickly yellow light. The animals were already fed and settled in for the night. His father was in the corner, raking the dirt floor. A useless task. His father never wasted time.

"*Daed.*"

Norman didn't look up.

"We need to talk. Now."

His father lifted his gaze. "Now, you say?"

"*Ya.* That's exactly what I said."

"I'm busy." He started raking again.

"Too busy to talk to your *sohn*?"

"It will have to wait."

Adam stepped forward, his hands clenched. "Too busy to be worried about your *fraa* too?"

Norman tossed the rake aside and put his hands on his hips. "*Geh* ahead. Talk. I'm listening."

"Emma and I are getting married."

Norman's lips thinned. "What?"

"I asked her to marry me. She said yes."

His father sucked in a breath. He looked away and touched his forehead with his thumb and middle finger, nudging his hat askew. "Did you tell your *mudder*?"

"*Ya.*"

"What did she say?"

"Not much."

He paused, then frowned. "You aren't ready for marriage."

Adam unclenched his fists. "I love Emma. She's going to be my wife. Whether you and *Mamm* like it or not." He shook his head. "I don't understand. I thought you would both be happy for me."

"I can't be happy with a foolish decision."

Adam stepped forward. "How is marrying the woman I love foolish?"

Daed didn't flinch. "How do you know you love her?"

"I know. And I don't have to explain it to you." He rubbed the back of his neck. "I can't believe this. Our families have been friends and neighbors since Emma and I were children. Emma and I were—are—best friends. Yet you and *Mamm* are acting like I want to marry a stranger."

"You've been back in Middlefield for, what, two months?" His father shook his head. "You nearly died a few weeks ago. This decision is rash."

"If anything, what's happened to me since I came back to Middlefield brought me to the right decision. I should never have left. I wasn't happy in the Yankee world."

"You weren't happy being Amish either."

"But I am now." He stepped toward his dad. "I've changed. God has forgiven me. The church has welcomed me back. Emma has agreed to be *mei fraa*. Why is none of that *gut* enough for you?"

His father didn't say anything. His gaze shifted, past Adam's shoulder. Adam turned around to see what he was looking at. The only thing behind them was the inside of the barn.

"What did you do while you lived in Michigan?"

Adam turned back to his dad. "It doesn't matter."

"*Ya*, it does. Did you have a *maedel*? A Yankee girlfriend?"

Adam's stomach turned. *"Ya."*

"Does Emma know?"

He swallowed. "She doesn't need to. It's—"

"In the past." His father's chin dipped as the corners of his eyes sagged. "Adam, were you with that girl?"

"With her?"

"I doubt you were innocent while you were gone. Your exact words, as I recall, were that you were determined to 'be your own *mann* and live life by your rules, not God's and not the Amish.' Do you remember telling me that?"

"More than once." Adam bit the inside of his cheek.

"I know what that means, especially when it comes to women."

Adam's mouth dropped open as he realized what his father was saying. Heat crept up his neck. He should tell the old man to mind his business. But he couldn't.

His father was right. Adam couldn't change the subject, ignore it, or, worse, deny what happened. Still, the humiliation he felt made it next to impossible to get the words out. "Twice. I slept with her twice."

Disapproval seeped into his father's eyes, making Adam feel lower than the dirt beneath his feet. "Were you ever going to tell Emma?"

Adam shook his head. "I don't want to hurt her."

"So you'll marry her with that secret between you?"

Adam turned around. Scrubbed his hand over his face. Sleeping with Ashley had been a mistake. He knew it at the time, but he was in rebellion and didn't care. He never thought about the consequences, other than making sure he didn't get her pregnant. Before he returned to church, he confessed that sin. *Privately*. He never wanted to think about it again.

Suddenly he felt his father's hand on his shoulder. Adam turned around. "What?"

The disapproval in his *daed's* eyes disappeared, replaced with sadness. Or was it sympathy? Adam couldn't tell. "If you're going to marry her, you have to tell her."

"I have to *protect* her," Adam said. "I promised I'd never hurt her again. I intend to keep that promise."

"Then you made another mistake. Never make a promise you can't keep. When you love someone, and live with someone, you *will* hurt her, whether you mean to or not."

"Like you're hurting *Mamm*?"

The frown reappeared. "We're not talking about your *mamm* and *mei*."

"Maybe we should."

"So we can avoid talking about you and Emma?" His father shook his head. "You've proven to me you're not ready to get married. Everything is not clear between you and Emma. If you believe you can keep this secret forever, you're wrong. It will come out. If not now, then later on down the road. How will you face her when that happens?"

"I'll deal with it when the time comes." Adam was making his father's point, and he detested himself for it. He leaned against the fence post, his head down. "If I tell her, I could lose her."

His father didn't say anything for a moment. Finally, he spoke. "Maybe. You'll have to take that risk. If you don't tell her and she finds out, you'll lose her eventually."

"That's not true. Once we're married, we'll be together for life. We can't divorce."

"There are other kinds of divorce within a marriage. You can live separate lives under the same roof. And that can lead to destruction, not only of your relationship, but of yourself."

Adam looked at him, trying to figure out what his *daed* wasn't saying. But the man's expression became hard. Unreadable.

"Do you really want to marry Emma?" *Daed* asked. "Do you love her enough to tell her the truth?"

Adam gulped. But he didn't have to think about it. "*Ya.* I do. I only hope that when I tell her, she can forgive me." He turned around and headed back to the house, his parents' problems fading into the back of his mind. How could he possibly tell Emma about his past with Ashley?

God, I don't want to lose her.

When he returned home to Middlefield and his Amish life, Adam had experienced both the consequences of his actions and the forgiveness of God and the community. He had expected that to be the end of it.

But it wasn't. He would still have to pay for his biggest regret—and Emma would pay for it too.

Norman leaned against the wall of the barn. His hat tilted back until it started to slip off his head. It landed on the ground. He didn't bother to pick it up.

Adam was right. He should be happy for him and Emma. But he couldn't be, not completely. He loved Emma like his own daughter. And at one time, he would have been pleased at the idea of the two of them together.

But now, although his love for Emma hadn't changed, the circumstances had. He had given Adam the right advice. Too bad he was too much of a coward to heed his own words.

Norman snatched his hat off the ground and brushed the dirt off. He picked up the rake and tried to block out the world, working at the menial task until he was too exhausted to do anything but fall into bed.

It was how he'd coped with Adam's *rumspringa*. There were times he would have lost his sanity if he hadn't been outside among his animals, working the land. Some days it was the only way he had any peace, a state of mind and soul that Adam had been chipping away at for years with a rebellion that culminated in leaving the Amish faith.

Now his son was back. Yet Norman was still avoiding the house, avoiding his family. If only the situation with his wife could be ignored as easily as his wayward boy.

Norman loved his wife. After twenty-five years, he still cared deeply for her. But he had made a mistake. One that made his son's rebellious indiscretion pale in comparison. And he didn't know why or even how, but he suspected Carol knew about it.

Shame filled him. He was a deacon. Held to a higher standard. Yet how could he acknowledge his sin to his wife, his son, possibly the church?

The rake fell out of his hands. He dropped to his knees. *God, forgive me . . .*

It wasn't the first time he'd asked for forgiveness.

It also wasn't the first time he didn't feel forgiven.

CHAPTER 10

"Are you sure you don't want me to go with you?"

Cora tapped her manicured nails on the edge of the leather seat. She looked at Kenneth Hamilton, her personal attorney. She had called him the night before, and he had met her at the penthouse before dawn. Now they were headed for the airport.

Cora retained several attorneys, but Kenneth had been with her the longest. She confided more in him than in anyone else. Even then, she only told him the minimum of what he needed to know. "I'm positive. This is something I need to do on my own."

Kenneth adjusted his glasses and looked over the open file folder of legal documents and forms. "Everything seems to be in order here, considering the rush job I put my paralegal through." He looked at Cora. "But I have to tell you. Since your grandson is an adult, there's not much you can do to make him come to New York."

"Which is why I wanted you to draft a new will."

"He can still refuse." Kenneth took off his glasses and set them on his lap. "I wish you would reconsider your final wishes, Mrs. Easely. I would hate to see everything you and your late husband worked for fall into the wrong hands."

"He's my grandson. This is his birthright." Cora glanced out the window as her driver weaved through early morning New York traffic. "I would not have my sizable fortune end up in some trust for strangers to siphon out until it was empty."

"We can make sure that won't happen."

"Don't worry, Kenneth. You'll get your usual fee. And you will still be on retainer. I have no intention of firing you."

He tugged at his collar. "The thought never crossed my mind."

"Perhaps you're more concerned about my *grandson* firing you?"

Kenneth touched a well-groomed, silvery sideburn. "If he's of the same fine character as his grandmother, then my concern would certainly be invalid."

Cora turned to her attorney. "I'm not on my deathbed yet. And I'm fully confident that Sawyer will return with me. I'll make sure he's trained in how to run our business concerns."

The same business his mother had turned her back on when she married that useless husband of hers. But Cora had made a mistake with Kerry. One she didn't intend to repeat with Sawyer.

"Well then." Kenneth put his glasses in his suit jacket pocket and gathered the papers. "I suppose there's nothing left to say except good luck. I hope you find everything in Middlefield agreeable to you."

Including your grandson.

Kenneth didn't have to say the words out loud. The silent thought hung in the air between them as they continued on to the airport.

Her child had been such a disappointment to her. But her grandson wouldn't be. Cora felt that deep inside, a truth she couldn't deny. Still, the thought did not help steady her nerves.

Cora wasn't used to slow taxis. She wasn't used to taxis at all, to be perfectly honest. She was used to a finely appointed limo with an experienced driver who knew how to negotiate the crowded streets of New York, weaving in and out of avenues and boulevards jammed with traffic.

There were few cars on this road in Middlefield, yet the driver was poking along as if caught in five o'clock gridlock. If they were doing ten miles an hour, she was the queen of England.

She should have paid the extra money, brought her chauffer, and rented a car. Luxury model, of course. But she didn't want to invite questioning, and this didn't seem to be the kind of town that would ignore an entourage. She wanted to slip in, retrieve her grandson, and fly back to New York without spending a moment longer in this backwater than absolutely necessary. With any luck, she'd be in first class with a glass of champagne, and her grandson beside her, before the sun went down.

If this infernal driver would get a move on, that is.

"Can't you hurry up?" When the driver didn't respond, she forced out the one word she rarely used. "Please."

The taxi driver talked over his shoulder. "We're in Amish country. No need to hurry."

"I'll be the judge of that."

From Cleveland to Middlefield was, Kenneth had told her, about forty-five miles. Yet they'd been driving for over an hour with no sign of arriving anywhere. The taxi fare from the airport was already exorbitant, but it was clear this driver needed more incentive. "I'll double your rate if you get me to my destination quickly."

"I'll do my best." He tilted back his baseball cap. A little cartoon Indian was embroidered on the front. "All depends on how many buggies we get behind."

Buggies. Cora fell back against her seat and scowled. She knew precious little about these people, except that they were incredibly backward, and deliberately so. One of her friends had once invited her on a tour of Amish country in Pennsylvania. "You'll love it," Isabel had said. "Everything is so peaceful. We need a break from the bustling city for a while."

But Cora had refused. The Hamptons were rural enough for her.

A black buggy appeared. Piles of horse manure dotted the side of the road. Cora wrinkled her nose. "And people say New York City is dirty."

"What was that, ma'am?"

"Nothing. How long is this going to take?"

"Like I said." He gestured a hairy forearm toward the

windshield. Even though it was getting close to winter, he wore short sleeves. "Depends on the buggies. You know, most people come to Amish country to relax."

She adjusted her cream-colored cashmere scarf around her neck. "I'm not most people."

The driver didn't respond. *Wise man.*

"Coming!" Anna Byler wiped her floury hands on a kitchen dishrag. Who would be here mid-morning, especially on baking day? Fortunately she'd just set all eight balls of dough to rise. She had at least thirty minutes before she'd have to attend to them again.

Anna left the kitchen and hurried to the front of the house. Another set of sharp, impatient knocks echoed through the house.

"Just a minute." She pushed back a loose strand of hair as she opened the door. An unfamiliar woman stood on the porch, a steady curtain of rain her backdrop. What had started as mist this morning had now turned into a full downpour. Somehow the woman managed not to have a drop on her.

"Hello," Anna said.

The woman held her umbrella away from her body and shook off the excess water. She didn't look at Anna when she spoke. "I'm here to see Mr. Sawyer Thompson." She leaned the umbrella against the side of the house. Without asking, Anna noted.

She stared at the Yankee woman. Anna had never seen any-one quite like her before. The collar around her coat had to be real fur. The woman's hair was short and silver, almost white. Long nails with white tips tapped on a gold watch. A cloud of floral perfume wafted from her in the damp air. "I hope you don't plan to keep me standing here all day. Is Sawyer here or not?"

"Would you like to come in?" Anna opened the door wider. "To get out of the rain?"

"Only if Sawyer is inside." Her accent sounded strange too. Anna wondered if she was from Ohio.

The woman sniffed and glanced around the porch. Her nose wrinkled, as if she smelled something foul. There was, of course, the usual scent of livestock in the air, heightened as it always was during and after a rain. Everyone in Middlefield was used to it.

"I'm sorry," Anna said. "Sawyer is at work. If you tell me your name, I'll let him know—"

"Where is his place of employment?"

Anna's brow rose, along with her guard. "What?"

"Where . . . does . . . he . . . work?" The woman's gaze slid down her nose as she looked at Anna.

Anna crossed her arms. She didn't appreciate being treated as if she were stupid. But she held her tongue and managed to remain polite. "He works with my husband. Like I said, I'd be happy to tell him you stopped by."

"I don't have time for this. You will tell me where he works. Now."

"I'm sorry, Miss . . ." Anna waited for her to respond. When she didn't, Anna stepped forward. Her bare feet hit the cold porch as the rain slowed. "I'm not telling you anything unless I know who you are."

The woman fiddled with a light tan scarf tied around her neck. She stared down at Anna's bare feet. Finally she looked up. "My name is Easley," she said. "Cora Easley."

"How do you know Sawyer?"

Cora lifted her chin, her look both confident and chilling. "I am his grandmother."

"Grandmother?"

"That's what I said."

"But Sawyer doesn't have any other family."

"Obviously you're misinformed." The woman lifted an eyebrow. "Now, will you tell me his place of employment?"

"I—" Anna hesitated, trying to comprehend what she'd heard. Sawyer had family? Why hadn't they known this before? If this woman was telling the truth, if she really was Sawyer's grandmother, why was she showing up now? Anna couldn't just send her to the shop, not like this. "I think it would be best if you talked to him after work."

"*You* think it would be best." Cora sniffed. "Who are you to make that decision?"

"His mother."

The woman lifted her chin and arched one eyebrow. "*Adoptive* mother. My daughter, Kerry, was his true mother."

Anna fought to remain calm. "Sawyer works with his *father* at our carpentry shop. It's the Christmas season, and—"

Cora's gaze narrowed. "Is this an attempt to put me off?

Because I assure you, no one will stand between me and my grandson."

"*Nee.*" Anna's panic rose. "I wouldn't do that. He'll be surprised to see you, that's all. I think it would be better for both of you to have some time to talk. Since it's the Christmas season, they're very busy at work right now."

"A carpentry shop." Cora frowned and shook her head. Then she looked at Anna. "I suppose I shouldn't have expected any better." She picked up her umbrella and returned to the car.

"Where are you going?" Anna asked.

Cora didn't answer. The engine was still running, the driver sitting in the front seat, reading a magazine.

Water dripped from the porch eave, splashing against Anna's dress. She barely noticed. Her son's only blood relative stood a few feet away. Clothed in fancy furs and expensive jewelry and possessing the disposition of a woman used to getting what she wanted. What would Sawyer do when he found out?

Anna rushed to the car, ignoring her bare feet and the pelting rain. "You're leaving?"

Cora Easley peered down her narrow nose. "If you won't tell me where my grandson is, I'll visit every carpentry shop in this pathetic town until I find him."

Anna looked at Cora. How could this woman be Sawyer's grandmother? Sawyer was kind, easygoing, compassionate—everything she wasn't. Besides that, where had she been when Sawyer was abandoned? When he had *no one*? She couldn't just stroll into their lives now and start making demands.

Anna crossed her arms over her chest and bit back the

words, for her son's sake. "Sawyer is an adult. He takes care of himself now."

"So you're saying he doesn't live here?"

"He does, by his own choosing. But his life is his own."

Cora looked at the driver. "That's because he doesn't know he has other options."

"How could he, when he has no idea you even exist?" Anna bit her bottom lip. The words had flown out of her mouth. She should have held her tongue.

The woman's eyes blazed. "Let's go," she said to the driver, her teeth clenched. She shot Anna a scathing look. "I will deal solely with my grandson from this point forward."

"Nee!" Anna touched her arm.

Cora jerked from her grasp. "Excuse me?"

Anna reined in her anger. She couldn't let it get the best of her. Not unless she wanted to alienate this woman, and possibly Sawyer.

"I'll take you to see him."

"I thought you said he was busy."

"He is, but—" Anna took in a shuddering breath. The last thing she wanted to do was take this woman to meet Sawyer, yet she didn't see any other choice. Cora was determined to find him. Besides, if they went to the workshop together, Lukas would be there. Anna needed her husband by her side. "It's not too far away."

"Finally, you're being reasonable." Cora looked around the driveway, searching over Anna's shoulder at the barn behind her. "Where is your car?"

Anna heard the taxi driver snicker. She shot him a quieting glance. He wasn't helping matters. "I don't have a car. It won't take me but a second to hitch up the buggy."

"Buggy?" Cora's voice faltered a bit.

"Looks like you don't need me anymore." The taxi driver opened the trunk and deposited three huge suitcases on the gravel driveway.

Cora's thin brows lifted almost to her hairline. "What are you doing? Be careful with that—it's all very expensive."

"You heard the lady," he said. "She'll take you where you need to go."

"But you can't leave. I still need to find suitable lodging for tonight."

The cab driver shut the trunk. "I think you'll find the hospitality here just fine." He got inside the car and backed out of the driveway.

"I never should have paid him in advance," Cora muttered.

Anna stared at the luggage, fine-grained tan leather with gold monograms on the outside. "I'll take those in the *haus*. They'll dry out there. Then I'll get my shoes and hitch up the buggy. You can come inside and wait in the living room."

Cora stared at the cab as it disappeared in the distance. "I don't suppose I have a choice, do I?"

She looked down at her baggage, now splotched with rain and splattered with mud. "No wonder no one wants to visit Cleveland," she huffed. "These people have no idea how to treat guests."

CHAPTER 11

During Laura's second day on the job, she learned more about the Bylers' business. In early November they geared up for the Christmas season. Sawyer was in charge of finishing the simple toys the shop sold as seasonal gifts, sanding them smooth, applying several coats of varnish, and in the case of small rocking horses, painting the eyes, bridles, reins, and saddles. She could see he had a talent for the job. His skill impressed her. She couldn't draw a stick figure, much less have the patience to do such detailed work.

She also dealt with her first customer, an English woman— or Yankee, as the Amish here called them—who had just ordered a small wooden sled for her grandson. Laura tried to steady her nerves as she wrote down the information, wincing as she saw her crooked handwriting and hoping the woman didn't notice.

"Your receipt." Laura handed her the slip of paper and waited. For the stare. The disgust. At the very least, pity.

"Thank you." The older woman put the receipt in her purse. She smelled like flowery perfume and mothballs. As she adjusted the bright red felt hat covering her salt-and-pepper hair, she smiled. "I always enjoy doing business with you folks. I admire your lifestyle so much."

Laura smiled, surprised. "Thank you. We appreciate your order."

"You're most welcome. I must be going. More shopping to do. I like to have all the grandchildren's gifts bought and wrapped by the first of December. My youngest grandson will just love that sled." The woman waved as she walked out the door. "You have a nice day."

"Same to you," Laura called out. She leaned against the small counter at the front of the shop. The woman hadn't blinked at Laura's scars. Was she blind? Laura shook her head, wishing her negative thoughts hadn't intruded. Why couldn't she appreciate the few nice moments she had?

"Another rocking horse?" Sawyer came up behind her.

"A sled."

"Ah. We haven't made too many of those. I'll let Tobias know." He moved, then paused. "How's it going?"

Laura nodded. "Fine." Surprisingly fine. The tension in her shoulders eased.

"Good."

"*Danki* for the ride this morning."

"You already thanked me. But I don't mind hearing it again." He grinned.

Her equilibrium faltered under the warmth of his smile.

She chided herself for her foolishness. He had to have a girlfriend stashed somewhere. He was too nice and good-looking not to.

Not that she cared whether he did or not.

She exhaled nervously, and the Yankee woman's invoice slipped off the counter and fluttered to the floor. They both bent over to pick it up. Her head smacked into his.

"Ow!" she said. She pressed her hand against the top of her *kapp*.

He stood, his face red. "Laura, I'm so sorry. Are you okay?"

"I'm fine." She rubbed her head.

"Are you sure?" He moved closer. "You don't have a knot or anything?"

"Really, Sawyer. I'm fine." She stepped back, disoriented by a fluttery feeling in her stomach.

"I'm okay, in case you were wondering." He leaned his hip against the counter.

"Sorry." How could he be so unaware of how attractive he was? Why couldn't she stop noticing it? "I s'pose I oughta get back to work."

Sawyer chuckled.

"What's so funny?"

"You." He grinned. "You're just very direct. When you do talk, that is."

"I don't believe in wasting time."

"I can see that."

Laura turned to go to her office before she made a bigger fool of herself. Initially, her biggest concern about the job had been dealing with the public. Now she was more worried about keeping herself immune to the charms of Sawyer Thompson.

"Wait," he said.

She turned. *"Ya?"*

"Would you like to go to lunch today? I can show you around town and we can stop and pick up a bite to eat."

Laura clung to the invoice. "I have a lot of work to do."

"You have to eat."

"I have lunch at my desk."

"Not much of a break."

"I don't need one."

He tapped his fingers against the smooth wood countertop. "Everyone needs a break."

"I'm sure you can find someone else to eat with."

"Ouch."

Laura closed her eyes. "I shouldn't have said that."

"But I understand why you did." He held out his hands. "Laura, I'd like to talk to you."

"We talk enough in the truck."

He laughed. Her skin tingled at the deep, throaty sound. "I talk in the truck. You listen. Or maybe you tune me out."

"I don't tune you out." She pressed her lips together. "There's not much for us to talk about, I guess."

"Not sure I agree with you on that."

His answer surprised her enough to meet his gaze. "We don't have too much in common, in case you haven't noticed."

"We have more in common than you think." He ran the pad

of his thumb along the counter. "I know what it's like to be in a new town."

"You've said that before. More than once." Her chin twitched. She clenched her hands, resisting the itchiness. It seemed to crop up at the worst times.

"Guess I have said it a couple times. But I also know what it's like not to fit in."

She let her gaze rake him from head to foot, taking in his short haircut. Blue jeans from the store. Machine-manufactured sweatshirt. Baseball cap with an orange football helmet on it. Today must be his English day. He switched from Amish to English clothes without any apparent logic. "I think I fit in better here than you do."

"On the outside, maybe."

His words forced her to look away. She barely knew this man, yet he somehow managed to peek inside her soul. The vulnerability unnerved her.

"Laura." He paused, his tone serious, soft. "If you plan to stay here awhile, you're going to need a friend."

"The Shetlers are *mei* friends."

"I'm glad they are. But I don't think they understand what you're going through. I do. I can help."

"Trust me, Sawyer. I don't need any help."

"That's what I used to say. Especially when I was pushing people away." His expression held a mix of concern and kindness. "Just remember, when you're ready to talk, I'm ready to listen."

Half an hour later, Laura heard a knock on the office door. She stood from her chair and looked through the glass. A young woman with red hair smiled and waved.

Laura frowned. Katherine Yoder? What was she doing here?

She opened the door. Katherine grinned. "Surprise!"

"Hello," Laura said. "This is . . . ah, unexpected."

"That's what makes it a surprise," Katherine said. "Today is my day off, so I stopped by Emma's to say hello." She came into the office, still bubbling. "Emma said you were working here. Congratulations on the job. Does this mean you'll be staying in Middlefield?"

"For a while." Laura spotted a stool in the corner and pulled it out for Katherine. "Do you want to sit down?"

"Sure." Katherine settled her thin frame on the stool while Laura sat in her office chair across from her. "I've never worked in an office before," Katherine said. "Just at Mary Yoder's restaurant. Is the work fun?"

Laura looked at Katherine's wide, bright blue eyes, filled with sweetness. And innocence. "I'm enjoying it so far, but it's only my second day. I used to work in my *familye's* bakery."

"Oh!" Katherine retrieved a letter from her purse. "Speaking of, Emma wanted me to give you this. She said it was delivered with the morning mail."

The return address was Etheridge, Tennessee. Laura hesitated before accepting it. Despite the homesickness writhing inside, she didn't want to read this letter. It would make everything worse. But she took the envelope from Katherine anyway and set it on her desk. "*Danki* for bringing it. And again, for the quilt. I have it on my bed at the Shetlers'."

"*Gut.* That's what it's for, to be used."

Laura watched Katherine's smiling, animated face. Did this woman ever have a bad day? Was she really that chipper, or simply unaware of reality? She seemed to radiate kindness and warmth, but as Laura well knew, compassion could be faked.

"I really enjoy making them," Katherine was saying. "Do you sew?"

Laura shook her head. "I can bake. Oh, and do office work." She returned Katherine's grin. "I've never been very *gut* with a needle."

"Oh, then I must teach you how. It's very easy. We can start with a prayer quilt."

Laura's smile faded. "I don't know . . ."

"Sewing is very important. Especially after you're married. You'll have all the sewing to do for the children, and the grand-children." Her gaze grew wistful. Then she shook her head, as if clearing a thought. "I've been sewing since I was a *kinn*. And knitting and crocheting. I taught my cousin Amanda how to crochet a few years ago. She sent me this scarf for Christmas last year." Katherine held up the dark blue scarf.

"It's very nice."

"She lives in Pennsylvania with her *familye*, but she stayed with us for a school year." Katherine brought her hand to her mouth. "I'm babbling again. I do that all the time. *Mei daed* said I was born jabbering and never stopped."

Laura chuckled. For a moment she forgot about her letter,

about Sawyer, about everything. "I'm glad you stopped by, Katherine. And I don't mind the chattering a bit."

"Oh *gut*. Does that mean we'll work on a quilt together? We can start with a lap quilt. We'll do something easy, like a rag pattern. I know the perfect fabric—spring colors. Teals, roses, whites. It will be beautiful."

"I don't know. I'd like that, but—"

"You let me get the materials, and we can meet at Emma's house. Maybe Thursday evening?" She stood. "I'd better go. See you Thursday. It'll be fun."

Katherine was still talking when the door closed behind her. And despite herself, Laura found herself smiling.

Then her gaze landed on the letter. Laura picked up the envelope. She'd written her parents one letter, and that was while she was in the hospital. She didn't go into details about the fire or the glass that shattered all over her face. She only told them where she was, that she was safe, and that she wouldn't be coming home for a while. She should have known it wouldn't be enough to assuage their concern.

She closed her eyes and bittersweet memories flooded over her. Supper with her parents. Working with her mother in their garden. Helping out in the family bakery. Going to Sunday singings with her friends. Sleeping in her own bed. She'd lived a peaceful life. Content with her family and with herself. Until Mark King appeared.

Seeing her mother's handwriting thrust the knife of pain and homesickness deeper. She ran a finger under the edge of the seal, pulled out a plain piece of white paper, and began reading.

Dear Laura,

Your father and I were very happy to hear that you're safe. We were so worried when you ran away. We don't understand why you left, but we feel it has something to do with Mark. You haven't been the same since he disappeared.

Please come back home. We miss you and love you. We're not mad, especially not at you. We just want our daughter back here with us, where she belongs. The past is gone, and all we can do is move forward. Please, Laura, come home.

Love, Mamm

Laura folded the letter, put it back in the envelope, and laid it on her desk. Her parents didn't understand. She couldn't expect them to. They were kind, open, and nurturing. Easy targets for a man like Mark.

She had trusted him. They had discussed marriage, so his questions about their bakery business made sense. But it was just a way to get his hands on the money. She'd been a fool to trust him. A fool about so many things.

But not anymore.

She could handle the homesickness. Much as she might miss her parents and her friends and church, she wouldn't go back to Tennessee. Not until she finished what she'd set out to do.

A knock sounded at the door, and before she could compose herself, Sawyer walked into the office.

"We just had another customer. I saw Katherine was here

with you, so I . . ." He frowned and moved toward her. "Are you okay?"

A tear spilled from her eyes. She averted her gaze and wiped it away. "I'm fine."

"You don't look fine." He shut the door and sat on the edge of the desk. "Katherine didn't upset you, did she?"

"Of course not." Laura sniffed and looked at Sawyer, feigning a smile. "She's so sweet and . . . cheerful. I can't imagine her upsetting anyone."

"I've never known her to." He scanned her face for a moment, then his eyes focused on the desk. He nodded. "A letter from home?"

Laura snatched the letter and shoved it into a desk drawer. "This really isn't your business."

"I know it isn't. But anyone can see you're struggling right now."

She sat up straight and clenched her jaw. "I won't let it affect my work. I promise."

"I know. That's not what I meant." He leaned forward. "Remember what I said. I'm here if you need me."

His words unlocked a dam inside, and the tears began to well up again. "We hardly know each other." She pulled back, covering her face with her hands. "I don't understand why you care."

"Because if there's anything I've learned from living with the Amish, it's that they care about each other. Isn't it that way in your community?"

Laura looked up. "*Ya.*"

"And if someone you knew was struggling . . . hurting . . ."

He swallowed and looked away for a moment. "Wouldn't you try to help, if you could?"

She stared at him. She'd been so consumed by her own pitiful, vengeful thoughts she hadn't given anyone else much consideration. She nodded.

He looked at her again. "You may not want to talk to me about what happened with Mark. And that's okay. I just wanted you to know that you're not alone." He smiled. "Everything is going to be all right, Laura."

"How can you be so sure?"

Sawyer shrugged. "Isn't that one of God's promises? Something about all things working together for good? I don't think that means everything that happens to us *is* good, but that somehow God brings good out of it if we'll only trust. That's what I've been told, anyway." He smiled at her again and left the office.

Laura's eyes fixed on the door.

Trust that God could bring good out of all that had happened to her?

If only she could.

CHAPTER 12

Emma stood at what used to be the front entrance of her grandfather's workshop. The rain had stopped, but gray clouds cloaked the sky. She held her thumbs together and created a frame, trying to visualize the animal shelter. Adam had given her a diagram he'd sketched out. They would have to get started before the weather made it impossible.

But what about the wedding plans? It was the beginning of November, and they planned to marry in January. Could they do both in such a short period of time?

"Emma."

She smiled at the sound of Adam's voice, and a warm rush of love rose up in her. Now that they were engaged, she didn't even try to hold back her happiness. *Grossmammi* had given her blessing, saying something akin to "It's about time."

Emma turned and looked at him, and all thoughts of romance flew away. His normally healthy complexion was ashen. "What's wrong?"

"I told *mei* parents. About the wedding."

A drop of rain landed on Adam's light blue shirt. Then two. "We need to go inside," Emma said. "I'll fix us some *kaffee* and—"

Adam took her hand and led her to the front porch. A crack of thunder split the air. Rain started to pour. "We need to talk. Out here. Alone."

"Adam?" She let go of his hand. A sickening lump formed in her belly. "You haven't changed your mind, have you?"

"*Nee.* Of course not." He shook his head so hard she thought he might hurt his neck. He took her hands in his. "I haven't. And I never will. Don't ever doubt that, Emma. I love you. I will love you for the rest of my life."

His passion soothed her doubt but didn't keep the panic at bay. "Is it your parents?" She gripped his hands. "They don't want us to get married?"

"They didn't say that."

"But they aren't happy about it."

Adam let go of her hands. "Emma, they aren't happy about anything." He pulled back a foot or two.

Distance. He was only a few steps away, but it felt like miles separated them. "I don't understand. I thought—"

"Emma, this isn't about *mei mudder* and *vadder*. It's about us." He wiped the back of his hand across his forehead.

Sweating? The patter of rain echoed in her ears, and she felt chilled to the core. Yet he was standing on her porch, pale as paper and perspiring.

"I have to tell you . . . I don't know how . . ." He swallowed hard. "I promised I'd never hurt you again."

"*Ya*, you did." She backed away from him.

"And I meant it." He closed his eyes for a moment. Then opened them. They were shiny. Wet with unshed tears. "I'm going to have to break that promise."

"What do you mean?"

"I have to tell you. When I was in Michigan, I . . . I had a girlfriend."

She clasped her hands and rubbed them together. Had she really expected him not to date when he broke away from the church? Her mind accepted it, while her heart lagged behind. But even though it stung to hear him say it out loud, he wasn't hurting her. Not in the way he thought. She went to him. "Adam, I understand."

"*Nee*, I don't think—"

"I do. Really." She reached up and touched his cheek. Felt the roughness of the stubble on his chin. "You lived another life in Michigan. You didn't think you would come back here. Dating . . . having a girlfriend. It's only natural." She forced a smile. "I can't be the only one to find you irresistible."

He closed his eyes again. Removed her hand from his cheek. "I didn't just date, Emma. Ashley and I, we were serious. We were—how do I say this? Intimate."

Emma's mouth dropped open. "You were . . . *with* her?"

"Only twice."

"Twice?" She brought her hand up to her mouth. "Why are you telling me this?"

"Because you have the right to know—"

"I don't want to know!"

"Emma, I'm sorry. You can't imagine how bad I feel about this."

"Imagine?" Her eyes flew open. "All I can do now is imagine. You didn't have to tell me, Adam."

"*Ya*, I did. I don't want any secrets between us."

"But now this . . . this *thing* is between us!"

"I had to be honest," he said.

"It's one thing to be honest." Emma glared at him. "It's another to throw your *maedel* in my face."

Adam went to her. "Ex-girlfriend," he repeated. "I never loved her."

"Then *why?*"

"Because I was stupid. Growing up, we were taught to stay pure until marriage. I know that. But I didn't care. Everyone does it. I wasn't even Ashley's first."

Her stomach turned inside out. "I didn't need to know that either."

"Emma, this doesn't change anything between us. Tell me it hasn't."

"I . . . I don't know."

"Emma."

"Don't push." Tears welled up in her eyes. "Adam, please don't push me. Not on this." She opened the door and ran inside.

The rain drummed against the top of the buggy. Cora shifted on the bench seat, trying to find a comfortable position that also kept her coat and pantsuit dry. There was no door on either side of the buggy. No windshield to keep the biting air at bay. And nothing hiding the full view of the rear end of the horse, which was only a couple of feet ahead of her.

"I'm sorry we don't have the winter cover on yet." Anna tapped the reins on the horse's backside. It did nothing to increase the buggy's speed. "It's been a mild winter so far."

"Indeed." Cora brought a handkerchief to her nose. At least she was sitting on the right side of the buggy. Every few minutes a car would whiz by on the left, splattering water and making her grip the edge of the seat. It was minimally padded, with a covering of shoddy velvet. Everything about these people was cheap, backward, and painfully *slow*.

The buggy rolled through a large puddle. Muddy water splashed on the hem of Cora's designer pantsuit. "This is ridiculous! I hope you have a dry cleaner somewhere in this town."

"I'm sure we do." Anna glanced at her but didn't apologize. She returned her gaze straight ahead.

Cora looked at her surroundings. Anything to avoid the back end view of the horse. There was nothing worth seeing. A few cars, houses, farmland—nothing that bespoke class and stature. As the rain beat a steady cadence outside, she grimaced. *Middlefield? More like Middle-of-nowhere-field.*

Pain twinged in her hip. She had left her medicine in her cosmetic case back at the Bylers'. At some point she had to find a suitable place to spend the night. Definitely not here.

"We'll be at the workshop in a short while." Anna pulled on the reins, bringing the horse to a halt at a stop sign.

"Define 'short while.'"

"Twenty minutes."

Cora brought her fingertips to her temple as Anna made a right turn. Twenty more minutes in this . . . *thing*? Next time she would insist on a cab. Of course there wouldn't be a next time. As soon as humanly possible, she intended to get out of here and back to New York, taking Sawyer with her.

A sudden stench filled the air. Cora looked up just as the horse relieved himself in the middle of the road. Repulsed, she turned away, only to get splashed again by a spray of dirty water.

She couldn't get out of this dreadful place soon enough.

"That's looking *gut, sohn.*"

Sawyer glanced up at Lukas. He smiled, then dipped the fine-pointed paintbrush into a small jar of black paint. "I think after about twenty of these rocking horses I've finally figured out how to get the eyes just right."

"Nothing wrong with a small flaw here and there. That's what makes them one-of-a-kind."

Sawyer swirled a bit of black paint on the side of the horse's head. "That's interesting, coming from you."

"Why?"

"You have some pretty high standards, in case you haven't noticed."

Lukas chuckled. "And you've never failed to meet them."

Sawyer grinned again as Lukas walked away. His gaze flickered to the office door. Shut, as usual. He thought about his conversation with Laura. He kept reaching out. She kept pushing away. Why did he bother?

But what would have happened if Mary Beth and Johnny had given up on him? If their family hadn't connected him with Lukas and Anna? If the Bylers hadn't come all the way to the group home to convince him to live with them?

What if all the important people in his life had walked away when he told them to?

He wouldn't be painting horses' eyes in his father's woodshop. He wouldn't have a feeling of accomplishment and, yes, pride when Lukas complimented his work. He wouldn't *belong* anywhere.

So he wasn't about to give up on Laura. Not as long as she was in Middlefield. However long she stayed, he would keep on reaching out to her, even if she didn't want him to.

A tinkling bell sounded, signaling the front door of the shop opening. Sawyer didn't look up. Tobias had left an hour ago to pick up an order of cherrywood planks, but Laura or Lukas would handle the customer. Sawyer needed to put the last finishing touches on this eye before it dried.

"Anna?"

The concern in his father's voice caused him to look up. His mother walked toward Lukas, her face drained of color. An older woman followed behind her. She was tiny—a good six inches shorter than Anna, yet her presence seemed to fill the entire workshop.

"Lukas . . ." Anna stood by his father's side.

"What is it, Anna?"

Then his mother did something he'd never seen her do in public. She took Lukas's hand.

Sawyer put down the paintbrush. He stood. "Mom?"

"She's not your mother."

His head jerked around at the commanding sound of this woman's voice. "Who are you?"

"Your real family." She shot Anna and Lukas a derisive look. "Blood family. And I'm here to take you home."

Sawyer's gaze narrowed. "I don't know you. And as far as me having any blood family—" He stopped short. Why was he explaining himself to this stranger? He moved to stand by his parents. "What is she talking about?"

"Sawyer." Anna put her hand on his arm. "This is—"

"Cora Easley." She walked to him, her heels clicking on the concrete floor. "I'm your grandmother. Your mother was my daughter."

A sudden roaring filled his ears. "My grandparents are dead."

"Your grandfather is. But as you can see, I'm very much alive."

Sawyer's head spun. "I don't believe you."

"I have proof." She looked around the room. "Do we really have to do this here?" She brushed the sleeve of her coat and sneezed. "It's dirty, and my allergies are flaring up."

"That's sawdust, not dirt." This woman couldn't possibly be related to him. His mother had never been snooty and had never been afraid of a little dirt. Every year they had planted a small garden together. He had a sudden flash of memory—a picture of her scrubbing her fingernails underneath the running tap water.

He even had vague memories of playing outside after a spring rain with both of his parents when he was a little kid. They would wear rubber boots and splash in the water and thick mud. Everyone needed a bath afterward, but the fun had been worth it.

This woman looked as if she'd never seen a mud puddle in her life.

"Mrs. Easley." Lukas stepped forward, Anna close beside him. "I'm Lukas Byler. Sawyer's father."

Sawyer looked at Lukas, pleased that he didn't hesitate in making sure this woman knew the score. These were his parents now. His family.

Lukas held out his hand. Cora ignored it.

She faced Sawyer. "Can we talk privately?"

"*Nee.* I have work to do." Sawyer turned and walked back to the rocking horse. He sat on the stool and picked up the brush. His hands shook, smearing black paint over what had until that point been a perfect horse's eye. He muttered an oath and tossed the brush aside.

"Sawyer." Lukas' voice was low but firm.

"Sorry." Tension clamped down on his gut like a vise. The walls of the workshop started to close in; the huge room seemed to shrink into a small box around him. If he didn't leave now, he would say or do something he would regret.

He shot up from the stool. "I have to get out of here." Without looking at his parents, he rushed right by Cora and out the door.

CHAPTER 13

Cora gripped her Hermes calfskin bag and resisted the urge to throw the four-thousand-dollar purse on the ground. "Is this how you raised my grandson? To be rude?"

"*Nee,*" Lukas said. He shoved his free hand in his pocket but held on to his wife's. How touching.

She looked at the woman's husband. Sawdust covered his clothes, his hat, even his hair and beard. This was what Sawyer had spent his teen years doing? Manual labor? She pinched the bridge of her nose. He should be attending Harvard or Yale. Even Stanford would be preferable than living with people who dressed like they stepped out of a John Wayne western.

"Go get him." She lifted her head and faced Lukas.

"What?" Lukas's dark eyes narrowed.

"I said, go get him." Cora tilted her chin. If this man thought to intimidate her, he wouldn't succeed. "And be quick about it."

The man didn't say anything for a long time. He stared at her, as if trying to see inside her.

And for a brief moment, Cora Easley was the one intimidated.

Foolishness. She owned paintings that cost more than this shop and house combined. She tapped her foot against the cement floor. A small cloud of sawdust lifted around her shoe. "I'm waiting."

"Sawyer will come back when he's good and ready." Lukas crossed his thick arms over his chest. "You can wait here if you like. I'll even bring you a stool if you want to sit down." He pointed to a tall stool in the corner.

Cora looked at the stool. Like everything else, coated with sawdust. "I'll stand." She adjusted the collar of her coat and looked away.

"Suit yourself."

Cora ignored Lukas and looked at Anna. She hadn't said much, yet her confused expression spoke volumes.

But sympathy was out of the question. This couple had Sawyer as part of their family—for a few years, anyway. She had missed out on a lifetime. If anyone deserved sympathy, it was Cora herself, not them.

The door to a room in the back of the shop opened. A young woman entered, wearing that white bonnet-looking thing just like Anna, and a hideous plum-colored dress that hung nearly to her ankles.

"Is everything all right?" the young woman asked.

She turned to look at Cora, and the sight sucked all the breath from Cora's lungs.

Her face was webbed with scars. A thick one ran across the

width of her chin. Razor-thin ones crisscrossed her cheeks. Cora knew she shouldn't stare, but she couldn't pull her gaze away. The scars were still pink. Fresh-looking. What happened to this girl?

"Laura," Lukas said. "Why don't you and Anna *geh* into the *haus? Mamm* should be home. I'm sure she'd be happy for the company."

He spoke a mix of English and some strange guttural language. German, but not exactly.

Laura nodded but cast Cora a quick look before following Anna out of the workshop.

After they were gone, Lukas took a step toward Cora. "Now. I believe you and me are gonna have a talk."

"I—"

"And you will listen."

His tone had changed, enough to catch Cora off guard.

Laura frowned as Anna took her hand. The woman's fingers were as cold as ice cubes. "Anna? Who was that woman?"

Anna didn't look at Laura. She kept moving toward Lukas's parents' house next door to the carpentry shop. Anna walked inside without knocking.

"Hello?" *Fraa* Byler, Lukas and Tobias's mother, came into the living room, wiping her hands on a dish towel. "Anna? What's wrong?"

"Sawyer's grandmother." Anna's voice broke on the last word. "She's here. She wants to take him with her."

"His *grossmammi?* But I thought—"

"So did we. So did the courts." Anna slowly lowered herself onto the couch. *Fraa* Byler sat down beside her.

Bewildered, Laura stood at the edge of the living room, unsure what to do. The fancy woman in the workshop, the one who had blatantly stared at Laura when she came out of the office, was Sawyer's grandmother?

"Tell me what happened, Anna." *Fraa* Byler glanced up. "Laura, please. Sit down."

Laura perched on the edge of a wooden chair near the couch as Anna explained how the woman, Cora Easley, had shown up at her door a couple of hours ago.

"She demanded to see Sawyer. Said he was her *grosssohn.*"

"Is he?"

"I don't know. She says she has proof." Anna's eyes dampened. "I have a feeling she is telling the truth. There's no reason for her to lie."

Fraa Byler pushed up her wire-rimmed glasses. "Does he know she's here?"

Anna nodded. "And he's not happy about it."

Laura sat back in the chair. Her heart went out to Anna and Lukas. Cora Easley looked like a woman who was used to getting what she wanted.

"Where's Lukas?" *Fraa* Byler's expression resembled calm, yet her voice rose with the question.

"Talking to Sawyer's . . . talking to Cora."

Fraa Byler sat up straight. "Lukas will get to the bottom of this."

"I hope so." Anna looked at her mother-in-law. "What are we going to do?"

"Sawyer's an adult. He can make his own decisions." She took Anna's hand.

"What if he decides to leave?"

The question unnerved Laura. She shouldn't care what Sawyer did. Or anyone else in Middlefield. But she did care. There was no point in denying it.

"Anna, we must give this to God." *Fraa* Byler stroked her hand. "Whatever happens, we must accept His will."

Laura averted her gaze. God's will again.

Everything always came down to God's will.

"We have nothing to talk about." Cora peered at the stocky, broad-shouldered man who claimed to be Sawyer's father. "I'm here for my grandson."

"You've made that clear," he said.

How dare he scrutinize her like this? She should be investigating them, especially since their rustic lifestyle was not exactly the ideal environment for a young man of Sawyer's quality.

But I should have been here for him.

She pushed the thought away. There was no room in her plan for guilt. It wasn't her fault her daughter had kept Sawyer away from her. She blamed her wretched son-in-law for that. If he hadn't been in Kerry's life, everything would be different now. She would know her grandson. She would have had influence over him. Now she couldn't even get him to talk to her.

Lukas's voice broke into her thoughts. "How do I know you're telling the truth about being Sawyer's grandmother?"

"You're accusing me of lying?" First she had to come to this godforsaken town. Now this simpleton was impugning her integrity. If only her daughter had listened. If only she hadn't destroyed Cora's life with her selfishness. If only—

"I don't know you." He crossed his arms again. "And Sawyer is my *sohn*. It's my job to protect him."

"He's an adult."

"I'll never stop being his father."

"You're *not* his father."

"The law says I am." He shook his head. "Look, we're getting nowhere. Sawyer was upset when he left. Shocked, if nothing else. I'm sure he'll come back after he's had some time to think. He's a smart young man."

"I hope so." Cora sniffed. Fine, powdery sawdust flew up her nose. She sneezed.

"Gesundheit."

She pulled a tissue out of her bag and wiped her nose. Allergies. Dust, mites, pollen, dander. So many she sometimes lost track. "I can't stay in this room much longer."

"We can wait outside." Lukas gestured to the door. "Or in *mei* parents' *haus*."

"Outside will be fine." She stood by the door. Lukas didn't hesitate to open it for her. *At least this man has some manners.*

They stepped outside. The rain had stopped again, but the

crisp autumn air still held a bite, along with that revolting animal smell that had surrounded her since she arrived. How did people live like this?

She pulled a blue-backed packet of papers, folded in thirds, out of the Hermes bag. "You wanted proof? Here it is."

Lukas took the papers. Looked them over carefully, turning each page with slow movements, his thick fingers running across the words. Time stood still as he read the legal documents. Finally he handed them back to her. She was thinking she might have to explain the legal terminology when he said, "These seem to be in order. So why are you just showing up now?"

"That's none of your business."

"I believe it is." Lukas stood askance. "Sawyer grew up believing he didn't have any family other than his parents. When they died, he had no one."

She wasn't about to admit to this man the reason why she hadn't known about Sawyer. She would not look like a fool. "Now he has someone. The details aren't important."

"I imagine they are to Sawyer."

She shifted on the heels of her pumps. Hopefully she hadn't stepped in anything offensive and ruined them—they were one of her most expensive pairs. "I will explain myself to him. *Only* him."

"I'm listening."

Cora turned at the sound of Sawyer's voice. As he walked toward her, her stomach turned. The nearly black hair. Square chin. Broad shoulders. He looked just like his vagabond of a father. The man Kerry had given up everything for.

Then she saw it, and one of the thick layers of ice around her heart started to melt. *His eyes.* His eyes were his mother's.

Cora blinked back the tears. No weakness. She couldn't afford it, not with so much at stake. "If you come home with me, Sawyer," she said, "I'll tell you what you need to know."

Sawyer shook his head. "You'll tell me now. Right here. Or I guarantee you'll never see me again."

CHAPTER 14

As Anna and *Fraa* Byler talked in low tones, Laura stood and looked out the living room window. She was at a loss to know what to say to this family, these loving people who had not only offered her a job, but extended kindness far beyond the call of Christian duty. Kindness she'd never fully appreciated, especially Sawyer's.

Until now. She pulled back the curtains and saw Lukas, Sawyer, and his grandmother standing in front of the workshop.

Laura homed in on Sawyer's face. His black eyebrows were set in a straight line, his square chin lifted. Anger. Resentment. She recognized those emotions—she had seen them often enough in her own reflection. But she had never seen Sawyer express them. Until now.

"Is something happening?" Anna came up behind Laura and peered over her shoulder. "What are they doing?"

"Talking."

"Sawyer is upset." Anna gripped the edge of the curtain

and pulled it farther back. "Hasn't he been through enough? I should *geh* to him. He needs me."

"*Nee.*" *Fraa* Byler extracted the curtain from Anna's grip. "Let Lukas handle this."

"But—"

"Anna." *Fraa* Byler touched her face. "I know how much you love Sawyer. But he's not a helpless *kinn* anymore. He's a *mann*, and you must respect that. You must also trust your husband's judgment. He'll be there for Sawyer."

Anna nodded. "It's just so hard . . ."

"I know." She lightly gripped Anna's arm. "Let's *geh* in the kitchen. We'll have some *kaffee* while we wait."

Laura looked out the window again. She'd join Anna and *Fraa* Byler in a minute. But not until she knew Sawyer was okay.

Sawyer didn't move. He looked down at this woman who claimed to be his grandmother. He saw the legal papers she handed to his father. Heard Lukas say that what she claimed was true.

But it couldn't be. If Cora Easley was his grandmother, his parents had lied to him. They would never have done that.

Would they?

"This isn't the place to discuss the matter." Cora looked past Sawyer to Lukas. "We should talk about this privately."

"Anything you have to say, you can say in front of my father."

"He's not your—"

"Father?" Sawyer glanced at Lukas. He loved his biological dad, but he also loved Lukas. And he wouldn't have her short-change this man. He faced her again. "He is my father, just as much as Ray Thompson was."

She pressed her lips together. "I'd rather not talk about that man. And as for your mother, she had her reasons for not telling you about me."

"What reasons?"

For the first time he saw doubt flicker across her features. Up to this point she'd been demanding. Confident. And prideful. Every inch of her reflected wealth and position. So different from his parents and in complete contrast to the life he lived now. Yet his simple question made her pause. A knot of anxiety formed in his gut. Suddenly he doubted everything his mother and father had ever told him.

"I will tell you those reasons when we get home."

He took a step back. "I am home."

Cora looked around. "This is not where you belong."

"Not true." He narrowed his gaze. "If you knew anything about me, you'd know better." He shook his head. "I'm tired of whatever game you're playing. Tell me the truth. Now. Or I'm walking into that house."

She opened her mouth to speak. Her bottom lip trembled. Only for a second, but he caught it. He steeled himself. He didn't want to feel sorry for this woman. He didn't want to feel anything for her.

He waited. She waited. A minute. Two. Five. Still she stayed silent.

"That does it," he said at last. "I'm going inside."

"Sawyer."

He turned at Lukas's voice. His father's mouth was barely visible through his thick, dark beard. But his eyes were intense. Never had he seen Lukas look so serious. Or so worried, despite how he tried to hide it. Sawyer could sense the strain radiating from his father.

"We need to talk about this," Lukas said. He stepped forward. Lowered his voice. "As a *familye*."

"No." Cora stepped between them. "What you need," she said, pointing at Sawyer with her long, artificial fingernail, "is to stop being ridiculous. You're wasting everyone's time."

"Did you really think you could show up in my life, after twenty years, and just expect me to jump at your command?" Sawyer said. "Do you actually think I'd walk away from the people who took care of me after my parents died?" He narrowed his eyes at her. "The police, the social workers, the lawyers . . . they all looked for a relative, anyone, to claim me." Sawyer's throat tightened. He forced out the words. "Not a single person showed up. Except for the Bylers. They were the only ones who cared enough to save me from the group home."

"If I'd known . . ."

"If you'd *known*?" He sneered at her. "You're rich. How hard could it have been to find me?"

She looked away. "You have no idea."

"You should have tried harder." He leaned forward. "I don't care where you go, just leave. I'm done here." He stormed past her and bounded up the front porch steps of his grandparents' home. His *real* grandparents. The ones who mattered to him. Not the woman who finally showed up when it was convenient for her.

He went into the house, letting the door slam behind him.

Laura was in the living room next to the window. She dropped the curtain, and the fabric swayed against the window. Her cheeks flushed, but the rest of her face was pale.

She'd been watching.

"Are you all right?" she asked.

Sawyer looked at her. Saw the concern in her eyes. And for some bizarre reason, he wanted to hold her. He wanted to wrap Laura Stutzman in his arms and keep her there. To draw from the well of strength he knew she possessed. Because right now, his well was running dry.

Instead, he walked away.

"Was that Sawyer?"

Laura turned to see Anna walk into the room. Her emotions reeled as her skin tingled. One look from Sawyer and she felt like she'd been inside his skin, experiencing a fleeting moment of shared emotions. Desperation. Confusion. Feelings she knew intimately. "He went upstairs."

"I need to see him."

Laura put her hand on Anna's arm. *"Nee."*

Anna whirled around, her face beet red with anger. "Why

is everyone trying to keep me from *mei kinn?* I'm his *mamm.* He needs me right now."

"He needs to be alone."

"How do you know? What makes you an expert on *mei sohn?*"

Laura knew she shouldn't have said anything. But Sawyer didn't need his mother. Or anyone else. She recognized that the minute he walked in the door. "I . . . I just know."

She wanted to tell Anna that she understood the anger. The frustration. But she kept her mouth shut. She wouldn't risk making things worse by saying the wrong thing.

Finally, Anna went outside. *Fraa* Byler came into the room as the front door shut.

"Sawyer?"

"Upstairs." Laura nodded at the staircase. "Anna went outside. I think Lukas and . . . what is that *fraa's* name?"

"Cora." *Fraa* Byler sighed. "Cora Easley."

"I think they're both still out there."

Fraa Byler rubbed her left temple. "This is so hard to believe. *Mei* Lukas and his Anna, they could never have *kinner* of their own. Sawyer was their only one. It's why Anna is so upset. She knows he's an adult. But in her heart he's still that young, scared *bu* who tried to hide his fear and grief. She's always tried to protect him, but still let him be who he is."

She looked at Laura and wrung her hands together. "Now everything has changed. If Sawyer leaves, I don't know what she'll do. Or what we'll do. He's a part of us. A part of our *familye* as much as if he'd been born into it. Even though we've never been certain he would join the church, we assumed he would always be close to us." She bit her bottom lip. "Now I'm not so sure."

Laura put her arms around *Fraa* Byler. "It will be okay."

"You have faith, *ya?*" *Fraa* Byler whispered in her ear.

Laura didn't respond. She couldn't. She wasn't sure she had faith in anything anymore.

But she'd let the old woman believe it, if it brought her comfort.

"How can my grandson refuse me?"

Lukas prayed for patience. He'd never met a woman like Cora Easely before. Yet he knew he had to tread carefully with her. The legal documents she'd presented him had been clear. First Cora's identification documents—copies of her birth certificate, her passport. Then Kerry's birth certificate, which proved Cora was her mother, along with the copy of Sawyer's birth certificate the lawyer had uncovered.

Cora was his biological grandmother. There was no doubt about it. And now she looked mad enough to snap in two. Somehow they had to work together and put Sawyer's interests and feelings first. Something this woman didn't want to do.

"Have you people brainwashed him?" She glared at Lukas. "I can't believe a grandson of mine would behave like this."

"Lukas?"

He saw Anna heading toward him. His heart twisted at the

pain in her eyes and the tension in her face. His beautiful, tender wife. She loved their son with every beat of her heart. And they had been through so much over the past five years.

All their married life, Anna had wanted nothing so much as to be a mother. Shortly after they married, they found out she couldn't have children. Then, like a gift from God, Sawyer appeared in their lives.

After Sawyer, they tried adopting more children, only to have them taken away. They had little Samuel for two months, and then his birth mother changed her mind at the last minute. With Curtis, they were in the final stages of adoption when his father asserted parental rights and the adoption fell through. And sweet baby Amanda, who won Anna's heart immediately, had been claimed by a distant relative.

Too much heartbreak. Too many dashed hopes.

But through it all they'd had Sawyer.

And they always would. He put his hand over Anna's. In this, as in everything, they would stand together as a united front.

"I have lawyers at my disposal." Cora's piercing gaze landed on Anna, then him. "Sawyer will come to New York."

Anna's grip tightened. "Why? This is his home."

"He has business interests to attend to."

"He works in our family business here." Anna glanced at Lukas.

Cora huffed. "We can hardly compare the two."

Lukas held up his hand. "Just a minute, Mrs. Easley. We don't have to argue about this. We all love Sawyer and want what's best for him. But if he doesn't want to leave, we have to respect that."

"And if he does leave? Will you respect that as well?"

Lukas hesitated. His wife's face went white. *"Ya,"* he said quietly, squeezing Anna's hand. "We will. But right now we need to give him time. He deserves that."

For once Cora didn't say anything. Then she gave him a curt nod. "Fine. I will wait for him at your house." She looked at Anna. "I'm ready to leave now." She whirled on her spiked heel and walked to the buggy.

"Lukas." Anna's voice trembled like a frail leaf in a gale-force wind. "What are we going to do?"

He faced his wife. "We must pray. Trust God. And above all, be there for Sawyer. This isn't about us."

"But—"

"Lieb. Please." He touched her face. "Remember, we have always trusted God with everything. This isn't different."

"Ya, it is." Fear entered her eyes.

He wished he could wipe away her anguish. Give her a tender kiss and she would know everything would be all right. But he wasn't sure of that himself. They both knew that God's will wasn't always their own. If it was, they would have a houseful of children, instead of being on the verge of losing their only son. Not only did Cora Easley seem determined to take Sawyer with her, she also seemed closed to compromising.

But there was an even worse fear. Sawyer already had one foot in the Amish life and one in the Yankee world. Once he left Middlefield behind, would he ever come back? Or would he become a part of his new family and forget about Lukas and Anna?

Lukas banished the thought from his mind. He was borrowing trouble, inviting worry, and doing exactly the opposite of what he told Anna. *I trust in You, Lord*, he said to himself. To his wife he said, "Be as kind as you can to this *fraa*. Where is she staying tonight?"

"Her suitcases are in our living room." Anna wiped her eyes. "She brought a lot of them."

"Then maybe she plans to stay for a while. To get to know Sawyer and where he comes from. Maybe she knew this wouldn't be easy and prepared for that."

"I don't think that's it." She looked at Lukas. "I think she just has a lot of stuff. You heard her. She can't wait to leave."

"Maybe she should stay with us."

Anna looked away. "I don't want her to," she whispered.

"I know. But this will give us a chance to get to know her better. And hopefully Sawyer will be open to learning about her too." He leaned close to her. "Be anxious for nothing."

She nodded.

"*Danki, lieb.*" He ran his hand over the back of hers before letting it go. "You should *geh*. Don't keep her waiting. I'll be home as soon as I can."

"With Sawyer?"

He nodded. "With our *sohn*."

CHAPTER 15

Cora placed her foot on the narrow, muddy step of the buggy and heaved herself upward. The slick sole of her shoe gave no traction; she slipped, lost her footing, and had to grab onto the front wheel to keep from falling. That was all she needed to complete this day—make an utter fool of herself by landing face-first in a pile of manure.

What did these people have against cars? Against decent clothing?

On the second try she had more success. She hoisted herself into the buggy and carefully checked the bench. Satisfied that it was relatively clean, she sat down and pulled a linen handkerchief from her bag. She flinched as she wiped the mud off her palm, then laid the handkerchief on the seat, as far away as she could. She wasn't about to put that nasty thing back in a four-thousand-dollar Hermes.

Cora leaned against the seat and looked out at Anna and Lukas, their heads close together. No doubt plotting how they would circumvent her attempt to convince Sawyer to come home.

It shouldn't even be an issue. He was her grandson. But Sawyer hadn't just inherited his mother's eyes. He also had her stubborn streak.

Cora's determination, however, ran deeper. Stronger. She would not be denied her only grandson. Not by anyone.

The sound of running water arrested her attention, and Cora realized with a lurch of disgust that the horse attached to the buggy was relieving himself. Again.

Cora cringed. She detested animals, had never had a pet, nor allowed Kerry to have one. The one time her daughter had brought home a puppy, Cora had promptly taken it to the pound. Animals were dirty. They made messes. And in the case of this horse, a huge, steamy puddle in the driveway.

Anna returned to the buggy wearing a strained, forced smile. Cora was used to seeing those. She didn't return it.

"It won't take long to get back to the *haus*," Anna said. She picked up the reins, snapped them smartly across the horse's rump, and started out of the driveway.

By now Cora knew that "not long" in Amish meant "whenever we get there." Horse and buggy, indeed. At least in New York the carriages were open. Decorative. And depending on your companion, romantic.

There was nothing romantic about the Amish.

"Do you like chicken and dumplings?"

Cora looked at Anna. "Pardon me?"

"Chicken and dumplings. That's what we're having for

supper tonight. Along with cabbage casserole and butter beans. With Ho Ho cake for dessert." She smiled again, although her face looked like it might crack at any minute from the strain. "That's Lukas's favorite."

Ho Ho cake? Cora looked out the window of the buggy. "As soon as we get back, I plan to call a taxi. As I said, I'll be returning to Cleveland tonight."

"You don't have to. You're welcome to stay." She paused. "With us."

Anna sounded anything but welcoming. "I would prefer to go." Cora crossed her legs. Arranged her scarf and fiddled with her collar for the sixth time since she'd arrived. Pushed the dirty handkerchief onto the floor of the buggy.

Her suit smelled like horse, and her shoes . . . well, better not to think about what her shoes smelled like. She ought to burn the whole lot. But first she had to find a hotel. With a spa. After the day she had, she needed the pampering.

"Sawyer will be home this evening."

She angled her head toward Anna, all thoughts of spa treatments fleeing her mind. "Are you sure?"

"Lukas will make certain of it."

That changed everything. If she had access to Sawyer again, she could apply more pressure. Hopefully gain the upper hand. She'd learned that skill not only in her business dealings but in her personal life. Always stay one step ahead of everyone else. The one time she hadn't, she'd lost Kerry forever.

She wasn't going to make the same mistake with Sawyer.

Anna didn't say a word the rest of the drive home. Cora preferred it that way.

Emma gazed out the window of her bedroom, blinking back tears. She couldn't believe Adam had told her about that Ashley girl and what happened between them in Michigan. She paced across the room and back again. And paced some more. With each step she prayed for clarity, for the pain of yet another betrayal to cease.

But had Adam really betrayed her? They hadn't been a couple when he was with Ashley. They hadn't even been friends at the time. He had turned his back on everyone and everything in Middlefield for those two years. So why did she feel so hurt?

She flopped down on the bed. The strings of her *kapp* bounced against the front of her dress. She knew why she was hurt, if she was just honest enough to admit it.

She wasn't his first. His one and only. Like he would be for her. That special, intimate moment, that first time, he had already experienced. With another woman.

Adam knew so much, and she knew nothing.

What if she disappointed him? What if she didn't measure up?

What if he wishes he'd married someone else?

Emma tried to push the anxious thoughts away. But she couldn't. She wasn't one of the pretty girls. Her hips were too wide and her face too plain. But since Adam's return, he had helped destroy the self-doubt that had always plagued her. When she was with Adam, he made her feel like the most beautiful woman in the world.

Now all those old insecurities came rushing back, smashing

her confidence to smithereens. She didn't know if she could regain it again.

"Emma?"

She heard her grandmother's muffled voice outside the door. She wiped the tears from her eyes and stood. *"Ya?"*

"Are you okay? It's nearly suppertime."

Emma opened the door. "I'm fine. I'm sorry, I just . . . lost track of time. I'll be right there."

Her grandmother peered at Emma's face and frowned. "You aren't all right."

Emma started to deny it, but she couldn't fool her grandmother. She never could. *"Nee,* I'm not. But I will be."

"Lieb, talk to me. You've been so happy the past few weeks." She smiled. "It's been so nice to see. What happened to change that?"

The old woman leaned heavily on her cane. Emma opened the door wider. "Please, come sit down."

Grossmammi shuffled to the bed and sat. She put the cane in front of her and placed both hands on the handle. She didn't say anything, just waited.

And suddenly Emma didn't know what to say. She walked to the window again. Dried raindrops smeared the window pane. She'd always confided in her grandmother. But how could she tell her grandmother about Adam and Ashley?

"Adam has something to do with this, doesn't he?" *Grossmammi* asked.

Emma nodded but didn't turn. She traced a line on the window ledge. Dust. She'd have to clean it later.

"Emma?"

Emma leaned her head against the window. "Adam . . . he told me something." Her cheeks heated. "Something I didn't want to know. I didn't need to know."

"All right." Her grandmother spoke the words in a measured tone.

She turned around. "The odd thing is, he told me because he thought he was doing the right thing."

"And was he?"

"I don't know." Emma crossed the room and sat next to her grandmother. She leaned her head on *Grossmammi's* shoulder. "Part of me believes he was right in telling me his . . . secret."

"But you don't believe that completely."

She lifted her head and looked at her grandmother, thankful the woman didn't press her for the details of her and Adam's conversation. "*Nee*, I don't. I'm so confused."

"Love is confusing, especially in the beginning." Her grandmother patted her knee. "Emma, you and Adam have been through a lot together. And not just in the past few weeks. You've been together almost your entire lives. As friends. Now as something more."

Emma nodded, close to tears again. "I wanted him to notice me for so long, *Grossmammi*. Then he left and I thought I'd never see him again." She looked at her hands, her fingers trembling.

"But he came back. He fell in love with you."

"And I love him."

"You always have." *Grossmammi* smiled.

"I didn't do a *gut* job hiding it, did I?"

Her grandmother shook her head. "*Nee*. But it doesn't matter now. You're together. You're getting married. This is what you prayed for, *ya*?"

"*Ya*." She looked away. "And then he had to tell me about Ashley."

Grossmammi paused. She nodded in her wise, knowing way. "I see. But, Emma, surely you aren't letting his past direct your future together?"

"I thought I came to terms with everything. I thought I was finally happy. And then he had to ruin it."

"So this is his fault."

"*Ya*, it is!" Emma jumped up from the bed. She put her hand against her chest. "I didn't leave Middlefield. I didn't date a Yankee *bu*. I didn't—" She turned away, unable to bring herself to say out loud what Adam had done.

"Goodness." *Grossmammi* tapped her cane against the floor. "If only we could all be as *perfekt* as you."

Emma spun around. "That's not fair. You know I don't think that."

"I do. But you would judge the man you love as if you have no blemishes of your own. That, *lieb*, isn't fair."

She drew in a long breath. "So I'm supposed to forgive and forget what he's done."

"*Ya*, Emma." *Grossmammi* stood. "You know that as much as I do. You know it here." She tapped Emma's temple. "And here." She touched Emma's heart.

"That's supposed to make it easier?"

Grossmammi shook her head. "It often makes it harder. The

easy way is to hang on to the pain. Because it makes us feel better."

"*Ya.* I feel so wonderful right now."

"It makes us feel better because it lifts us above another. It protects us from further hurt." She moved closer to Emma. "And it drives a wedge between us and the people we love."

Emma thought about Adam's parents. How separate they'd been from each other. There was something unsettled between them. She didn't know what it was, but it made both of them miserable. Now she could see Adam was trying to avoid that in their relationship.

And she would hold his honesty against him.

"I have to see Adam." She headed for the door but stopped short and looked over her shoulder at *Grossmammi.*

"*Geh* on," her grandmother said. "I'll make a sandwich. I wasn't that hungry to begin with."

Emma smiled. Then she turned and went to her grandmother, wrapping her arms around *Grossmammi's* frail shoulders. "*Danki,*" she whispered in her ear.

Her grandmother stepped back. "*Geh* see your *yung mann, lieb.* He's waited long enough. You both have."

Sawyer paced the length of the bedroom at his grandparents' house. He'd gone into the first one at the top of the stairs, which happened to be Lukas's old room. As a teenager he'd spent the night here several times, when the family would get together for church, picnics, singings, and other gatherings. It had taken him a couple of years, but he eventually became a real part of this family.

Then here came Cora Easley. How could she, a stranger to him, expect him to just leave everything behind and follow her to New York? He knew nothing about her, other than he would bet his pickup truck that she was hiding something. Maybe a lot of things.

A knock sounded on the door. "Sawyer?"

Get it together, Sawyer. He'd acted like a child since Cora Easley showed up. Time to man up. He opened the door and looked at his father. "I'm sorry about all this, Dad. Don't worry, I'll be right down and back to work. There's so much we have to get done. We didn't need this interruption."

Lukas shook his head. "Don't worry about it. I closed the shop for the day."

"What?" His father never closed the shop, except for Sundays, holidays, and weddings.

"After what happened today, we can't *geh* back to work and pretend everything is normal. We need to settle some things, *ya?*"

Sawyer turned around and went to the bedroom window. He looked at the backyard, now cloaked in darkness. Memories poured over him, and he sank down on the bed. How many times had he played baseball and volleyball here at the Bylers' with his friends? Watched over his young nieces and nephews as they learned to walk and toddle around in the thick green grass?

"There's nothing to talk about," he said. Then, with a sudden desire to prove he belonged here, he added, *"Nix."*

"Sawyer."

He felt his father's strong hand on his shoulder. The strength of his touch broke something inside of Sawyer. "Why?" He swallowed, nearly choking on tears. "Why did they lie to me?"

"I don't know." Lukas squeezed Sawyer's shoulder. He let go. "But from everything you told me about your parents, they were *gut* people. I'm sure they had a sound reason for not telling you about Mrs. Easley."

"Is there really any reason for lying? For letting me think I didn't have any other family?" He gritted his teeth, then rolled up his shirtsleeve and pointed to the burn on his forearm. "I wouldn't have this if—" He covered his face. "I just don't understand."

The bed creaked as Lukas sat down. "You'll get your answers, *sohn*. Although you have to prepare yourself. They may not be what you want to hear."

"Then maybe I don't want to know." He looked at Lukas. "Things were perfectly fine here before she showed up."

"Were they?"

Sawyer blinked. "What does that mean?"

"You're comfortable here, that's true. But can you say you're content?"

"What's the difference?"

Lukas expelled a long breath. "The difference is that if you were content with our way of life, you would have made your decision about the church by now. But there is a part of you that is still pulled by the Yankee world."

Sawyer opened his mouth to speak, but his father continued.

"That's not a wrong thing for someone in your situation,

Sawyer. You spent more years in that world than in ours. There are Amish who have lived in this community all their lives and still question whether they belong here. Some decide they don't. Your mother and I were prepared for you to tell us that you didn't either."

"But what if I am?" He shot up from the bed. "What if I'm ready to join the Amish?"

Lukas looked at him intently. "Can you say that with honesty? With a clear heart and conscience?"

Sawyer sucked in a breath. He couldn't lie. Wouldn't be dishonest with the man who had saved him from living in foster care. "No. I can't."

"Then maybe this is God's way of helping you decide. What if you had joined the church and your grandmother had shown up?"

"She's not . . ." Sawyer sighed. "Your *mamm* is *mei grossmudder.*"

Lukas nodded. "All right. But that doesn't change the question. What if Mrs. Easley had shown up after you were baptized? You would be faced with an even more difficult choice."

"There's no choice. She can do whatever she wants. I'm staying here."

"You don't want to find out why your parents never told you about her?"

"No."

But it was a half-truth, and Sawyer knew it. Part of him wanted to understand the reason for his parents' deep secret. Yet a larger part wanted things to return to the way they were before Cora Easley entered their lives. But that would never happen.

Lukas rose. "We should *geh* home. Your *mamm* offered Mrs. Easley a place to stay tonight."

"In our house?"

"*Ya*. I know you're upset about this. We all are. But that doesn't mean we change who we are and how we behave. If she were anyone else, we'd offer the same hospitality."

Sawyer huffed. "All right." He thought about Anna at home. Alone with Cora. "We should leave now. I'll meet you downstairs." Then he remembered Laura. He couldn't leave her to walk alone in the cold darkness. "Laura—"

"I'll meet you at the *haus* after you take her home."

After Lukas left, Sawyer leaned against the door frame. What was he going to do now? He dreaded going home but didn't want Anna to be alone. Maybe if Cora saw how happy the three of them were, she'd get her fancy self on the next plane out of Cleveland and back to whatever high society she belonged to. That was her world. This one was his.

Somehow he had to convince her of that.

CHAPTER 16

Laura straightened up the paperwork on her desk in the office. Once Lukas had told her he was closing down the shop, she made sure everything was put away, not just in her workspace, but in the shop as well. She returned the tools to their places on the pegboards, closed the cans of paint and varnish and set them on their respective shelves, and took a broom to the floor. By the time she finished sweeping the sawdust and depositing it in the storage bin, it was already dark.

The days were getting shorter. Colder. And tonight she would have to walk home. She didn't expect Sawyer to drive her after what happened today.

She put on her coat, picked up her purse and took out the flashlight. Then she turned off the gas lamps and locked the workshop door. *Fraa* Byler had invited her to stay for supper, but Laura declined. Her husband, Joseph, had come home, and she knew they had a lot to talk about. She didn't want to impose.

As she walked out of the shop, her skin instantly chilled. She turned on the flashlight. At least she knew her way home this time. She just didn't realize how accustomed she was to getting a ride from Sawyer. Her fingers were cold and stiff, and her breath hung in the air like a puff of stretched cotton. Would she ever get used to the cold in Ohio?

Then the rain started again. It had been raining on and off all day, as if God were twisting a water spigot on a whim. She sank inside her coat, prepared for the cold, wet walk home.

Headlights shone behind her. She turned, shielding her eyes. The driver's side door opened. Sawyer poked his head above it. She could barely see him through the blinding light.

"Hop in," he called to her.

Laura walked toward the truck. The passenger door sprang open, and she slid in. "I thought you left."

"Not without taking you home."

"You don't have to." But the gesture touched her. Even in the midst of his turmoil, he hadn't forgotten about her.

She held her cold hands in front of the heating vents, thankful she didn't have to walk home. *"Danki."*

"Welcome." Sawyer's tone was sharp, yet she could tell it wasn't aimed at her. Questions whirled in her mind. How had the conversation gone with his English grandmother? How were Anna and Lukas holding up?

And when did she suddenly become so interested? When did she start to care?

She drew her hands back. She couldn't afford to care about Sawyer or his family.

But she did. All the effort she'd expended trying not to

become attached, and once again she'd let her heart overrule her mind.

Sawyer slowed down the truck. He pulled over to the side of the road, almost completely on the grass shoulder in front of a wide pasture, and put the truck in park. He flicked a switch and the hazard lights started blinking and clicking.

"Is something wrong?" Laura asked.

In the dimness of the dashboard lights he faced her. "Can I ask you a question?"

Laura nodded, too surprised to do anything else.

"What are you doing?" he asked.

"Right now I'm sitting in your truck—"

"In Middlefield. Why are you here and not back home with your family?"

She pushed back one of the ribbons of her *kapp*. "Why are you asking me this now?"

"Because I want to know. I *need* to know. You have a family. You're choosing to stay away from them." He gripped the steering wheel. "I never had that choice before. Not until now."

Laura wasn't quite sure what he meant. But it didn't matter why he asked the question. She had vowed never to tell anyone.

Yet the desperation in his voice, in his eyes . . . She couldn't refuse him.

"I can't *geh* home. Not until I can make things right with my parents."

"How can you do that living here?"

"By making money. That's why I needed the job. I owe them a lot of money."

Sawyer kept silent. Maybe that answer satisfied him. But it wasn't the complete truth. And for some reason she felt she owed him that.

"I fell in love with Mark King." The words flew out of her mouth, and she couldn't have retrieved them even if she wanted to. "Almost at first sight." Her stomach twisted into a knot at the words.

"So you and Mark were together."

There was something strange about his tone. A mix of surprise and . . . jealousy? No, that couldn't be. He had nothing to be jealous of. Of course it was so like her to read into something that wasn't there. She had done so with Mark. "Falling for him was the dumbest thing I'd ever done. All he wanted was my money.

"I had been working since I was fourteen in our family business. *Mei* parents ran a bakery and delivery service. A very successful one. I had saved quite a bit of money for when I would get married." She looked down in her lap. "I thought Mark would be *mei* husband. You see how that turned out."

"What did he do?" Sawyer's voice was low. Almost menacing.

"I gave him *mei* money. I did it willingly. He was going to be *mei mann*. But he started asking questions. About the business, the way *mei* parents ran it. How they took care of the money. I thought it was because he wanted to learn about the bakery. He had already started working part-time, going on deliveries with *mei daed*.

"*Mei daed* didn't trust banks. For years *mei mudder* tried to convince him they were safe and necessary. But *mei daed* wouldn't listen. *Mei grossvadder* was the same way; never used a bank in his life. *Daed* kept all the savings in a box buried behind the barn. Just like his *daed* before him."

"And you told Mark where to find it?"

She shook her head. "He found it himself, after he figured out the money was somewhere on the property. He took everything—their whole life's savings. Not long after that he disappeared. I thought he had changed his mind about the wedding." She closed her eyes against the humiliation of that day, when she discovered he had left Etheridge without a word to her. "A few days later, *Daed* discovered the missing money. By that time Mark was long gone."

"And you followed him here."

She couldn't see Sawyer's expression very well in the dark cab. But she could imagine how foolish he thought she was. She'd thought that enough about herself.

"Laura. You know it's not your fault he's a thief."

"It's *mei* fault for bringing him into our lives! He stole every penny from them. Almost thirty years of savings, gone. I had to do something."

"And you thought if you found him, that would help?"

"*Ya*. I'd hoped to talk him into returning the money. If that didn't work, I was going to report him to the police. I know that's not what we're supposed to do. We're supposed to pretend *nix* happened."

"But you couldn't."

"*Nee!*" She took a deep breath. Raindrops splattered

against the windshield, first just a couple, then a steady stream. "I couldn't ignore what Mark did. *Mei* parents refused to seek any justice. But they were devastated. They kept saying, 'This is God's will.' What they really meant was it was my fault."

"Laura." Sawyer let go of the steering wheel and moved closer to her.

"You know the rest." Involuntarily, her hand went to her face. Heat suffused her cheeks underneath the raised ridges. She closed her eyes. Scarred for life, both inside and out.

Sawyer took her hand. "You didn't deserve that."

The sound of rain pounding against the truck echoed in her ears. She opened her eyes and looked at him. "Maybe I did."

"Laura, I'm sure your parents want you to come home. Do you really think you'll be able to replace what Mark took? We don't pay you that much. It will take you months. Probably years."

"I have to try." She looked away. "I can't face them until I do." She glanced down at her hand in Sawyer's. A tingle passed through her, a little shock. She pulled away. "I should get home."

He nodded. "Me too." He leaned back, not putting the truck in gear right away. He let out a long sigh before reaching for the gearshift.

When they reached her driveway, he turned and stopped the truck close to the house. She opened the door and started to get out. Then she stopped and closed it, keeping the rain at bay for another moment. "Sawyer, please don't tell anyone what I said. No one knows. Not even *mei mudder* and *daed*. I didn't tell them why I left."

"I promise I won't say anything. Thank you for trusting me. I know it wasn't easy."

She nodded. "I'll have my own way to work tomorrow."

"No, I'll pick you up."

"Sawyer, I'll walk. You need to work things out with your *familye*."

"Nothing's changed. We both have to work tomorrow."

"Your grandmother's here."

His eyes narrowed. "Like I said, nothing's changed. I'll see you in the morning."

Laura climbed out of the truck. As usual, he waited until she got inside. She peered out the window as he drove away. *Nothing has changed.*

She'd just told him about Mark. Not everything she planned to do, but more than she'd ever thought she'd tell another soul.

Oh, Sawyer. Can't you see? Everything has changed.

Emma gripped her umbrella as she trudged through the rain to Adam's house. The umbrella shielded most of her body, but the bottom of her dress was soaked. She didn't care about her dripping hem or the cold, wet wind whipping at her. Her only thought was Adam.

Grossmammi was right. She'd kept them both waiting too long.

She knocked on the door, folded the umbrella, and leaned it against the side of the house. The Ottos' small front porch roof sheltered her from the downpour. But it didn't shield her from the chill seeping through to her skin.

The door opened. Adam's eyes widened. "Emma."

She didn't say anything for a moment. Their gazes met, and the chill disappeared. She loved him so much; she could forgive him anything. Now she had to be honest with him, and herself.

"You're shaking. Come inside." He opened the door wider.

But she didn't move forward. She hugged her arms around her body. She didn't want to risk his parents being there. What she had to say was for Adam's ears only. "Can I talk to you privately?"

"The living room. *Mamm* and *Daed* are both upstairs."

She shook her head. "We need to be alone."

His brow lifted. He shut the door. "The barn?"

Emma nodded. She reached for her umbrella, but he grabbed it before she could. He opened it and put his arm around her shoulders. They rushed to the barn. Despite the cover, they were almost soaked through.

"Just a minute." He went to the wall where a lantern hung on a peg. Next to it was a matchbox holder nailed to the wall. The moment he lit the lantern, the barn glowed with a dim amber light.

She tried not to shiver, but she couldn't help it. Behind her she could hear the horses stirring. The barn was warmer than the front porch, but not by much.

"Emma, you're freezing." He went to her, rubbed his hands up and down her arms. A droplet of water ran down the side of his face. "We should have gone inside the house."

His touch warmed her just as much as his nearness. For the past few weeks they had come so far in their relationship. She felt secure with him. Cherished. Then he had told her about Ashley, and everything changed again. She was tired of it. And only after speaking with her grandmother did Emma accept her own blame.

She put her hands over his and removed them from her arms.

He closed his eyes, his lips pressing inward. When he opened them, she could see his pain.

"I'm sorry," she said.

The pain changed to confusion. "You're sorry? I'm the one who messed up."

"You made a mistake."

"*Ya,* "he said. "A big one."

"And I shouldn't have made you feel worse because of it."

Adam moved closer to Emma. Already she felt the tension draining from her body.

"You didn't make it worse for me. I did that myself. I just hope you understand how much I regret being with her. But it's not only that."

Emma steeled herself. "What do you mean?"

"I was unfair to Ashley too. I did care for her at one time." He looked down at the strands of hay strewn on the barn floor. "I took advantage of her, and I shouldn't have." Adam looked at Emma again. "I won't have the opportunity to tell her I'm sorry. But I can make it up to you."

"You don't have to. That relationship is in the past. Let it stay there."

"The wedding—" A flash of uncertainty crossed his face. "Is it still on?"

She wiped a raindrop off his forehead and brought her lips to his. "It never was off," she said.

She stepped into his embrace and leaned her ear against his chest, feeling his heartbeat race. She felt him kiss her temple, just below the edge of her *kapp*.

When they drew apart, Emma's smile dimmed. There was only one thing that stood in the way of their happiness. "Your parents."

"What about them?"

"Do you think they'll come to accept our marriage?"

Adam rubbed his thumb against her cheek. "They don't have a choice. Whatever is going on between them, we can't let it affect our life together." He traced the edge of her jaw before letting his hand fall to his side.

Emma nodded. She trembled again. Adam grinned. She could see he was willing to draw her back into his arms.

She was eager to accept him. Too eager. "Adam . . ."

"I know. You have to *geh* home." He sighed and stepped back. "Soon enough it will be our home. I hope."

"What do you mean?"

"With everything going on, we haven't talked about where we're going to live after we're married." He put his hands in his pockets. "I thought I would move in with you and Leona, if that's all right with you. I could still work with *mei daed*, and take care of you and your *grossmammi*."

"The *haus* would stay in the *familye*."

"That's the idea."

"She'd like that." Emma smiled.

"And you?"

"I like it too."

"I was hoping you'd agree. Makes everything easier. I'll be close to work, the *kinner* will be near their grandparents." His honey-colored eyes twinkled. "It's what I get for marrying the *maedel* next door."

Giddiness made her move toward him. She caught herself. If she stayed here much longer . . .

"I need to get back home."

Adam drew her into his arms one more time. She didn't resist.

"I can't wait until you're *mei fraa*," he said.

"It won't be long."

"It will be long enough."

CHAPTER 17

Sawyer pulled his truck into his driveway, parked, and turned the engine off. He leaned his head against the steering wheel. It was hard to absorb everything he'd just learned—not only about Cora Easely, but about Laura.

She and Mark were involved. He felt a pinch of jealousy at that. And more than a pinch of anger. The man's cruelty knew no bounds. He'd not only used her, but stolen from her and permanently scarred her.

Sawyer understood her anger, her desire for justice. But couldn't she see how impossible it would be to pay her parents back? He was certain they'd rather have Laura there with them than the money.

Yet he had seen her determination. Nothing he said would change her mind. And he wasn't exactly thinking straight himself right now.

He sat up and looked toward the house, the outline dim in the dark, pelted by a few lingering droplets of rain. He didn't want to go inside and face Cora. Then again, he couldn't leave his parents to deal with her.

He exhaled and opened the door. The sudden rainstorm had stopped, leaving a damp chill hanging in the air. He stood at the back door, which led to the kitchen. Paused before turning the knob. Then did something he hadn't done in a long time, except superficially, when it was expected.

He prayed.

God, help me. I don't know what to do. Please . . .

He couldn't finish the prayer. He didn't know what to ask. Didn't know what to do. Didn't know anything.

Sawyer removed his muddy shoes in the small room just off the kitchen, hung his jacket and hat on the peg rack. Every movement was in slow motion, putting off the inevitable. But he was done running away from this.

He expected to smell the delicious aroma of whatever supper Anna had prepared, but as he entered the kitchen he didn't detect anything. He frowned, there saw Anna sitting at the table. *"Mamm?"*

Anna looked up. She stood. "Sawyer. I'm glad you're home." Her smile trembled. "Can I fix you something to eat? You must be starving."

"I'm not hungry." He went to her.

She looked down at the empty kitchen table. "No one else was either."

"Where's *Daed?*"

"In the barn. He's taking care of the animals. But he's been out there awhile."

Sawyer nodded. His father was probably praying. The perfect example of a godly man. Sawyer had always known that, but it wasn't until tonight that he appreciated it. Perhaps his father's prayers would reach God's ears. He certainly didn't expect his own pathetic attempt to make any difference.

"Cora? Is she still here? Or did she hightail it back to Cleveland, since Middlefield is so beneath her?"

"She's still here. She said she had a headache and went upstairs. I haven't seen her since." Anna sat down. She gestured to the chair beside her.

Sawyer sat. He'd never seen his mother so red-eyed. Or so tired. He touched her hand. "It will be okay."

"That's what Lukas says." She gripped Sawyer's hand. "I wish I had his faith."

Sawyer wished he did too. "*Mamm*, it doesn't matter what that woman says. I'm not leaving you or *Daed*. I'll always be here in Middlefield. I'll always be a part of the family."

She ran her fingertips along the smooth surface of the kitchen table. He remembered when Lukas had made it for her. Big enough to seat ten adults, plus a couple of smaller chairs for kids. A table built of love and hope.

But it was only the three of them in this large house. "You say that now—"

"Because I mean it," he said.

"Sawyer. We both know it's not as simple as that." She released his hand. "No matter what you decide, you will always be welcome here. This is your home."

He nodded, ignoring the growing lump in his throat.

"But you do have a decision to make," Anna continued. "More than one. You need to figure out what you want to do with your life, with the church. With your relationship with God."

He rubbed his chin. "I know. *Daed* said the same thing. He thinks maybe Cora showing up is God's way of pushing me along."

"He might be right." She gave him a half-hearted smile. "I pray for you. Every day. But especially harder this past year. You can't have one foot in each world. Not for much longer."

"I know." Sawyer let his hand drop on the table. The slamming sound was louder than he intended. "Sorry."

"It's okay." Anna threaded her fingers together. "I understand."

But she really didn't. They both had to know that. She'd never been in his position. No one had. "Once Cora leaves I'll give it some more thought."

"Not just thought." She took his hand. "This isn't just about deciding to live in the Yankee world or ours. It's a decision about God. You can't make a choice without knowing what His will is for you."

He swallowed. "How am I supposed to figure that out?"

"Prayer." She squeezed his hand. "Lots of prayer. For wisdom in discovering what He plans for you."

Prayer. He should have known she'd say that. It seemed to be the Amish answer for everything. But he rarely felt God's presence, much less thought God really listened to the pitiful attempts he made at prayer. Still, Sawyer nodded, desperate to give his mother some comfort.

His mother ran her hand over the smooth wood table and

continued. "Once we accept that God is in control of our lives, then we can work on understanding His will."

"So you're saying it's God's will that my parents' lied to me?" Sawyer fought to keep the edge out of his voice.

She paused. "I don't believe that God is ever the author of sin or deception," she said. "But God uses many ways to reach us. Even other people's bad choices." Her gaze met Sawyer's. "Often we don't understand why something happens. But you can't pick and choose. You have to accept what happens and trust in God's mercy and love. It's not easy to do." She gripped her fingers together. "I'm struggling with it right now."

Sawyer leaned back in his chair. As little as a few days ago he would have dismissed his mother's words as more Amish rhetoric. But he sensed the wisdom in what she was saying. And she was right—he didn't like it.

But was that a reason not to believe? Not to trust the Lord?

"Are you sure you don't want a sandwich?" Anna stood. "That's what your *daed* had for supper."

"Maybe later. And I'll fix it." He rose and went to his mother. Kissed her cheek. "You look exhausted."

"I am."

"Go on to bed."

"But what if Cora comes downstairs? She'll want something to eat—"

"And she won't be happy with anything you give her."

Anna nodded. "True. She seemed less than thrilled with the bedroom upstairs. Said something about her bathroom being bigger than the whole room."

Sawyer rolled his eyes. He couldn't wait for this woman to leave his parents alone . . . and to get out of his life.

The next morning Leona made her way slowly up the gravel and dirt driveway to the Ottos' house. She hadn't been over here in a long time. Distance had grown between her and the Ottos.

She knew why, but hadn't felt it was her place to get involved. Norman and Carol were both hurting. When Emma and Adam's attempts to help them failed, Leona couldn't stand by and do nothing. Norman and Carol didn't seem to be able to find their way out of the abyss alone.

She bypassed the house and kept walking through the backyard to the pasture. Her hip started to ache. Cold weather always intensified the arthritis, and the air was thick with the dampness of last night's rain. She ignored the aches, like she ignored every other pain shooting through her body. Over the years she faced a choice—accept the pain and deal with it, or let it take over her life. The only One she would allow control of her life was the Lord. Everyone and everything else, including the vestiges of old age, were kept captive by Him.

She saw Norman standing by the white fence, watching his cattle graze on the last of the grass in the pasture. She had expected to find him here. He was never far from his herd, from the land. He was a good farmer. A good deacon. A good man who somehow lost his way.

He turned before she arrived, as if he knew she was coming. He faced her, leaning back against the fence. Crossed his arms over his chest. "Leona."

"Norman." She stood beside him, gripping her cane in one hand and the wood fence with the other. "Fine herd you've got this year."

"*Ya*. Will bring a *gut* price at the market."

"I'm sure they will. Where do you sell them?"

"Bloomfield, usually. They'll be ready in the spring." He turned and looked at her. "You're not here to talk about my cows."

"*Nee*. I'm not."

Norman sighed. "You know, don't you?"

Leona nodded. "Mary told me just before she died."

His face turned gray. "What . . ." He swallowed. "What did she say?"

"Does it matter?"

"I guess not." He glanced at Leona, peering at her from beneath the brim of his straw hat. His beard lifted slightly in the chill breeze. "Whatever she said, it was enough."

"Emma's worried you'll never accept her as a daughter-in-law."

Norman shook his head. "That's not true, Leona."

"Then why can't you be happy for Adam and Emma?" Leona shifted her weight to her cane. "Is it because you're unhappy in your own marriage?"

He sucked in a breath. "*Mei* marriage is fine."

"We all know it isn't. Including your *sohn* and *mei grossdochter*."

Norman turned and faced the field again. She saw how much he and Adam resembled each other. Same sandy-brown hair, although Norman's was threaded with gray. Hazel eyes that could be both kind and piercing, depending on the man's mood. A long, angular face.

But father and son were not only similar in looks. They both had the same stubbornness and pride. Yet while Adam was making steps to release those sins to the Lord, Norman continued to cling to them like a lifeline. Why couldn't he see that hanging on only made him sink further down?

"You're overstepping your bounds, Leona."

"I am. But you've never known that to stop me before." She touched his arm. "When will you make this right?"

He swallowed hard. "I don't know if I can."

"You're the only one who can, Norman. It's up to you to make your *familye* whole again. Isn't that what you want, now that Adam's returned?"

"Of course it is." He closed his eyes. "Mary said she'd never speak about what happened between us. Not with anyone."

"She was dying of cancer. She was in extreme pain near the end. But that wasn't the only way she suffered."

Leona winced at the memory. Her *sohn's* death had been quick. Mary's had dragged on. "The doctors gave her medicine for the pain. Most of the time she didn't make sense. But there were moments of clarity. She needed reassurance that she had been forgiven."

He gripped the fence rail. Stared down at the ground. "Weak. I was weak, Leona. After James died—" He lifted his head. "I knew she was lonely. Trouble was, so was I. Doesn't make it right, though."

"That's why we need mercy."

"I don't deserve it."

Leona shook her head. "None of us do, Norman. If we deserved it, it wouldn't be mercy. You know this as well as I do. You're a deacon—"

"And I should have known better!" He wiped the back of his hand across his mouth. "I let everyone down. God, *mei fraa* . . ." His voice shattered on the last word.

"Then make it right. Talk to Carol. Tell her what happened."

He looked at Leona. His eyes were red. Shiny. "What if she doesn't forgive me? How can I live with that?"

"How can you live with this secret?"

Norman shook his head. "You know, I told Adam the same thing. I can't seem to take *mei* own advice." His shoulders hunched, as if a heavy weight had slammed upon them.

Compassion filled Leona's heart. She could see why Norman couldn't move on, why he couldn't take responsibility for his actions and the state of his marriage. It wasn't easy. It might, in fact, be the hardest thing he'd ever done. But until he did it, he would continue to be at odds with his wife, his son, and soon, Emma.

"Norman, stop giving your guilt the upper hand. When are you going to accept God's forgiveness?"

Tears welled up in his eyes. "How can He forgive me for what I've done?"

"When did you become the authority on who and what and

when God will forgive? You know the scriptures. God grants mercy to those who repent. Who truly repent with their heart and soul. But if you don't accept it, how can He give it?"

He choked on a sob and turned to Leona. "I don't know. All I know is I love my wife."

She gripped his hand. "Then *geh* to her. Show her. Fix what's broken between you. Let God mend both your hearts."

CHAPTER 18

Cora squinted against the sunlight streaming through the window. Just as quickly the sun disappeared behind the clouds, casting the room in gray light. She reached for the lamp on the end table. She didn't find one.

Then she remembered where she was. *In the nineteenth century*.

She sat up, fully expecting the headache that plagued her last night to return. Instead, she actually felt refreshed. The single bed she slept in didn't look like much, but the mattress was soft, the way she liked it. The sheets and blankets smelled fresh and clean. She hadn't slept that well in a long time. She'd even forgotten to take her Valium.

But the refreshed feeling disappeared as she became fully awake. She picked up her phone and checked her voice mail. Nothing. She thought about calling Kenneth and asking him to be on the next flight here. Maybe with legal muscle behind her, Sawyer wouldn't be so stubborn.

She set the phone down. Sawyer wouldn't be impressed with

her high-priced attorney. Nor would threats make him change his mind. She'd have to find another way to convince him to leave. She could see that he was attached to this place. If she didn't pry him free of the strange grip these people had over him, she'd never be able to direct him to reach his full potential. And that certainly wasn't painting crude rocking horses for a living.

Cora slipped on a light pink cashmere sweater and slim gray wool pants. For a moment she considered a bath, but she'd catch her death of cold. Was there any heat in this house? No lights, no heat. How did these people live under such barbaric conditions? This life definitely wasn't suitable for her grandson.

She freshened up in the upstairs bathroom—at least she found a battery-operated lamp on the counter—and went downstairs. Oddly, her heartbeat quickened as she headed toward the kitchen. She had missed her chance to talk to Sawyer last night. Maybe she could see him this morning.

When she entered the kitchen, she found it empty. An ancient, battered coffeepot sat on the stove. She walked over to it and touched the side. It was still hot.

She hadn't seen a stovetop percolator in years. It took her back to her mother's kitchen, and the heavy scent of the dark roast coffee her mother liked. Black. Unlike the hazelnut coffee Cora preferred.

Not that she made her own coffee at home. That was Manuela's job.

But the Bylers didn't have a maid. Given the primitive conditions they lived in, she was surprised they had running water.

A white coffee mug sat by the stove. Next to it was a small

bowl with sugar, a tiny white pitcher that presumably held milk or cream, and two huge cinnamon rolls on a plate covered with cellophane. She ignored the cinnamon rolls. She preferred wheat toast, no butter.

She poured herself a cup of coffee, liberally adding the sugar and milk, and sat down at the table. She laced her cold fingers around the mug and let the warmth seep into her skin.

While she sipped at the coffee, Cora looked around the kitchen. No décor to speak of. Nothing to critique or pique her interest. An utterly boring room.

"I see you finally decided to wake up."

Cora jerked to attention and looked up at Sawyer. He stood in the doorway, leaning against the jamb. His eyes pierced her with accusation. Didn't he understand that she was as much a victim in this as he was?

"I don't appreciate your tone, young man." She set the coffee cup on the table. The clattering sound echoed in the bare kitchen. She smoothed the side of her hair with her hand. "But I'm glad you're here. I thought I might have missed you."

"I thought you might have gone home."

She lifted her chin. Impertinent young man. Again, a reminder of his father. *And Kerry.* "We have unfinished business."

"It's finished, as far as I'm concerned." He remained still, arms crossed over his body his black brows straight. Yet for all his calmness, she saw he was on edge. The muscles in his cheek twitched. He blinked a little too rapidly. He was unnerved.

A chink in the armor. She could take advantage of that.

"If you're still questioning the validity of my claim, I can show you the legal documents. They will give you all the proof you need about my daughter, Kerry Easley."

"Kerry Thompson." Sawyer moved from the doorway. He went to the table and placed his palms on it. Leaned toward her. "My mother's name was Kerry Thompson."

Cora leaned back, fighting the sudden lump in her throat. The verb struck her like a physical blow: *was.*

His mother. Her daughter. Dead. Gone. Past tense. Kerry had been absent from Cora's life for so long. But Cora had never once considered she might not be alive. Even getting the news from the detective hadn't hit her as hard as her grandson hovering over her, his eyes cold as he drove the spike of truth into her heart.

Sawyer stepped away from Cora. His anger cooled as he saw the grief that suddenly raked across her face. She looked away, clutching the coffee cup.

"When did you find out about my mother?" Sawyer asked.

Cora didn't look at him. "The same day I found out about you." Her hands trembled as she brought the coffee cup to her lips.

"When was that?"

She looked at him. "Three days ago."

Sawyer tensed. He'd had years to accept the reality of his parents' death. She'd had three days. And as soon as she found out, she had come to find him.

Despite himself, he said, "I'm sorry."

"Thank you." She set the coffee cup on the table. "Why aren't you at work?"

"After I dropped Laura off at the workshop, I took the morning off."

"Laura?"

"She's the office clerk at the shop."

Cora paused. "The one with . . ."

"The scars?" Sawyer shoved his hands in his pockets. "That's her."

"Is she your girlfriend, then?"

Sawyer frowned. "You look horrified at the thought."

"No, no, that's not what I meant." But the guilt in her eyes said something completely different.

"She's a friend. Not that it's any of your business."

"It is. I want to get to know my grandson." Cora looked up at him. "You look a lot like your father."

"I take that as a compliment."

"It wasn't meant as one." She quickly added, "I also see Kerry in you. That *is* a compliment." Cora stared at the inside of her coffee cup. "What was she like?"

"Who?"

"Kerry." She looked at Sawyer. "Your mother."

"You didn't know?" He pulled out a chair and sat down.

"I knew her as a child. A young adult. Not as a wife. Or a mother." Cora sighed. "Please, Sawyer. Come to New York with me."

She touched the pearl necklace strung around her thin neck. No doubt it was real and cost a fortune. The woman reeked of money. "This place may have been your home. But I'm taking you back where you belong."

Where you belong. Wasn't that what he'd been yearning to discover—his place in the world? For a long time he had felt torn. Did he belong with the Amish or the Yankees? And now he had this stranger who claimed to be his grandmother telling him he belonged in New York.

"You've wasted a trip." He said the words with as much conviction as he could muster, but even as he uttered them, he felt a tiny fraction of his resolve melt.

"You might change your mind."

"Not a chance."

She sat up straight and looked him directly in the eye. He saw the change in her, from grieving grandmother to calculated businesswoman. "You haven't heard what I have to offer."

"We're losing him." Anna stepped away from the kitchen doorway and looked at Lukas.

"*Nee.*" Lukas put his arms around Anna. She leaned against him, her chin resting on his shoulder. Sawyer wasn't the only one who took the morning off. The shop was in good hands with Tobias and Laura. She was glad her husband was able to put his work aside to tend to his family. It was one more reason she loved him.

And because she loved him, she also knew him. "You're worried too."

He sighed. Held her tighter. "I'm trying not to. We have to trust that Sawyer will make the right decision. I believe God will guide him."

"I thought he might Yank over eventually." Anna pulled away from Lukas and stared at his face. "I was never sure if he would join the church. But if he had, at least he would live here. He could still work with you. We'd see him all the time. But if he goes to New York . . ." She pressed her fingertips against her lips. "We may never see him again."

Lukas cupped her face with his hand. "Anna, don't fret about something that hasn't happened yet."

"But he's our only *kinn*." A tear slipped down her cheek, followed by several more. "You always wanted a house full of *kinner*. I couldn't give that to you. I'd hoped—I'd prayed—that at least we would have *grosskinner*."

"And we still might. But if we don't, then that's God's will." Lukas wiped her tears away with his thumb. "*Lieb*, that woman in there, she's Sawyer's *familye*. She has a *grosskinn* she's never known."

"Then she should understand how we feel." Anna tore away from Lukas's embrace and went back to the doorway. Cora and Sawyer had lowered their voices. She couldn't hear what they were talking about.

Lukas's hands covered her shoulders. She leaned against him. He was hurting too. But as she'd done in the past, she put herself first. After years of marriage, she should have learned by now. "I'm sorry."

"I understand." He pressed a kiss to her temple. "I don't

want to lose him either. But we have to pray that Sawyer allows God to lead him. And we have to support whatever decision he makes."

She nodded. Lukas was right, of course. They had to abide by God's will. And Sawyer's decision.

Yet if he chose to go with Cora, how could she say goodbye to her only son?

CHAPTER 19

"I don't want your money."

Sawyer stood up to leave. This was one cold-blooded woman. She could go from compassionate to icy before he had a chance to blink. Even the way she sat made the simple hand-crafted chair at the kitchen table seem like a throne.

He tried to reconcile the regal woman in front of him with his down-to-earth mother. He couldn't remember his mother ever dressing fancy or wearing a lot of jewelry. She was simple and plain, at least by Yankee standards. But not Cora. There was nothing plain or simple about this woman.

She twisted a huge emerald ring around her thin middle finger. Blue veins showed beneath her smooth, nearly transparent skin. "This isn't just about money, Sawyer." She wrinkled her nose a bit. "Why on earth your mother chose that name—"

"There is nothing wrong with my name. You've been here less than a full day and you've criticized everything." He crossed his arms over his chest. "I can see why my mother ran away."

"I wasn't the reason your mother ran." Her gaze flicked away.

She was lying. But he wouldn't call her on it. He just wanted her to leave. "Like I said, you wasted your time coming here. I don't want to go to New York."

"You've never been there."

"And I don't plan on going." He unfolded his arms. "You can't offer me anything that would change my mind. I have a good life here."

"I can see that." She sniffed. "Of course it makes perfect sense that you would choose poverty and hardship over comfort and security."

"Sarcasm doesn't flatter you."

The left side of her mouth lifted up in a half smile, half smirk. "You have a lot of your mother in you. Especially the stubbornness."

Her smart phone interrupted her train of thought. She tapped the screen. "Kenneth. No, now isn't a good time. Yes, everything is under control. I will keep you posted." She clicked off without saying good-bye.

"Who's Kenneth?"

"Kenneth Hamilton. My attorney."

"What did he want?"

Cora leaned back in the chair. "So you *are* curious."

Sawyer paused. "Who wouldn't be?" He grimaced. "You're doing this on purpose. Dangling little hints here and there like a carrot in front of a horse."

To his surprise, she smiled. "You're very intelligent. A quality you inherited from my side of the family, I might add."

"Your legacy is important to you, isn't it?"

She gave him a pointed gaze. "Yes. And it should be important to you too." She gestured to the chair beside her. "I wish you'd sit down. I'm getting a cramp in my neck having to look up at you."

He hesitated, then sat at the opposite end of the table. "Satisfied?"

She folded her hands together. The stones in her rings glinted in the sunlight streaming through the kitchen window. "Sawyer, you're accusing me of playing a game and not being honest with you. Here is some truth for you—you are the heir to a very large fortune, and first in line to run a multinational corporation. Your intelligence, your instincts for people . . . I'm more convinced than ever that this is your destiny."

Sawyer didn't say anything as he let her words sink in. Finally, he spoke. "Was my mother your initial heir?"

Cora nodded. "She was."

"What about my father? What was his role in your plans for world domination?"

She looked away, but not before he saw the sharpness in her eyes. When she faced him again, it was still there. "Easley Industries is a *family* company."

"Yet my mother didn't want anything to do with it."

"She had other . . . interests."

Sawyer pushed away from the table. "So do I. I don't care about your company or your inheritance. I'm sure there are lots of more qualified people who can take over your business interests."

The full force of her gaze bored into him. "Don't be foolish, Sawyer."

"I'm not foolish." He laid his hands flat on the table, resisting the urge to clench them. "I just don't want the same things you do. I don't know how I can say that any clearer."

Cora pressed her lips together. When she finally spoke, her voice was tight. "If that's how you feel."

Sawyer blinked. She was giving up that easily?

"That's how I feel."

She stood. Lifted her chin in that imperious way of hers. "Then there's nothing more for us to say."

He stared at her. "I guess not."

Cora picked up her phone. "I will call a taxi at once to take me to the airport." She walked out of the kitchen.

Now he was confused. And, unbelievably, a little guilty. All this trouble, all this cajoling and upsetting his parents, and she was calling it quits? It didn't make any sense.

He'd wanted her gone. Now he was getting his wish. The tension should be draining out of him, not increasing.

Anna and Lukas appeared.

"Where is she going?"

Sawyer turned and looked at Anna. He could see the strain in her eyes. "Home. Back to New York."

"Are . . . are you going with her?"

He shook his head. "No. I'm not. I doubt we'll see her again."

"But she's your *grossmudder*."

He shoved his hands in his pockets. Pain radiated through

him. He brushed his hand against his forearm and felt the familiar cigarette scar beneath the fabric of his shirt. If she had all this money, all this power, why didn't she find him earlier? Why did he have to endure that foster home?

Why did she suddenly care?

She wanted an heir, that's why. Nothing more.

Without a word of explanation to either Anna or Lukas, he stalked out of the house, slamming the door behind him. He revved the truck and peeled out of the driveway, his thoughts a blur.

Before Sawyer knew it, he had zipped right past the workshop. He muttered an oath as he turned around in the neighbor's drive. There was no place else to go; he might as well go to work, even though he had the morning off. Throwing himself into his job might get Cora and her will out of his mind.

Yeah. Right.

But when he stopped at the rear of the driveway behind the workshop and threw the gear stick into park, he couldn't make himself go inside. He left the engine running and sat there with his head in his hands.

He was fourteen years old again, confused, hurt, and lost.

Laura heard the sound of a car pulling into the driveway. She waited for the customer to come inside. When no one came, she left the office and walked outside. She heard the hum of a familiar engine.

Sawyer was here. But why was he sitting in his truck in the driveway?

She rounded the workshop and saw the truck idling. As she neared, she could see him resting his head on his hands. She twisted one of the strings on her *kapp*. Slowly she approached the driver's side. Knocked gently on the window.

Sawyer's head shot up. He turned to her, glaring. She stepped back. She'd never seen him lose his temper before.

His shoulders slumped as he turned off the motor. He opened the door and jumped out. "I'm sorry."

"You're sorry? I'm the one who startled you."

"Yeah, but . . ." He leaned against the truck. The chilly wind picked up, ruffling his thick black hair. It brushed against the collar of his shirt. She realized she hadn't put on her jacket. Her thin, dark blue sweater did little to protect her against the cold.

"It's cold out here." He stepped toward her. "Let's go inside."

She nodded and they headed for the shop. He didn't try to make conversation with her, which heightened her alarm. Normally she couldn't get him to stop talking.

When they entered the shop, he walked past her, leaned his hands on one of the work tables, and ducked his head. Since the day she met Sawyer Thompson, Laura had wanted nothing but for him to leave her alone. To stop prying, to stop acting like he understood her. To let her be. Now that he was doing just that, she couldn't stand it. She could see he was suffering. And despite knowing she shouldn't, she went to him. "Are you okay?"

He lifted up his head. Stared at the sawdust on the table. "*Nee*. I'm not."

She rarely heard him speak *Dietsch*. On instinct she reached out to touch him. Then she drew back. She had no right to be this close to him. But when she started to move away, he turned and faced her.

"Don't."

"Don't what?"

"Don't go off and hide in the office." He looked down at her. "Stay here. With me." His voice shook. "I need you."

"Sawyer, I . . ."

He shook his head and ran his hands over his face. "I don't know why I said that. Never mind. Forget I said anything."

But she couldn't forget it. "Sawyer, talk to me. What happened?"

"It doesn't matter."

"*Ya*, it does." She took a breath and said the one true thing on her mind. "It matters to me."

The more he told Laura about his conversation with Cora, the more Sawyer felt like a fool. Like a fourteen-year-old fool. He should be over this. His grandmother's appearance shouldn't affect him, not this intensely. "I must sound stupid."

"*Nee*. You don't."

"It's just that she had her chance, you know? When my parents died. Before they died." He sat on one of the wooden stools by the work table. "Why show up now?"

"You said she just found you. Maybe that's the reason."

"The woman has more money than Fort Knox."

"Fort what?"

"Never mind. She's rich. *Very* rich." He looked at Laura. While he still felt dumb, he also felt relief at being able to talk about this. She was the only person who could be objective. "She could have found me if she really wanted to."

Mark entered her thoughts. "Not everyone is easy to find."

"Except when you have endless resources." His thick eyebrows knotted. "Whatever. I don't care. She and her stinky perfume and fancy jewelry can hop on the next plane to New York. Or private jet." He let out a bitter chuckle. "Can't imagine her flying coach."

Laura frowned. "Sawyer, sometimes I don't understand you."

He lifted his gaze. "You understand me better than you think."

His typical confidence returned in that one statement, and the tone of his voice sent a flow of warmth through her. He continued to look at her, the chestnut color of his eyes turning a darker brown. Her breath caught. Mark had never looked at her like that.

"Laura." He leaned forward. Her pulse quickened as he brushed his finger against the top of her cheek, touching one of her scars.

She drew back. "What are you doing?"

"You had some sawdust there." His eyes widened and he jumped off the stool. "I'm so sorry. I don't know what's wrong with me."

Laura placed her hand where his finger had touched. Felt

the raised bump. She shut her eyes. How could he bear to look at her, much less touch the ugly scars on her face?

"I—I've got to go."

She opened her eyes to see him rushing out of the work shop. "Sawyer!"

He didn't come back.

Laura started after him, but her way was blocked by Tobias coming in the doorway. She heard Sawyer's truck start up. "Where is Sawyer going?"

Tobias shrugged. "I don't know. He brushed right past me. Didn't say a word. I'm surprised he's even here." He looked at Laura. "Did something happen while I was gone?"

Laura paused. Tobias was part of Sawyer's family. She probably ought to tell him what happened. He'd find out anyway. But instead, she felt compelled to go after Sawyer. "Can I take my lunch break early?"

"Sure. Looks like we're not gonna be busy today."

"Danki." She ran out of the workshop and onto the driveway, and turned just in time to see Sawyer's truck barreling toward her.

CHAPTER 20

Sawyer slammed on the brakes. His body pitched forward as the truck screeched to a halt within inches of Laura's body. He threw the truck in park and leaped out of the vehicle. "Are you all right?"

Laura didn't move, her blue eyes round with fear.

His stomach dropped. He grabbed her shoulders, fighting the urge to shake them. But she wasn't responding. "Laura?"

"What happened?" Tobias hurried up beside him. "Is she okay?"

Laura slowly nodded. "I'm fine."

Sawyer expelled a long breath. "Thank God. I nearly hit you."

"You did what?" Tobias moved closer to Laura. "Are you sure you're all right?"

"*Ya.*" She looked at Tobias, then at Sawyer. "I'm okay. "Y'all stop fussing. You didn't hit me."

"I could have." Without thinking he squeezed her shoulders tighter.

"But you didn't." She glanced down at his hand.

He pulled away. "This day keeps getting better and better."

"Anyone want to tell me what's going on? And where's Lukas? He hasn't missed a day of work since he had chicken pox when he was a *kinn*."

Sawyer looked at his uncle, his head pounding. How could he sum up the events of the past two days in a sentence or two?

"I reckon Lukas is still at home," Laura said. "He's taking care of something with Anna."

"She's not sick, is she?"

Laura shook her head. "Everything's okay. I'm sure he'll explain it to you later. Is it still okay if we *geh* eat now?"

Tobias's gaze darted between Laura and Sawyer. He looked at his nephew. "That's how you pick a *maedel* up for lunch?"

"Uh, sorry. Wasn't thinking clearly."

"I can tell." Tobias waved them off. "*Geh* on. Be back in an hour."

"We will." Laura looked at Sawyer. "Ready?"

"For what?"

"Lunch. Remember you promised you'd take me to get one of those sandwiches you like so much."

"Right." He glanced to see where Tobias was, but his uncle had already gone inside. Sawyer leaned against the truck. "Laura, I'm so sorry."

"You can tell me on the way there."

"To Middlefield Cheese? You're serious. I thought you were covering for me." He wasn't hungry. But he didn't want to be alone either. After nearly running over Laura, he didn't need to be left to his own devices. At least not now.

"I didn't want to lie to Tobias." Laura moved closer to Sawyer. "We don't have to *geh* eat. We can just *geh* for a drive. Or a walk. Whatever you want."

This was a new side of Laura. He thought for sure she'd be mad at him for touching her. Which he'd been an idiot to do in the first place. He knew how sensitive she was about the scars, even though she didn't let on. But the look of fear in her eyes as he'd brushed the sawdust off her cheek convinced him that she wasn't over the trauma. Although her confidence seemed to grow with each day, there were some wounds that took a long time to heal.

He thought about the pond behind Johnny's house. In the past few years it was his fishing hole, but the pond held more meaning than that. When he was hiding in the barn, he would pick up clothes and other items there from Johnny and Mary Beth. It was their drop spot, meeting spot, and eventually where they hung out with their friends. But over time, as Mary Beth spent more time with Christopher and Johnny with his job, he'd gone there alone. To fish. To think.

He turned to her.

"I know exactly where I'd like to go."

Emma was preparing lunch when she heard a knock at the door. She set aside the bowl of chicken salad and answered the back door. "Clara," she said. "I'm surprised to see you."

Clara twisted her fingers together. "Can I come in?"

"Of course. You don't have to ask." She wasn't used to Clara being so subdued. In the past she would have barged in, making some demand or another. Emma closed the door.

Clara's smile was uneasy. "Can we talk?"

"*Ya.*" Emma led Clara to the couch. Her sister perched on the edge of it. "Nothing's wrong, is it?"

"*Nee.*" Clara shook her head, looking away. She glanced back at Emma. "I . . . well, I wanted to know . . ."

"Know what?"

She took a deep breath. "Do you need help with the wedding?"

Emma's eyes widened. Despite the improvement in their relationship, her sister still didn't care for Adam. She never had, not since he had left Middlefield.

"I thought you might be surprised," Clara said.

Emma nodded. "I know how you feel about Adam." When Clara didn't say anything, Emma added, "But I could use the help." She sighed. "I don't really know what I'm doing. *Grossmammi's* helping, of course, but neither of us is as organized as you."

Clara smiled for the first time since she arrived. "Peter might disagree with the organization part," she said. "But since I've been through this before, I thought I could help you with a few things."

"How about the whole wedding?"

Clara laughed. "Is it that bad? Isn't Adam's *mudder* giving you advice?"

"Not right now." Emma didn't say anything about her talk with her grandmother. While she didn't want to keep secrets, everybody didn't need to know what happened between her and Adam. "I think once it gets closer to the date, she'll be more help."

Clara nodded. "I also think we should put off building the shelter until after the wedding. Maybe even until the spring. If that's okay with you. You should be spending time with your *mann*."

Emma grinned. "Don't worry, I will be. I agree about waiting until after the wedding, but I don't think we should put it off until spring. The shelter will be a warm place for the animals during the coldest months of the winter."

"All right. That's up to you. It's your shelter." She smiled again. "Your dream."

Emma smiled. "*Danki*. I know how hard it was for you to say that."

Clara pressed her lips together. "It's hard for me not to feel protective of you."

"Or boss me around." Emma tried for a good-natured tone, but a slight note of sarcasm slipped in. Years of resentment couldn't disappear in a few months.

"You call it bossing, I call it guiding." Clara shrugged, a half grin on her face. "Peter says I can be heavy-handed sometimes."

"Sometimes." Emma leaned forward. "Before we make any plans, I need to know something."

"What?"

"I love Adam. I can't wait to be his wife. I need to know that you can accept that. We'll be *familye* soon."

"Emma, your happiness is important to me. I can see he makes you happy."

"He does. He makes me very happy."

"Then I'm glad to have him as a *schwoger*." Clara suddenly reached over and hugged Emma. "I'm glad this is all happening for you."

Emma hugged her back. "Some days I have to pinch myself to believe it." She pulled back. "I never thought I'd feel so wonderful."

Clara held her sister's hand. "Enjoy that feeling, Emma. You deserve it."

Leona stood in the doorway of the kitchen, watching Emma as she sat at the table. Emma was humming a slightly off-key version of a church hymn as she wrote in a small notebook. From the smile on her face and the rosy hue of her cheeks, Leona could tell she was thinking of Adam.

Emma looked up at her and smiled. "You just missed Clara. She came by to offer her help with the wedding."

"Miracles never cease." Leona leaned on her cane as she moved into the room and lowered herself into the chair across from Emma. "What are you doing?"

"Starting a list for the wedding." She glanced up at Leona. "There's so much to do in such a short time."

"*Ya*. That's usually how it is with weddings."

"I remember Clara's." Emma tapped her chin with the eraser end of the pencil. "How perfect she wanted everything to be."

"I thought your *mammi* was going to have a fit from all the stress."

Emma's expression turned somber. She put down the pencil. "I wish *Mamm* was here."

"Me too, Emma."

Leona gripped the edge of the table. Emma's comment made what Leona had to say that much harder. As if it wasn't hard enough. "I have something to tell you."

Emma frowned. "I know that look, *Grossmammi*." She leaned forward. "What's wrong?"

Leona hesitated. Maybe she shouldn't do this. She had prayed for guidance last night, once Norman had agreed to talk to Carol. Did Emma really need to know about her mother's weakness? Would that taint her memory of her? Yet how much worse would it be if she found out some other way, and found out that Leona knew?

Emma had experienced enough betrayal and loss in her young life. There was no guarantee that she wouldn't deal with more. But Leona didn't want to be the source of it. Like ripping off a bandage, it would be painful now, but quick.

The secret had festered long enough.

Emma's chest tightened. What else could go wrong? She finally had what she wanted, what she'd prayed for. Adam's love. His promise to marry her. A better relationship with her sister. For the first time in years she looked forward to the future.

Yet the ache in her grandmother's eyes promised to bring more pain. When would enough be enough?

"It's about your *mammi*, Emma." *Grossmammi* cleared her throat. Her grandmother continued speaking. About Emma's mother. Adam's father. Their indiscretion. A buzzing sound grew loud in her ears as she heard the words.

Emma couldn't sit still any longer. She got up and paced across the room. "How do you know this?"

"Mary told me. Norman confirmed it when I confronted him."

It made sense. Adam's parents' strange behavior when they heard about the wedding. Carol's distance and noticeable despair. Everything finally fit. "Does Adam's mother know?"

"I think she does."

"I think so too." Emma gripped the back of the chair. "What about Adam?" Was he keeping another secret from her?

Grossmammi shook her head. "I doubt it. Emma, I'm so sorry. Sit, *lieb*. Please." When Emma sat down, *Grossmammi* reached for her hand.

"I didn't want to tell you. I don't want you to think badly of your *mudder*. She was a *gut* woman. And your *vadder* had just died."

"You forgave her that easily?"

"It wasn't my place to forgive her, Emma. She didn't wrong me. She didn't even wrong your *vadder*. She needed God's forgiveness. Not mine."

Emma's eyes stung. She closed them, trying to hold the

tears in. She should be angry, but she wasn't. Her mother had endured so much suffering, so much loss. Emma remembered how much she missed Adam when he left Middlefield. Her mother and father had been married for years, had loved each other since they were teenagers. In her own grief over losing her father, she'd never thought about how hard her mother had grieved over her husband.

Emma opened her eyes. "I'm tired of secrets. I'm glad you told me."

"Then you understand?" Her grandmother's blue eyes held hope.

"*Ya.* I do. *Mammi* didn't wrong me either. And I know she sought God's forgiveness."

"She did, *kinn.*"

"Which is all that matters." Emma released her grandmother's hand. Picked up the pencil. A touch of pain lingered in her heart, mostly grief that her mother wouldn't be there for her wedding.

She smiled at *Grossmammi.* "Will you help me plan?"

Grossmammi grinned. "I would love to."

CHAPTER 21

"Whose house is this?" Laura asked.

Sawyer put the truck in park. "The Mullets'."

"You want me to meet the Mullets?"

"No." He opened the door. "Come with me."

Laura walked next to him as they cut through the yard behind a large white house with a wooden play set in the back. They made their way to a pond at the edge of the property, near a small grove of oak and maple trees.

"Reckon we should let them know we're here?"

"They don't mind me coming here. They're good people."

They reached the edge of the pond. Sawyer stood on the bank, the toes of his work boots dangling over the edge, hovering above the murky water. Brown leaves floated on the surface. A gaggle of geese flew overhead, their honks breaking the silence as they headed south.

Laura waited for Sawyer to speak, to tell her why he'd brought her here. It was an ordinary-looking pond, but she figured there was something special about it. Special to Sawyer, anyway.

Finally he spoke. "I come out here a lot. Mostly to fish. It's a pretty good fishing hole."

Laura folded her arms across her chest. The wind kicked up and she shivered, but tried to hide it from Sawyer.

"Cold?"

"A little. But I'm all right."

"I've got a jacket in the truck."

Before she could protest he hurried away. She turned and looked at the pond again. Wind blew leaves against the water, forming little waves that lapped against the grassy edge. More geese flew overhead, a common sight and sound now that winter was approaching. Despite the chill and the cloudiness of the day, a sense of calm enveloped her. She was starting to understand why Sawyer came here.

He appeared behind her and put his jacket around her shoulders. She looked down at the dark blue fabric and realized it was an Amish jacket.

"You look surprised," he said.

"I am. I figured you'd have an *Englisch* jacket. Not an Amish one."

"I have as many Amish clothes as I do Yankee ones. Anna made sure I would fit in no matter where I was. That was important to me when I was a kid."

"And now?"

He shrugged. "Now I don't know." He squatted down by the edge of the pond and ran his fingertips across the grassy edge. "I don't know anything anymore. Feels like my entire life has been a lie."

Laura paused. What could she say to that? She didn't know his entire story, yet she could see he'd been through so much. Her heart reached out to this gentle, wounded man.

He looked over his shoulder and up at her, giving her a half grin. "I'm not sure why I brought you here."

"I'm glad you did."

"Johnny and I used to fish here a lot. Mary Beth sometimes joined us."

"That's Johnny's twin sister, right?"

"Yes. The one who just got married." Sawyer gazed out over the water. "When I started high school, he asked me lots of questions about what it was like. He was curious, but not enough to want to try much outside of the Amish life. He always seemed to understand his place in the world. I have no idea what that feels like."

Laura reached out to put a hand on his shoulder, then pulled back. She had no comfort for him, because she felt the same way. Confused. Torn in two directions. The only thing that came to mind was what her mother used to say whenever Laura asked for advice: *"You must pray."*

But prayer never seemed to be enough. Eventually Laura quit trying to talk to her mother—and to God.

"I shouldn't have bothered you with this," he said.

"I don't mind." She snuggled deeper into Sawyer's jacket. The fabric held the scents of wood smoke and sawdust, mixed in with a smell that was unidentifiable, but made her stomach flutter. "I wish there was something I could do to help."

"My mom always said it was good to talk things out."

He picked up a small rock and threw it into the pond. Ripples parted the water, sending the leaves floating in different directions. "Funny how she never told me anything about her life."

"You grew up without knowing your grandparents?"

"Grandparents, aunts, uncles, cousins. No brothers or sisters either. It was always just the three of us. I remember asking my mom about it. Why we didn't ever visit any relatives and no one came to see us. All she said was that her parents and my father's parents were dead."

He swallowed. "My father went along with everything she said. I wonder how many more lies they told me?" He stood and faced her. "We should get back. I'm sorry I touched your cheek earlier. I didn't mean to upset you."

"It's okay. I was just . . . surprised." She looked away. "The scars—"

"They're barely noticeable."

"Now look who's lying."

"I'm not. You might think they are when you look in the mirror. But I hardly see them." He took a step forward. Opened his mouth as if to say something more. Instead, he turned and headed for the truck.

Laura followed him. They were halfway back to the Bylers' shop when he spoke again.

"You know, you're really impressive."

More surprises. A man who wasn't afraid to say what was on his mind. She appreciated that, just as his compliment warmed her. "That's kind of you to say, but the job is easy. The office is very organized."

"I'm not talking about your job." He glanced at her. "Your attitude. The way you don't let what happened to you bother you."

She folded her hands together. *"Danki,"* she whispered.

If only he knew how she really felt. He had confided in her. Could she trust him enough to bare her secrets?

She'd never know unless she took the risk. But she couldn't bring herself to tell the truth.

Not to him. Not to anyone.

"You sure you don't want me to pull up any farther?" The driver turned his head and looked at Cora. They were pulled over on the side of the road a few feet away from a large white house. A line of laundry hung on the front porch. But Cora barely noticed.

"No," she said. "This is fine."

Perfect, actually. She had an unobstructed view of Sawyer and Laura standing by the pond. He had just put his jacket over her shoulders. How sweet. And how telling.

For all his bluster about Middlefield being his home, how he didn't care about money and couldn't leave his *family*, Cora now knew the real reason Sawyer didn't want to go to New York. Even from this distance she could see how close they stood together. For some unfathomable reason, he cared for her. And not as a coworker or a friend. Something much more was going on between them.

Sawyer wasn't the only one who had insight into people.

Sawyer and the woman turned around and left the pond. Cora leaned forward. "We're finished here."

"Are you—"

"Drive!" She looked out the window. She couldn't risk Sawyer seeing her here.

"You don't have to be rude about it." The driver yanked on the gearshift and pulled onto the road. As they drove away, Cora knew exactly what she needed to do. By tomorrow, she would be on a plane to New York.

With her grandson.

After dropping Laura off at the shop, Sawyer went on home. As much as he'd like to use work as a distraction, he couldn't seem to manage it. Couldn't focus. Besides, he and Laura had spent more time than he thought at the pond. It was near quitting time. Even if he could work, he wouldn't get much done.

At least he wouldn't have to face Cora.

Questions about his past still whirled inside his head. He just wasn't willing to meet her terms to find out why his parents had lied.

But when he walked into the house, he found her seated in the living room. Alone.

"I thought you were gone."

He didn't move far from the door. Or take off his hat. He wouldn't get comfortable with her.

"I changed my mind." She gestured to the chair next to the couch. "Sawyer. Join me. Please."

He perched on the edge of the chair. "I haven't changed my mind."

"I understand. I know now we started off on the wrong foot." She looked at him. "I'm used to having things my own way."

"I didn't notice."

She smirked. "I'm also used to sarcasm. And digs. And thinly veiled insults. There's not much you can say to hurt me, Sawyer."

Sawyer looked up. "I don't want to hurt you. I just want you to leave."

"But I want to start over." She held out a blue-backed packet of papers, even thicker than the legal papers she had presented to him yesterday. "I want you to look at this."

"What is it?"

"My will. I had it changed when I found out about you."

He started to shake his head, but she held the papers out to him. "You were right about legacy being important to me. But it's not just about my legacy. Your grandfather worked hard to build Easley Industries. I don't want the business he loved to end up in the hands of a group of investors who have no personal stake in the company's success or failure."

Sawyer paused. He took the documents but didn't open them. "What did your original will say?"

She gave him a rueful smile. "I left everything in a trust. Kenneth is the executor."

He stared at the papers on his lap. Then he looked at her. "You said you wanted to know more about me. Here's the first thing: I don't care about money. Mom and Dad never did. The Bylers don't. So it doesn't matter how much money you bribe me with—"

"It's not a bribe. It's what you deserve. I know I've been less than polite toward you and your adoptive family." She twisted the pearl necklace around her fingers. "I want to apologize for that."

"Apologize to them."

"I already did."

Her admission surprised him. What was she up to? This wasn't the same woman he'd left this morning. "Cora, what do you want from me?"

"I want you to give me a chance. To give New York a chance. Just visit. I promise I'll tell you everything. About my relationship with Kerry. How she met your father. All your questions will be answered."

"And then?"

"And then, if you choose to—" She glanced away. "You can come back to Ohio. I won't stop you, if that's what you want."

He leaned back in the chair and scrutinized her expression. She was serious. The curiosity lingering at the edges of his mind slammed into him full force. If he went with her, he would find out why his parents lied to him. He would know his family history.

Sawyer opened up the will. His hands started to sweat as he read it. By the time he was done, his mouth dropped open.

"Understand now?"

He nodded. Looked at the will again. Yet he couldn't bring

himself to say yes. Something was still holding him back, and he wasn't sure what it was. "I'll have to think about it."

"Take your time." She didn't seem surprised by his answer. Or upset. It was almost as if she'd anticipated his response. For someone who had been in such a hurry to whisk him out of Middlefield, her sudden patience seemed suspect.

Or maybe she really was trying to be conciliatory. He couldn't be certain.

Only one thing was sure: when it came to Cora Easley, nothing was uncalculated.

Carol took off her *kapp* and unpinned her hair. It fell to her waist. She twisted the thick strands into a loose braid and laid it over her left shoulder. She changed into her nightdress and climbed into bed, slipping between cool, crisp sheets that smelled of autumn air. For a minute or two she looked at the empty place in the bed where Norman slept. Then she rolled over and faced the wall.

A short while later, she heard the bedroom door open. She closed her eyes, feigning sleep. The steady thud of Norman's boots against the wood floor made her flinch. She heard him undress and prepare for bed. Every night was the same. He would lie on his side, his back to hers, a wide vertical space between them. She waited for him to turn off the battery-powered lamp on his nightstand.

"Carol?"

She held perfectly still, holding her breath and waiting for him to leave her alone.

He touched her arm. "Carol."

Her eyes opened at the sound of his voice. It had been ages since she'd heard him use that soft tone. So long since she'd felt the warmth of his touch, like she did now, the heat of his palm seeping through the thin fabric of her white nightgown. Still, she couldn't bring herself to turn over. But if he demanded that she did, she would comply.

She waited for him to do just that. Instead, he lightly ran his hand up and down her arm.

"Carol. I know you're awake. It's all right if you don't want to look at me. I understand. Please, just listen."

Why was he being so kind? So gentle? Curiosity overwhelmed her. She rolled over and looked into his hazel eyes. Tears glistened in the corners.

"Carol, I have something to tell you. Something I should have told you long ago. But I was ashamed."

She put her hand to her chest. Her pulse beat beneath her palm, yet it felt like her heart had stopped. "Ashamed of what, Norman?"

He wiped his eyes with the pads of his thumbs and drew in a breath. "I've wronged you, *mei fraa*. I have wronged you in so many ways."

Anger suddenly took control. Carol sat up and turned on him. "Are you talking about Mary?"

He gaped. "You knew?"

"*Ya*. I knew."

"How?"

"Does it matter?"

He shook his head. "*Nee*. It doesn't."

"How could you do this to me?" She tried to fight back the tears. She failed. "How could you be with another woman? With *mei* best friend?"

"I didn't . . . It wasn't like that." He hung his head and didn't speak for a moment. "*Nix* happened."

"Don't lie to me, Norman."

"I'm not. After James died, I did go to Mary. She needed help, as you know. Two young *maed* to take care of, plus James's *mudder*. Animals to look after. I was doing my job as a deacon. Taking care of a widow. I was doing what the Lord called me to do."

"The Lord did *not* call you to have an affair."

"We didn't have an affair. It never came to that. But it could have." He sighed. "She kept telling me how lonely she was. How much she missed James. She wondered how she could go on without him. Then Adam started acting out." He looked at her. "It seemed like you were always taking his side."

"So that made it okay?"

"*Nee*. None of it was okay. Or right. I knew I shouldn't have done it, but I put my arm around her." He closed his eyes. "And then . . . we kissed. Once."

One kiss? Pain shot through Carol's heart. Hearing Mary's confession had been bad enough. Imagining what might have happened between Norman and Mary had been excruciating. All the pain, all those years, for one kiss?

Yet even if it was only one kiss, that didn't make it easier to accept.

"We both knew we had sinned. That what we'd done was wrong. We both carried so much guilt. We promised not to speak of it. We didn't want to hurt anyone."

Carol got up and stalked to the end of the bed. "You hurt me."

Norman moved to her. "I know. And I'm so ashamed, Carol. I was ashamed of what I'd done, and I couldn't tell you. Mary couldn't either. We thought if we kept quiet and pretended like it never happened, we could both forget."

Carol's whole body shook. Yet a small sense of relief penetrated her anger. She covered her face with her hand. Then she turned and looked at him. "This was my fault too."

"*Nee.*" He came to her and gripped her shoulders. "Is this what you've been doing all these months? Why you've been so distant? So upset? You're blaming yourself?"

She couldn't speak as the tears continued to flow. She nodded. "If I had been the *fraa* I was supposed to be, it wouldn't have happened."

"That's not true."

But she saw a flash of agreement in his eyes. "We've been drifting apart for a long time, Norman. We can blame it on Adam, on Mary, on life." She looked down. "It's so easy to blame everyone but ourselves."

"You're right." Norman sat down on the end of the bed. His shoulders slumped. "I don't know how to fix this."

Carol sat next to him. "I don't either."

"I do love you, Carol. That's never changed." He reached out and took her hand.

"I love you too." She looked into his eyes. "But is it enough?"

He nodded. "Until we get through this, it has to be."

CHAPTER 22

Cora fluffed her short layered hair with her fingers and thought about her conversation with Sawyer the evening before. She could tell he had been suspicious about her sudden change of attitude. If she had been in his position, she would have felt the same.

She looked in the small standing mirror on top of the bureau. Leaned forward and put a few dabs of expensive anti-aging cream under her eyes. And ignored the tremor in her fingers as she smoothed it out.

As she dressed, she pondered the ease with which her grandson could turn his back on such a rich legacy. On so much money. Just as Kerry had done. And he was doing it for the same reason.

For love.

Even if he couldn't admit it. Even if he wasn't aware of it, only something as strong as love could motivate the rejection of a massive fortune, unending opportunity, and a chance at freedom millions could only dream about.

The freedom only millions could buy.

A short while later, the taxi pulled into the Bylers' driveway. One thing she could say for Middlefield, there was no shortage of available drivers. She handed the middle-aged woman a hundred-dollar bill. "Wait until I come out."

The woman's eyes widened behind her glasses. She looked at the bill, then back at Cora. "Are you sure you didn't mean to give me a ten?"

"When it comes to money, I never make a mistake." Cora stepped out of the cab as the driver turned off the engine. She took a deep breath as she headed for the woodshop. Her grandson might have a rebellious streak that rivaled his mother's, but Cora had something else.

Resources. And she wasn't afraid to use them.

The small bell over the door dinged as she strode inside. She held her shaking hands together until the movement stopped. She couldn't appear weak. She was here to meet with a poor Amish girl, not some major stockholder of her corporation. Bolstered, she looked around at the empty workshop.

Where was everyone? To hear Sawyer talk, these people worked nonstop. The scent of wood and varnish penetrated the air and irritated her allergies. Nauseating. Not to mention dusty.

"Can I help you?"

Cora glanced up at the soft Southern accent and quickly adjusted her expression from one of disdain to pity and concern.

Laura froze when she saw Sawyer's grandmother standing just inside the door to the woodshop. The woman was finely dressed, as usual. Hesitating, Laura finally looked at Cora's face. She saw what she had been afraid of seeing since the day of the accident. Pity, bordering on revulsion.

No one had looked at her like that before. But then again, she'd only had dealings with the Amish community and a few English visitors. Sawyer's grandmother was different from any other woman she knew. Cora didn't bother to hide her reaction.

Was this how people really saw her? As someone to be pitied?

She forced the hurt aside. "Can I help you?" she repeated, determined to treat Cora like any other person who came into the shop.

"I was looking for Sawyer." Cora's chin lifted, her gaze drifting down the bridge of her nose. "Is he here?"

"He went on a delivery with his father." She made sure to put emphasis on Lukas's role in Sawyer's life. "When he comes in, I'll tell him you were looking for him."

"Actually . . ." Cora stepped forward. Her thin lips formed a tense smile. "Since we're both here, I thought perhaps you and I could talk."

Laura paused. "What would we have to talk about?"

"You'd be surprised." She glanced around the shop again. "Is there a place where we can converse in private?"

Laura didn't answer right away. This woman had to be up to something. She could sense it. Finally, she said, "In my office."

"Oh, you have an office? How . . . professional."

Laura bristled at the subtle dig. No wonder Sawyer didn't want to have anything to do with this woman. She could hardly believe they were blood family.

"Follow me." She opened the door and gestured to the simple chair at her desk. "You can sit here, if you'd like."

Cora nodded. She brushed off the seat of the chair before sitting down. Even while looking up at Laura, she managed to look down on her.

Laura folded her arms across her chest. "What did you want to talk about?"

"An opportunity. One you won't want to turn down."

"Puttin' the plow ahead of the mule, don't you think?"

Cora laughed. "Lovely accent. Where are you from?"

"Tennessee." She leaned against the wall.

"And why are you in Middlefield?"

"I don't think that's any of your business, Mrs. . . . ."

"Easely. But you can call me Cora." She placed her purse on the desk. "I apologize if I've overstepped."

Laura doubted the apology was sincere—or that the woman had ever uttered the words "I'm sorry" with anything like genuine remorse. Every word, every movement was calculated. In a subtle, unnerving way, Cora Easely reminded her of Mark. "You should get to the point. I have work to do."

"Ah, yes." The pity had returned to her eyes. "It's utterly awful what happened to you, my dear. I know how much a paper cut hurts, so I can only imagine what you've been through. Not just physically, but emotionally. Facing every day, knowing you're permanently disfigured."

Laura flinched.

"Our society . . . well, people can be so cruel." Cora crossed her slender legs. "And you're so young. Do you mind me asking how it happened?"

"Yes. I do." She couldn't believe the woman's nerve.

"Ah. I suppose that was rather nosy of me." The woman's smile held no warmth. "How do you do it?"

"Do what?"

"Live with knowing that each day could bring a nasty comment about your face?"

"Like the one you just made?"

Cora's smile grew. "That was merely a statement of fact. You seem to be a smart girl. Very direct. I can appreciate that. I can also see why Sawyer is . . . attracted to you."

Her words took Laura off guard. Sawyer? Attracted to her? Had Sawyer said something to his grandmother? The whole idea was ridiculous.

It was also wonderful. But she didn't believe a word of it.

"I see what you're thinking." Cora adjusted the jeweled bracelet around her thin wrist. "You're wondering how I know. I just do. A grandmother knows her grandson."

"Even one she just met?"

The woman's smile shifted. Not much, but it was visible if you looked close enough.

"Yes. He's very much like his mother. He misses her still. You never fully get over the death of a family member. You eventually accept it and move on, but there's an empty place inside that remains forever."

Laura dropped her arms. Despite not trusting Cora, she did have sympathy for her when it came to her daughter. "I'm sorry for your loss. I know how much Sawyer's parents meant to him."

"Yes. Family means everything. True family, that is." Cora leaned forward. "But I'm afraid Sawyer is letting his emotions interfere with what's best for him."

"Which is?"

"To return to New York. To learn about his past. To accept his true role in life. Surely you can understand that's what he needs to do?" She settled back in the chair. "But he's refusing to listen to reason."

"He's an adult. He can make up his own mind."

"Of course he can. But there are things holding him back. His adoptive parents, for one. Yet I'm hoping they can convince him that coming to New York to learn more about his real family is the wisest choice." She peered at Laura. "And then there's you."

Laura shifted on her feet. "Me?"

"You care for my grandson, don't you?"

She rubbed her forehead with her fingers. She couldn't lie, not about Sawyer. "*Ya.* I do."

Cora slowly rose from the chair. She stepped forward, closing the space between them. "Then I can count on you to talk to him?"

"You want me to convince him to leave Middlefield? To leave the family he loves?"

"He can come back to visit. Other than appreciation for what the Bylers have done for him, what is really tying him here? Unless you think there's a future for you?"

Laura inched away until her back pressed up against the wall.

Cora's intense gaze pinned her in place. "You realize that's not possible."

"Sawyer might join the church." Desperation forced her to voice the thought out loud. But with each passing moment she realized Cora was right. What kind of future would she have with Sawyer? Even if he cared for her the way she hoped? Although she struggled with some aspects of her faith, she had no plans to leave the Amish. And he wasn't sure he wanted to join.

"Laura, you're a sweet girl. A kind girl. If you really care for Sawyer as much as you seem to, you won't make him feel like he has to stay here with you. My grandson has a sensitive side to him. Kerry was like that. She used to take in strays. Feel sorry for her friends who were less fortunate. She always wanted to fix what was wrong." Cora's gaze traveled over Laura's face. "Do you really think Sawyer can fix you?"

Tears sprang to Laura's eyes. She glanced away.

Cora took a step back. "Do what's right for Sawyer, Laura. Let him go. Set him free to be the great man he's supposed to be."

Laura wiped her damp cheek. Sawyer was already a great man. But she understood Cora's meaning. He was destined for more than being a carpenter's apprentice. He deserved more than a scarred, flawed woman.

"All right. I'll talk to him," Laura said.

Cora smiled. She walked to the desk and pulled a checkbook and a gold pen out of her purse. "I believe in rewarding loyalty," she said. She signed the check with a flourish, tore it out of the book, and handed it to Laura.

"I don't want your money."

"I know you don't. But I want you to have it, as a token of my appreciation." She held out the check. "There is enough here to pay for plastic surgery. If you need a recommendation, I know several good surgeons, both in New York and Beverly Hills."

Laura didn't know who Beverly Hills was, and she didn't care. The reality of what Cora offered sank into her. No more scars. No more worrying about what others would say and think about her. She'd have a chance to be whole again.

But could she be whole without Sawyer?

The thought stunned her. But before she had a chance to examine what it meant, another idea occurred to her, one that couldn't wait. "I'll talk to Sawyer," she said. "But before I do, I need another favor."

Surprise colored Cora's features. "More money? I thought you people didn't care about wealth."

"This isn't about money," Laura said. "It's about justice."

CHAPTER 23

Laura paced back and forth in her office. Anxiety coiled and writhed like a snake inside her. Cora had left more than thirty minutes ago, and Sawyer hadn't returned. What had she done, agreeing to Cora's plan? She looked at the check on her desk. More money than she had ever imagined. Plus the woman's promise to help her, once Sawyer was in New York and away from Middlefield.

Away from her.

She picked up the check, and for the briefest of moments she thought of ripping it to shreds. She remembered her talk with Sawyer yesterday. How he gently touched her scar. Opened up to her. She had never known anyone like him before. When they first met, she wanted him to leave her alone. Now she looked forward to seeing him every morning. The rides home in the evening. Standing by his side as he went through this difficult time with his grandmother.

Her feelings for him weren't the crazy infatuation she'd felt for Mark. Instead, it was something deeper. More satisfying.

Real.

But once he went to New York, then what? He wouldn't come back, at least not for her, not after he had a taste of what money and the city had to offer.

She put the check in her purse. Cora was right. Laura couldn't hold him back. She wouldn't. And although it was tearing her heart in two, she and Sawyer were both getting what they needed—his future, and her revenge.

She heard the familiar ring of the bell. Through the glass in the door she saw him heading straight for the office. She closed her eyes, took a deep breath, and opened the door. "Hey."

He frowned at her. "What's wrong?"

"I saw you coming and I opened the door. What's wrong with that?"

"Nothing, except that you look white as a sheet."

Sawyer took her by the elbow and led her into the office. He closed the door behind them and put a clipboard on the desk. She recognized them as signed papers for the furniture delivery.

"I'll file those as soon as—"

"Don't worry about the papers." He squared his body to her. "Talk to me. What happened while I was gone?"

She took a shuddering breath. "I have something to tell you."

"I'm listening."

"I . . . I think you should go to New York with your grandmother."

"What? She was here, wasn't she?"

Laura nodded. "She was looking for you."

"Unbelievable." He turned away from her, clasping both hands behind his neck. "She said she'd give me time."

"So you were considering going?"

"I was *thinking* about it. But not seriously. And definitely not anytime soon."

"But why would you wait?"

He spun around. "The question is, why are you in such a hurry for me to go?"

Sawyer couldn't believe what he was hearing. "You *want* me to leave?"

She nodded, not looking him in the eye. "It's for the best."

"Not for me." He stepped closer. "Not for *us*."

"There isn't an us." She moved away. Turned her back to him. "Did you really think there was?"

"Cora put you up to this, didn't she?"

He saw Laura's shoulders slump. "She didn't have to." When she turned around, he could see the tears in her eyes. "Everything has changed."

"No, it hasn't. So what if she showed up? She should have been here six years ago, when I didn't have anyone. Now I have parents. A family." He reached for her. "I know it sounds crazy, but I also feel like I have you. Remember when I said I understood you?"

She nodded but remained silent.

"I also know that you understand me." He cupped her

shoulders with his hands, felt her body trembling beneath his touch. "You understand me better than anyone else could."

She pulled away from him. "I'm goin' back to Tennessee. Tomorrow."

The words hit him like a punch to the gut. "When did you decide this?"

"I been thinkin' about it for a while. You were right, I need to let Mark go. I need to get on with my life." She looked up at him. "Just like you need to get on with yours."

"I will. I am. This is my life. Here, in Middlefield. Not New York. And definitely not with Cora Easely."

"She's your grandmother."

"She's a snooty old woman—"

"She's blood. And she deserves a chance."

Sawyer reached out. She tried to pull away, but he clasped her hand. "What about us? Don't we deserve a chance?"

Laura averted her gaze. She let out a long breath. "Look at me," she whispered.

"I am." He stepped toward her. Cupped her face with his palm. "I'm looking at you right now. I like what I see."

She met his eyes. For a fleeting moment he saw his emotions reflected in her gaze. He opened his mouth to say something else, but she pulled away from him again. "I 'preciate you sayin' that."

"I don't want you to appreciate it. I want you to believe it."

"Sawyer, I . . ." She shook her head. "I'm goin' back home. *Mei* parents need me. I was selfish to leave them." She took another step back. "Cora needs you."

"Cora doesn't need anyone. Or anything. She's got enough money to *buy* a grandson."

Did he imagine it, or did Laura flinch?

"She wants you. She lost her daughter, Sawyer. Can you blame her for wantin' to get to know you? I'm sure there's a *gut* reason why she's shown up now. Don't you want to find out why?"

"Yeah, but not . . . not at the cost of losing you."

"Sawyer." Laura swallowed. "You . . . you never had me." She turned and walked away.

"Laura!"

She didn't answer. He watched as she grabbed her coat and purse.

"Laura, please—"

She disappeared out of the office. He followed her out of the shop, ignoring the stares of his father and uncle. A few flakes of snow floated down. Small ones. Almost insignificant.

The way Laura felt about herself.

He didn't buy what she was trying to sell him. He knew she cared. Could see it in her eyes, hear it in the cracking of her voice. But her words held a grain of truth. He did need to give his grandmother a chance, despite his anger toward her. And Laura's walking away made it easier.

That's it! he thought. *She's denying herself, denying our feelings for each other, so I can discover my past.* He stopped at the end of the driveway and let her go. The terror of losing her eased. He understood her, just as he always had. She was doing this for him.

And he would let her. Because while they might be apart for a short time, he wouldn't let her push him away forever. He would go to New York, listen to what Cora had to say, then go to Tennessee. If Laura thought she could get rid of him this easily, she thought wrong.

There was hope for them after all.

Laura fought the tears as she walked toward the Shetlers' home. Snow fell on her cheeks, her lips, chilling her skin. But that was nothing compared to the coldness she felt in her heart.

She had walked away. From her job. From the people who had been kind to her. Most importantly, from Sawyer.

For a moment she didn't think she could do it. The tender way he looked at her when he spoke. The truth that he wasn't bothered by her scars. The hope that bloomed like fresh clover when he drew near to her.

But she had to do what was best. For both of them. She thought about the check in her purse. Tonight she would say good-bye to Emma and Leona. Then she would pack. By morning she would be ready to leave.

But she wouldn't catch the bus to Tennessee. She was going somewhere else.

Finally, it was time to finish what she started.

"So you are leaving?"

Sawyer flinched at the tears in his mother's eyes. They had

just finished supper. Cora hadn't joined them, saying she had another headache. Fine with him. It had taken everything he had to eat the few bites on his plate. Now he and his parents were sitting at the table, each nursing a cup of coffee none of them seemed to want.

He nodded. "But I'll be back, *Mamm*." He looked to his father. "I just need a few days. Maybe a week, tops, to get everything sorted out with Cora."

His dad nodded. Little emotion shone in his dark brown eyes. "We understand. And we'll be fine." He turned to his wife. "Won't we, Anna?"

She nodded, then jumped up from the chair and went to the stove. "Anyone want coffee?" Her voice was as thick as the dregs in the bottom of the cold percolator. She seemed to have forgotten their mugs were still full.

"Mom." Sawyer went to his mother and put his hands on her shoulders. She stiffened for a moment, then turned and hugged him.

"I understand why you need to leave." She wiped her eyes and moved away. "And I'm sorry I'm not making it easier for you."

"It's okay. I'm only going for a visit. I'll be back. I promise."

She nodded but didn't look convinced. She turned away and fiddled with the coffeepot. Sawyer returned to the table and sat down.

"I suppose Laura isn't coming back?" Lukas said.

Sawyer shook his head. "She's going home to Tennessee."

Lukas sighed. "I thought she'd stay longer." He shook his head. "She was a *gut* worker. Learned the business quickly. I liked her. And I would have thought she'd do better than just walking out on the job."

"Don't be angry with her. She's had a rough time of it."

"So have you."

"We all have," he said. He looked at his dad and smiled. "I'm glad you like her. I like her too. And if I have anything to do about it, she'll be back."

Both his parents looked at him in surprise. "You're going to Tennessee?" his father asked.

"As soon as I'm finished in New York."

He leaned back in the chair and took in a breath. "But before I can do that, I have to commit to something else. When I get back from New York, I want to join the church."

Lukas didn't say anything. Sawyer looked over his shoulder at his mother, who was still standing by the stove.

"I thought you'd both be happy."

"We are." His dad looked at him. "As long as you're joining the church for the right reasons."

"I am. I know this is something you both wanted—"

"It doesn't matter what we want."

"It does to me."

His mother came back to the table and sat down. "Your *daed* is right. You can't join the church because you think it's what we want. Or because you feel it's the right thing to do." The sorrow in her eyes had changed to intensity. "Or because you're in love with a *maedel*."

Sawyer looked away. He was in love, but he couldn't admit it to anyone, not until he could convince Laura of his feelings.

"That's not the reason I'm joining. I know I belong here. With you. With the Amish."

"You think that now," his father said. "But when you *geh* to New York, you may change your mind."

"Cora will definitely try to change it for you," his mother added.

"She can do what she wants, but it won't work. I'm only agreeing to go with her to find out why my parents lied to me. And why it took her so long to find me. Why she let me . . ." He swallowed.

"Go to foster care?"

He nodded. "You saved me from that."

"Because we love you. And we love you enough to tell you the truth." She straightened. "Sawyer, if you join the church—"

"When."

"*If* you join, you have to do it freely, just as God wants us to come to Him freely. Being a member of the church isn't something to take lightly."

"I'm not." Sawyer gritted his teeth. "I've been thinking about this for a long time."

"Have you prayed about it?" his father asked.

Sawyer drew in a breath.

"I see." His father leaned forward. "Sawyer, this isn't a matter of thinking. It's a matter of the heart. Once you join the church, you can't leave."

"Not without being shunned." Once again his mother's voice wavered.

"You don't have to worry about that." He reached for his

mother's hand. Hesitated. Then held out his other hand to his father. After a pause, his dad took it. "I love you both. I love being a part of this family. Of this community. This is where I want to spend the rest of my life. Cora Easley isn't going to change that." He squeezed his parents' hands, then pushed away from the table. "I'm going to tell Cora I'll leave with her."

"She doesn't know?" his mother asked.

"Not yet. I wanted you and *Daed* to be the first."

His father stood. *"Danki, sohn."*

Sawyer nodded. He started to leave the kitchen but stopped and looked over his shoulder. "I meant what I said."

His mother nodded. His father remained stoic.

Sawyer could tell neither one of them fully believed him.

CHAPTER 24

Sawyer looked around the spacious first-class cabin. He tapped his foot against the floor of the plane as it drifted farther into the clouds. He yanked down on the window shade.

"Relax." Cora settled back into the plush leather seat. "I know this is your first time flying, but you'll be well taken care of here in first class."

"If we crash, it won't matter what class we're in."

"We're not going to crash." She motioned to one of the flight attendants. "Glass of champagne, please. Make that two."

"We don't have champagne, ma'am. Would white wine be all right?"

Cora sighed. "I suppose." She looked at Sawyer. "White or red?"

"I don't drink."

"It will help you relax."

"No, it won't." He tapped his foot faster.

"One glass, then." Cora crossed her legs and placed one

hand on her knee. Sawyer noticed the emerald ring glistening in the light of the cabin. He nodded at it. "My grandfather give that to you?"

"This?" She twisted the ring around her finger and shook her head. "No. I bought it myself. Your grandfather had terrible taste in jewelry."

"Tell me about him."

Her thin brows lifted as she paused. "In due time. I don't want to get into the family business."

"Why not? We have all this time to spend together. Alone." The plane gave a little jerk and dropped a couple of feet. Sawyer gripped the edge of the seat. In contrast, his grandmother seemed unfazed.

He glanced around the cabin again, trying to keep the claustrophobic feeling at bay. He'd rather be crammed into a buggy than stuck in a plane thousands of feet in the air. At least he could get out of the buggy when he wanted to.

"Ma'am?"

The flight attendant passed a glass of white wine to Cora. She accepted it. Took a sip. Looked at Sawyer.

"You really should try one of these."

"I said I don't drink."

She frowned. "I heard you the first time." She leaned back against the headrest. "This is a short flight. We'll land at La Guardia in less than an hour. My driver will meet us at the terminal." She smiled. "I can't wait to show you what New York has to offer."

Sawyer didn't respond. The cadence of his foot sped up.

Getting through the packed city traffic took longer than the flight from Ohio. Three hours later, Sawyer was standing in the middle of Cora's penthouse. The place reeked of money, from the lush white carpet to the highly polished antiques. Lukas would be impressed by the craftsmanship.

Paintings hung on the walls, and even Sawyer's untrained eye could see they were originals, not prints. The only thing that surprised him was the décor. Animal print fabric everywhere, a riot of zebra, cheetah, tiger, leopard skin. He thought it looked tacky.

"Now we can have champagne. Manuela?"

A short, plump Hispanic woman with graying black hair appeared. Sawyer couldn't believe it. She actually wore a black-and-white maid's uniform. He thought those went out in the nineteenth century.

Obviously, he had flown out of Cleveland and landed not just in a different city, but in a different world. One he disliked more by the minute. He scratched the back of his neck.

"*Si?*" Manuela said.

"Champagne, please." Cora looked at Sawyer. He shook his head. "And sparkling water for my grandson."

Manuela looked at Sawyer. He saw the surprise in her face. Guess Cora hadn't told her about him. Then again, Manuela was only the maid. Not an attorney or some other *important* person. "Plain water will be fine. And I can get it myself."

"Nonsense. That's what I pay Manuela for." Cora gestured

to her maid with her hand. "Afterward, please settle Sawyer's things in the guest room. Then you may attend to mine."

"Yes, ma'am." Manuela disappeared.

Cora sat down in one of the chairs. She held out her hand to Sawyer. "Make yourself at home."

He didn't think he could ever be at home here. But he sat down anyway, lost in a huge overstuffed chair, and watched as Cora clicked on the fireplace with a handheld remote control. Manuela appeared with two glasses on a tray—a champagne flute for Cora and a tumbler of ice water for him.

"Thanks," he said, taking the water.

Manuela smiled and nodded her head. Then she disappeared again.

So Cora had a driver and a maid. No telling how many other servants she employed. But he didn't wonder too much about that. "Now will you tell me about my family?"

Cora sipped her champagne. He noticed the glass trembled slightly in her hand. She set it down on the coffee table. "Patience, Sawyer. Let's just enjoy the afternoon before we get caught up in business."

Sawyer rubbed his neck again. "I don't appreciate being put off."

"That's not what I'm doing." She turned to him. "You will find out everything, I promise." She touched her fingertips to her temple. "But at the moment I have a splitting headache."

"Alcohol will do that."

Cora frowned. "I'm going to lie down. Feel free to take my driver and have him show you around Manhattan." She fished inside her purse and pulled out her wallet. "Here is some spending money."

He looked at the four hundred-dollar bills in her hand. "I'm sure I don't need that much."

"Take it. You might want to see a play. Go to a museum."

"Cut off my right hand. It would be just as enjoyable."

"No need to be vulgar." She scowled. "Fine, go to a club, or whatever it is you young people do."

A tiny spasm of guilt stabbed at him. "Sorry. I didn't mean to be rude." He took the money. "Maybe I'll get something to eat."

She brightened. "That's the spirit." She rose, taking her champagne glass with her. "Don't get too full. I'm ordering something extra special for supper."

"Okay." He stood as she walked out of the room. Manuela came in seconds afterward.

"Can I get you anything, Mr. Thompson?"

"Call me Sawyer." He stared at the fire for a moment. A gas fire with fake logs behind a glass. He suddenly longed to smell the smoky scent of real burning wood. But like everything else here, the fire was superficial. He turned to Manuela. "You don't have to wait on me."

"I don't mind. It's my job."

"Yes, but—"

"Mr. Thompson, it's my *job*. Señora Easely would be upset with me if I ignored my duties."

"I see." He didn't want to be the cause of her losing employment. "I think I'll go out for a while."

"I'll ring for the driver."

He held up his hand. "I think I'll walk."

She nodded. "Do you know your way around? I can get you a map if you need one."

"I have a good sense of direction."

Moments later, Sawyer was standing next to the doorman on the sidewalk. Cars, taxis, people—the noise was overwhelming. He looked up at the tall buildings.

No farmland, no fields, no fishing ponds. No grass. No winding roads.

Just endless concrete and exhaust and noise.

A couple of hours later, Sawyer returned. He had walked aimlessly around the city. It was easy not to get lost. There were no turns, other than at the corners of intersections. He remembered going to Cleveland a couple of times for an Indians game. But nothing compared to the size of this city.

He longed for home. His real home, back in Middlefield. More than ever he knew he didn't belong here. Nothing fascinated him or drew him in. By the time he returned to the penthouse, he was agitated. And determined to pin his grandmother down and find out what he came here to learn.

He waited impatiently in the lobby while the doorman called the penthouse and announced him. The elevator ride to the top of the building seemed endless. He walked down the hallway to the apartment. Knocked on the door. Manuela opened it.

"Surprise!"

Sawyer's mouth dropped as he saw the penthouse full of people. Cora wore a glittery jacket and black trousers. He stood at the threshold of the doorway as half-a-dozen gazes, filled with curiosity, assaulted him.

"Don't just stand there." Cora, holding a champagne flute, grabbed his arm. "Come inside."

"What's going on?"

"Just having a little dinner party in your honor." She lifted up on tiptoe and whispered in his ear, "There is suitable clothing in your room. You can freshen up and change. But don't be long."

Bewildered, Sawyer looked around the room. "Who are these people?"

"Some close friends. They're dying to meet you."

"Any family?"

Cora paused. "No. But I consider my dearest friends family. Hurry up. Don't keep us waiting."

"You promised we'd talk."

"After the party." Cora took a sip of champagne and smiled. But her eyes filled with impatience.

"What if I refuse? I can just turn around and leave, you know. I have money. Catch a cab to the airport. Spend the night there if I have to."

Her expression grew cold. "You wouldn't embarrass me like that."

They stared at each other. Sawyer shook his head. "No. I wouldn't."

Cora's smile returned. "Now, go get changed and meet us in the dining room. I've ordered an exquisite meal. No more chicken hash or whatever it is you've been eating for the past few years."

"I've eaten very well."

"And now you'll eat better." Cora turned. "Oh, there's Kenneth waving me to him." She glanced at Sawyer. *"Hurry up."*

Sawyer walked into the bedroom. Just as he figured, a brand-new suit, neatly pressed, lay on the bed. He picked up the purple silk tie. He couldn't remember the last time he wore a tie. He knew for sure he had never worn anything purple.

"Dear Lord," he said aloud. "Help me get through tonight."

It was the first sincere prayer he'd said in a long time.

CHAPTER 25

When the penthouse door shut behind the last guest, Sawyer yanked off his tie and unbuttoned the top button of his starched shirt. For the first time in hours, he felt like he could breathe again.

"Glad that's over." He sank down in the zebra-striped club chair. Manuela and two other maids, whom Sawyer assumed had been hired just for the party, were cleaning up the crystal glasses and glass plates. Many of them were half full of champagne that hadn't been drunk and food that had been barely touched.

What a waste.

He folded the tie and placed it on the arm of the chair. Maybe Cora could take the suit back. Or at least donate it. He never intended to wear it again.

"What a lovely party." Cora waltzed into the room. Her eyes were glazed, her smile wide. "It's been so long since I've had something this important to celebrate." She looked at

Sawyer, her smile slipping a bit. "I do wish you would have been a little friendlier."

"I thought I was friendly enough, considering you blind-sided me."

"Clearly you need some lessons in the fine art of small talk." Cora sat down in the chair beside him. "But you have an innate charm of your own. Kerry had it too."

"Didn't I inherit anything from my father?" Sawyer challenged her.

Her smile disappeared. "Nothing of import."

Sawyer nodded. He suspected the relationship between her and his father hadn't been a good one, since she never mentioned him. Now she had confirmed it.

"I don't want to talk about your father," she said, leaning back against the chair.

"Then let's talk about my mother, and why she never told me about you."

Cora sighed. "Not tonight, Sawyer."

He popped up from the chair. "Then when? Tomorrow? Next week? Three months from now? How long are you going to put me off?"

"I'm not putting you off. And I don't like your tone. Apparently the Amish don't feel the need to respect their elders."

"You're wrong. You don't know anything about the Amish. Or about me. Or, for that matter, about respect. You haven't asked a single question about my childhood. Or what it was like after the Bylers adopted me." He sat back down and tapped a fist against the arm of the chair. "I'm not sure you even care."

"I do care." She tilted her head to one side. "If I didn't, you wouldn't be here."

"I think you care that you have an heir."

Cora stood. "I don't have to listen to this. I know you're tired. After the day we had, we both are. Let's get a good night's sleep. Things will look different in the morning."

"And will you answer my questions then?"

But she was already walking out of the room. "Good night, Sawyer."

Sawyer stared at the gas fireplace. His mind went to home, and to Laura.

Had she left for Tennessee yet? Had she reunited with her parents? He was glad she decided not to pursue Mark anymore. But he missed her. And she was so far away.

He tried to imagine the Bylers in this posh place. His grandmother's "friends" at the party had mostly been people in her employ—her attorney, accountant, and CEO of her company and their wives. How would they have reacted to Laura? Would they have accepted her?

He knew the answer without thinking. They barely accepted him, wouldn't have given him the time of day if he hadn't been Cora Easley's grandson.

Dinner had been some kind of weird duck liver covered in a savory foam. He didn't know which fork to use. Which glass to drink out of. What he wouldn't give for some chicken and noodles. Even a pizza.

He had to get out of here. His grandmother's attorney, Kenneth Hamilton, had given Sawyer his card before he left. Well, if Cora wasn't willing to give Sawyer the answers he needed, he'd find them somewhere else.

The next morning he headed straight for the living room, expecting to see Cora there. He'd slept in later than usual, past eight o'clock. Surely she was up by now. But the living room was empty. So was the dining room, and the sitting room that opened up to a balcony overlooking the city. He followed the scent of coffee into the kitchen, where Manuela was placing a cup on a tray.

"Good morning, Mr. Thompson. I was just bringing you your breakfast."

Sawyer looked at the food-laden tray. Bacon, eggs, toast. This was something he could dig into. Without thinking he reached for the toast. At Manuela's questioning glance he shrugged. "I'm starving."

"Would you like to eat in here?"

"Where else would I eat?"

Manuela gave him a quizzical look. "Señora Easley always has breakfast in bed."

Was that how his mother grew up? Eating breakfast in bed? Getting dressed up and going to parties? She never mentioned any of that to him. She and his dad never talked about their childhoods. Looking back, he could see how they had deflected his questions, deftly changing the subject each time he asked about grandparents, aunts, uncles, cousins—any family member. Eventually he stopped asking.

"I hope you'll find this satisfactory. Señora Easely usually has dry toast and a boiled egg each morning. When she called and said you were coming, I figured you would want a little more than that."

"Thank you." He sat down at the bar, a smooth granite slab that probably cost more than he could make in a decade working at the Bylers'. He polished off the breakfast. Much better than the chintzy supper he'd had last night.

His mind drifted to Anna and Lukas. They would have already had their breakfast. His father would be at the shop, downing his third cup of black coffee. Christmas was in a couple of weeks. Who would paint the rocking horses? He shouldn't have left them right before the holiday.

Homesickness assaulted him. He shouldn't have left them at all.

Sawyer stared at his empty plate. He'd leave for Middlefield tonight. Even if he didn't have answers. If he couldn't get a flight, he'd rent a car. He couldn't wait to get home.

He rose and walked into the living room, his bare feet sinking into the soft carpet. Other than the echo of Manuela doing the breakfast dishes, he was surrounded by silence. Emptiness. The fancy decorations and expensive furnishings couldn't hide the coldness here. The Bylers might not have much, but that was by choice, and their house was filled with warmth. With love.

That's what he wanted. Not money. Not some company

that would own him and consume his life. He wanted to be surrounded by his family and friends.

Lord, thank You for showing me the way.

"Is there anything else you need, Mr. Thompson?"

He turned at the sound of Manuela's voice. "Is Cora—my grandmother—still sleeping?"

"No, sir. She went out early this morning."

"Probably on another shopping trip," he muttered.

"Not shopping." Manuela frowned. "She's at the doctor."

Sawyer's brow lifted. "Doctor? Why?"

"I don't know, Mr. Thompson. Señora Easley, she is very private about those things."

"Do you know when she'll be back?"

"No, Mr. Thompson. Can I help you with anything else?"

He shook his head and she left. He walked to the doors that opened up over the city. He pressed his hand against the cold window. Snatched it away. Great, a handprint Manuela would have to clean later. He took the tail of his shirt and wiped the print off.

Was his grandmother sick? If so, he hadn't been able to tell. She had plenty of spunk. Then he thought about her hand shaking as she held the champagne glass. The number of drinks she'd had at the party last night. She never lost her poise. But she couldn't have been sober either.

Sawyer shoved his hands into the pockets of his jeans. It was probably just a routine checkup. Nothing to worry about. And nothing to keep him here. He would still go back to Middlefield—and then on to Tennessee, to find Laura.

Sawyer couldn't spend the morning sitting in the apartment waiting for Cora to return. She had a TV, but he hadn't watched one since he was a kid. Even in high school he hadn't gone to the movies, preferring to save his money for other things.

Against his better judgment, he went out for a walk. Once again the city closed in upon him, frantic, rushed, claustrophobic. When he returned, he saw Cora sitting in the living room. The fireplace wasn't on, but she wore a thick sweater with fur trim. He didn't doubt the fur was real. He walked toward her, yet she didn't turn to look at him. Just stared at the empty fireplace in front of her.

"Hello," he said, feeling awkward and uncomfortable. He didn't know what to call her. Mrs. Easley? Cora? Grandmother?

No. She didn't deserve that title.

Her head jerked. She looked at him as he went to sit down. She smiled. "Did you enjoy your walk?"

"I wouldn't say I enjoyed it. But it was nice to get fresh air." Sawyer frowned. "What little I could find."

"Doesn't the city invigorate you?" Her grin widened. She shivered.

"Want me to turn on the fireplace?"

"I'll take care of it." She picked up the remote and clicked it on. "That's better."

"So why were you at the doctor? Are you sick?"

Cora seemed taken aback by the question. "You're being nosy."

"Nosy?" He leaped up from the chair and paced across the room. "You won't tell me about my mother. Or my father. Now you won't let me know why you went to the doctor. Did you ever plan to tell me anything?" His gaze narrowed. "Or was this just a ruse to get me here?"

She put her fingertips to her temple. "I have a headache—"

"Another excuse."

"I will not be spoken to like that in my own house."

"Don't worry. I'm leaving." He started to stalk away.

"Sawyer. Wait."

He turned. "What?"

Her face seemed to have aged ten years. "I'm not used to answering . . . personal questions. If you must know, my appointment was a routine checkup. Nothing more than that. And as for your other questions . . ."

He crossed his arms, waiting.

"I really do have a headache. If you'll indulge me for a couple hours longer, I'll tell you all you need to know." She moved toward him. "Please. I need to lie down for a little while."

He looked down at her. Her ramrod-straight posture had slumped a little. Perhaps she wasn't faking the fatigue. "All right. But when you wake up, I want to know everything."

"You will. I promise." She touched his cheek. "You should shave," she said. "You look so . . . uncivilized."

CHAPTER 26

Sawyer paced. It had been an hour since Cora had gone to her room. He was tired of waiting. His nerves felt like they were about to break through his skin. Manuela had disappeared too. Antsy, he walked into the kitchen. Opened one of the cupboards. It was almost empty, save for a couple jars of caviar, three jars of green olives, and a box of water crackers. Did this woman not have any real food? Then again, she probably ate out, when she wasn't having food brought in.

He shut the cabinet and turned around. Cora's purse lay on the counter. He was surprised she hadn't taken it to her room. He stared at it, arguing with his conscience. He'd never gone through someone else's personal belongings in his life, with the exception of things he'd found in the Mullets' barn. But he'd been desperate then.

Wasn't he desperate now?

His grandmother hadn't kept her promises, and he had a right to know what she was so determined to hide. Ignoring the stab of guilt, he glanced around for Manuela. She was nowhere in sight. Cautiously he picked up Cora's purse and began looking through it.

He took out her wallet first—soft leather, matching the pale pink purse. She'd been holding out on him. Five hundred-dollar bills, plus a few twenties and a ten. He shrugged and moved on to the card pockets. She must have every credit card ever produced. Nothing here. He was about to snap the wallet shut when he noticed a white card poking out, as if it had been hastily shoved inside. He pulled it out.

Dr. Frederick Henry. Neurologist.

A neurologist? He flipped the card over. An appointment for next week was written on the back. Why would she be seeing a neurologist? He tucked the card back in the slot, careful to make sure it was askew the way he found it, and shut the wallet.

Frustration and curiosity gave way to concern.

Maybe she was sick. Seriously ill. Then again, she was over sixty. Maybe a neurological checkup was normal for a woman her age.

He was about to abandon his search and close the purse when he saw her checkbook. He looked around. No Cora. No Manuela. He opened the checkbook. On top lay a carbon copy of the last check she had written. He froze at the name written on the line.

Laura Stutzman.

Sawyer stared at the check. Gaped at the amount. Why on earth would his grandmother have given Laura money? And so much?

But he knew exactly why. She had paid Laura off. Paid her to go away and leave Sawyer alone. Now she had the money she needed to pay her parents back. She could go home.

Fury welled up in him. He didn't blame Laura for taking the check. He blamed his grandmother for doing something so vile and underhanded.

Sawyer tossed the checkbook back into her purse and headed for her bedroom. As he neared, he could hear Cora talking, her voice faint through the partly open door.

"Kenneth, I don't know how long I can stall him. I thought once he came to the city he would realize his place here."

Sawyer crept to the door and leaned his ear as close as he dared.

"I know he's an adult. You've made it very clear I don't have a legal right to keep him here. But I have to do something. He's ready to leave."

He peered through the crack. She was sitting on her bed, her back to the door. Her back was straight and tense. She barely moved as she talked.

"I can't tell him about Kerry yet. Why? Because it's not the right time!"

"Mr. Thompson?"

Sawyer jumped at the sound of Manuela's voice. He stepped away from the door. "Um, hi."

"Do you need something?"

"I was checking to see if my grandmother was up from her nap." He moved farther from her room.

"Is she?"

"Yes, but she's on the phone."

Manuela nodded. "I will get started on lunch. Is there anything special you want, Mr. Thompson?"

To go home. "Nothing for me, thanks."

She turned, then stopped. "Mr. Thompson, I . . ." Manuela looked at her white leather shoes. "I . . ."

"What is it?"

The maid lifted her gaze. "I really don't want to pry into Señora Easley's business."

"I understand." He stepped forward. "But if you have something to tell me, I promise I won't let my grandmother know we talked. I'll make sure you won't lose your job."

"I'm not worried about that." Manuela scratched the back of her hand. "I care about Señora Easley. She's not the easiest woman I've worked for, but life has been difficult for her."

Sawyer doubted that. How hard could life be when you had enough money and power to do anything you wanted? To make people do your bidding? But she hadn't been able to control his mother. "I'm glad she has someone looking out for her," he said.

"*Sí.* I know she won't like this, but I think you should have them."

He frowned. "Have what?"

"Wait here."

A few moments later, she returned holding a packet of letters wrapped in a rubber band. She handed them to him. "These are from your mother."

Sawyer took them. He pulled one out of the package. It

was unopened. He flipped through the rest of them. Still sealed. "She never read them?"

Manuela shook her head.

"Why?"

"I don't know. But I think you should read them."

Sawyer looked at the letters. His pulse started to pound. He might find the answers he'd been searching for—without Cora's help. "Thank you, Manuela." Without waiting for a response he rushed into the guest bedroom, shut the door, and sat on the edge of the bed. He opened the first letter.

Dear Mother . . .

CHAPTER 27

Cora hung up the phone. The call to Kenneth had been pointless. Her attorney couldn't help her with Sawyer. And Cora could tell her grandson couldn't wait to leave.

She thought the party might have broken the ice between them. But Sawyer had kept to himself. He was polite when spoken to. Smiled when necessary. She was impressed with his manners. Yet he was clearly ill at ease not only around the guests but in her apartment as well.

She'd also hoped that exploring the city on his own might have piqued his curiosity. Instead, he seemed more irritated than ever. But she couldn't blame his mood solely on being away from home. She was putting him off, and he didn't hesitate to let his frustration show.

Cora stood and walked to the bathroom. The pain in her hips had increased over the past few days. After downing two pain relievers, she looked in the mirror. Tried to discern what the doctor claimed he saw during her appointment. She looked normal. Maybe she needed a little more Botox to keep her brow line lifted, but nothing alarming. Nothing to warrant the battery of blood work and tests the physician insisted on.

As she turned away from the mirror, she pushed her pain and physical issues out of her mind. Sawyer was her priority. Somehow she had to say or do something to convince him to stay. A private tour of the city, perhaps. She had access to places most New Yorkers only dreamed of seeing. During the tour she could find out what his interests were. Get to know him better.

A chill ran through her. She'd have to tell Manuela to turn up the heat. Her hands trembled as she pulled her cashmere cardigan closer to her body and left her bedroom. She'd treat Sawyer to lunch, anywhere he wanted to go. Anything he desired. Whatever it would take to keep her grandson in New York, she was willing to do it.

Anything but tell him the truth.

She gathered her reserves and walked into the living room. "Sawyer?" she called. Then she saw him, sitting in the chair near the cold fireplace.

She crossed the room. "You can turn this on whenever you—" The chill in her body shot straight to her heart. Her gaze went to the letters in her lap. "Where did you get those?"

"Does it matter?" His jaw tightened, the muscle pulsing back and forth.

"Yes, it does." She walked over and reached for the letters. He pulled them out of her reach. "That is my personal property. You have no right—"

"No right to know the real reason my parents left?" He

held up the letters. "Too late. I already know. And I'm sure you weren't planning to tell me."

She grasped at any remnant of calm, trying to maintain her composure. But confronted with the truth she'd tried to hide not only from everyone else but from herself as well, she couldn't maintain her control.

She dropped to the chair. "I threw those letters away." Then the truth hit her. "Manuela!" she gasped.

"Don't blame her."

"I will fire her this instant."

Sawyer held up his hand. "If you do, I will walk out that door."

Cora paused. She could see he was serious. "All right. I won't fire her." *Not yet.*

"How could you do this?" He stood. Paced in front of the fireplace. Stopped and glared at her. "How could you throw away my mother's letters?"

She gripped the arms of the chair. "I was . . . I was angry with her."

"She reached out to you." Sawyer snatched a letter from the chair. "*'Dear Mother. This is my fifth letter to you. I know you must be angry with me, but I had hoped to hear from you by now. I shouldn't have left the way I did. I apologize. But I love Ray. I didn't love Trenton Babbitt. Our marriage would have been a sham.'*"

"She didn't even give him a chance." Cora looked at Sawyer. "She left the morning of the wedding. Ran off with that ragamuffin of a man."

"That man was my father." Sawyer's voice shook. "He was

a good man. He took care of me and Mom. We didn't have all this." He gestured to the penthouse. "But we had fun together. We had love. That's all my mother wanted, was to love and be loved." He clenched the letter. "But you didn't care about that."

"I cared!" Cora rose. "I cared about her welfare. Her future. I didn't want her to struggle. With Trenton she would never be—"

"Poor?" Sawyer tossed down the letter. "She wouldn't have been happy either."

"Happiness isn't everything. It isn't security. And she could have learned to love Trenton, and her place in society." Cora looked away. "She never appreciated what I tried to give her."

"Oh, but she did." Sawyer's razor-sharp tone cut through the air. He picked up another letter. "She said so right here. *'Mother, I now understand what you were trying to do for me. I have to be honest, I never would have married Trenton. But I miss you. I want us to be a family again. I have a son. His name is Sawyer.'"*

Sawyer paused. *"'He's three now. Soon he'll want to know about his grandmother. His family. I want you to meet him. Please say you forgive me. If not for my sake, for your grandson's.'"*

Cora felt the color drain from her face. Out of anger and betrayal she had thrown away Kerry's letters. Her embarrassment over her daughter's behavior had encased her heart in layers of bitterness over the years.

Her daughter had wanted forgiveness. But it was Cora who needed it. "Oh, Kerry," she whispered, tears rolling down her cheeks. "What have I done?"

She heard Sawyer sigh. He went to her. Knelt down in front of her. "Grandmother," he said.

Her gaze lifted. Through her tears she smiled. "You haven't called me that before."

"I know."

"Does this mean you're staying?"

He shook his head. "I can't stay. I don't want to."

"Oh." She reached for a tissue in the box on the glass end table. "After what you know, I suppose you wouldn't."

"I don't belong here. This penthouse. This city. Everything about this place proves I should be in Middlefield. With the Bylers."

"Your *real* family." She blew her nose.

"Yes. They're my family." He suddenly reached for her hand. "But you're my family too. And even though I'm angry with what you've done, I know my mother would want us to have a relationship. For her sake, I will do that."

Hope sprang within Cora. "Does that mean you'll be back?"

"In due time." He let go of her hand.

"Irritating phrase, isn't it?" She shook her head. "I'm so sorry, Sawyer. If I'd only opened those letters . . ."

Sawyer stood up. He gathered the letters and brought them to her. "They're open now. Read them. This is how I remember my mother. Kind. Funny. And sometimes a little sad. Now I understand why."

Cora took the letters. She put them in her lap, running her hand over her daughter's handwriting. She looked up at Sawyer. "You'll be leaving soon, then?"

"Not yet. There's something else you haven't told me. About Laura. Why did you give her money?"

"How did you—? Never mind." She waved her hand at him. "You should forget about that girl."

"I can't. I care for her."

She could see he was sincere. And deluded. "Please, listen to me, Sawyer. She doesn't deserve you."

His dark brows furrowed. "Why? Because she's Amish? Because she's poor? Because she's not physically perfect?"

"Because she was so easily bought."

His grandmother's words struck Sawyer's heart like an arrow hitting a bull's-eye. He fought for every ounce of patience he possessed. He failed.

Lord, give me strength, he prayed. Since he'd arrived in New York, he'd been sending up these quick prayers, at first purely out of desperation. Now he knew they worked. He had prayed for his anger to diminish enough to allow him to reach out to his grandmother. Now he needed to be just as calm so he could find out the truth.

Cora's tears had dried up. Her usual cool mask was in place. "Sawyer, she took the money without hesitation." She leaned against the chair, crossed one leg over her knee.

"Why did you give it to her in the first place?"

"To protect you."

He shook his head. "I don't believe you. Try again. This time, with the truth."

Her façade slipped. "All right. Have it your way. I wanted her out of the way. I offered her enough money to take care of her face."

He frowned. "Her face? You mean the scars?"

"Of course I mean the scars."

"There's nothing wrong with her face." Sawyer let out a deep breath. "And you don't understand the Amish. They're not vain. She wouldn't have plastic surgery unless it would save her life."

Cora shrugged. "Be that as it may, she took my money. And she asked for something else."

Confused, he went to her. "What?"

"The services of my private investigator."

"So she didn't go to Tennessee?"

"Tennessee? Sawyer, Laura is in New York. Not the city— upstate somewhere. She is looking for a man named Mark Something."

"Mark King?" He tightened his fists.

"King. Yes, that may be it. I don't know for certain. I supplied her with what she needed to find him. All she had to do was make sure you came to New York with me. She kept up her end of the bargain." Cora looked away. "I certainly can't blame her for you leaving me."

But Sawyer barely heard his grandmother's last words. Laura had lied to him.

Was everyone around him filled with deception and deceit?

Then the realization struck him full force. Laura had gone after Mark. Alone.

He had to find her.

"Where is she?"

"You're going after her?" Cora said. "Why on earth would you do that? She betrayed you. She—"

Sawyer silenced her with a glance. "Those scars on her face? Mark King caused them. Who knows what else he's capable of?"

His grandmother turned even paler than usual. "Sawyer, I had no idea. I just gave her the information she asked for." She rose from the chair and disappeared into the kitchen. A moment later, she returned with a business card. "This is the private investigator I hired. He'll know where she is."

Sawyer took the card. "Thanks." He headed for the door.

"You're leaving?" She trailed him into the foyer. "But you've left your bag here."

"Send it to Middlefield."

"What about money?"

"I have enough." He opened the door.

She gripped his arm. "But you'll need to rent a car. Money for lodging—"

"Grandmother." He faced her. "I've been working since I was fifteen. I have money."

"Oh."

He hurried out the door.

"Sawyer?"

Impatient, he spun around. "I have to go!"

"Will you . . . please let me know you're all right? Laura too."

He paused. "Yes, Grandmother. I will."

CHAPTER 28

Laura looked out the window as the limo zipped down the freeway. Here, as in Ohio, brown leaves carpeted the landscape. The last remnants of sunlight dipped behind the horizon.

"This is your exit." The driver gestured to the right. "There's the sign for your hotel."

"Is this Jasper?"

The driver shook his head. "This is Corning. The Radisson's the closest decent hotel. Jasper's about thirty miles west on 417."

"But I need to go to Jasper."

"I got my instructions," the man insisted. "I was to bring you here. When you're ready in the morning, I'll take you wherever you need to go."

"Thank you." Laura clutched the door handle until her knuckles cramped. Cora had kept her word. During the past two days she'd managed to keep Sawyer in the dark while she made arrangements for Laura. First the detective. Then the information. Finally a car and driver, and hotel accommodations. By this time tomorrow she would be face-to-face with Mark King.

And she had no idea what she would say to him.

Later that evening she settled into the hotel room. Modest by Cora Easley's standards, she supposed, but lavish enough to make an Amish girl feel out of place. King-sized bed, flat-screen TV, marble bathroom. Who needed such luxuries?

Laura laid her suitcase on the low dresser and sat on the edge of the bed. Her stomach rumbled, but she wasn't hungry. And it wasn't because of nerves over her upcoming confrontation with Mark. All she could think about was Middlefield.

Saying good-bye to Leona and Emma had been almost as difficult as leaving Sawyer. She had lied to them too, telling them she was going back home to Tennessee. Instead, she had cashed the check, then called Cora on the prepaid cell phone and asked how she could wire money to her parents in Etheridge. That debt was now paid, with enough left over to see to her needs until she could get back home again.

Laura stood, fingering one of the strings on her *kapp*. The clerk at the front desk had looked at her strangely, but his curiosity could just as easily have been about the scars on her face as her Amish clothing.

Her first time in a hotel. Her first time using a phone. And she was now farther from home than she'd ever been.

Far from home, and far from God.

She had broken so many rules to get here. Lied to her friends. To the man she had begun to fall in love with. Deceived her family—more than once. Allowed herself to be bought off by a rich woman who didn't care a thing about her, just about what Laura could provide.

All for a chance to get even with Mark King.

The goal that had consumed her for months was within her reach. She should feel satisfied. Instead, she felt cold. Empty. Afraid. Most of all, alone.

A knock at the door made her jump. Except for the driver, no one but Cora and the detective knew she was here.

The knocking grew more insistent. Standing on tiptoe, she peered through the round peephole. She couldn't see anyone.

The knocking increased. "Laura?" a voice said. "Open up."

"Sawyer?" She opened the door to the length of the safety chain and looked out. If she was surprised to hear his voice, she was even more shocked by the angry look on his face. Then again, he had a right to be angry. "How did you find me?"

"Let me in."

He wasn't supposed to be here. Didn't need to be here. "*Nee. Geh* back to your grandmother, Sawyer. That's where you belong."

"I'm sick and tired of everyone telling me what to do. Now, let me in."

Laura pushed the door shut and unlatched the chain. He stormed in and slammed the door behind him.

"What are you doing here?" she said.

Sawyer turned, his brown eyes burning into hers. "Stopping you from doing something stupid."

"You have no right—"

"I have every right. I care about you." He moved closer to her. "I thought I made that clear in Middlefield. When you pushed me away." He lowered his voice. "Even though you didn't want to."

Her lips trembled. "I . . . I thought it was for the best. I still do."

Sawyer held up his hands. "It's amazing how everybody else knows what's best for me. What I need. You, my parents, my grandmother. Nobody thinks I have a brain of my own."

"That's not true. You're one of the smartest people I know."

"Then why won't you let me make my own decisions?" He drew nearer. "What do I have to do to make you trust me?"

Laura licked her lips. "I do trust you."

"But not enough to take a chance on us."

She stepped back. "I took a chance, and look where it got me."

He shook his head. "Revenge got you here. That and my grandmother."

Her eyes widened. "She told you?"

"It wasn't too hard to figure out. I knew you pushed me away on purpose. And when I found out she paid you, I knew why." His expression suddenly dropped. "You needed vengeance more than you needed me."

"Nee." She went to him. She had to make him understand. "I wasn't lying to you when I left. You do deserve better than me."

"Stop saying that!"

He reached out and pulled her to him. And before she could catch her breath, he kissed her.

Her kiss was as sweet as he'd imagined. It filled him, comforted him. He'd expected her to pull away. Instead, she leaned into him. His arms tightened around her shoulders. Then, before he reached the point of no return, he pulled away.

"Don't expect me to say I'm sorry," he said. "Because I'm not." He drew in a deep breath, gratified to see that she was also struggling for air. After that kiss she could never deny she cared for him. He knew her true feelings now. And they matched his own.

She backed up a step or two. "This won't work."

"Yes, it will." Sawyer tempered his tone. "We can make it work, Laura."

And he knew it was true. He knew it because he had risked everything to come and get her.

His grandmother's detective had told him where to find her. She was headed to Jasper, a small town in Steuben County, New York, just across the border from Pennsylvania.

All during the four-and-a-half-hour drive from Manhattan, Sawyer had steamed and stewed, furious with Laura, with his grandmother, with his birth parents. Sick of all the lies and betrayal. Sick of the incessant restlessness, the confusion about his place in the world. Sick of the years of grief and pain over his parents' death.

His life had never truly been his own. He was twenty-one years old and others were still making decisions for him. Still telling him what to do.

No more.

He looked at Laura, gazed into blue eyes filled with a mixture of pain and love. This was it. If he didn't convince her they belonged together, he'd never have another chance. He wasn't going to let her go. "Laura, listen to what I'm saying."

"You're not listening to what I'm saying!" Tears rolled down her cheeks. He wanted to wipe them away, but he didn't dare. "I'm broken, Sawyer. Inside and out."

"So am I."

"Not like me." She ran her fingers down her face, over the scars, over the tears. "I don't understand it. I did everything *right*. I followed the rules. I loved my family. I joined the church. I worked hard."

She turned her back on Sawyer. "I fell in love. The man I loved stole money from my *familye*. Then when I wanted him to pay, he tried to destroy me. He tossed a firebomb through that window. I still have nightmares from it, Sawyer. The glass, the pain. The fear. Why did God let this happen?"

He came up behind her, put his hands on her shoulders, and turned her to face him. "My parents died. I was in foster care. I was abused." Despite himself, he felt his eyes well up and his throat tighten. "The two most important people in my life lied to me until the day they died. Why did God let that happen to me?"

Laura sobbed. She touched his cheek. "Sawyer . . . I'm so sorry."

"We're all broken, Laura. And we're all looking for someone to blame. God's the easiest target. We let ourselves believe that if He loved us, things would be perfect. But we both know that's not true."

She nodded.

He led her to the edge of the bed. They sat down. "Since I was adopted, I've heard the same words over and over: *God's will. God's plan.* I never really understood what that meant. Until now. And I'm not sure I fully understand, but I know this much: Everything that's happened in our lives has brought us to this moment. To each other." He took her hand.

She gripped his hand. "You really believe that?"

"I do. Despite the mistakes we've made, the pain we've gone through, God has given us each other. You don't have to face Mark King alone."

"You're not going to stop me from seeing him?"

He shook his head. "No. We need to end this. Tomorrow. Mark needs to pay for what he's done. But not out of revenge. Out of justice."

Laura sighed. "I wasn't even sure what I was going to do. If I could even face him." She looked at Sawyer. "I'm scared."

He put his arm around her shoulders. "You don't have to be, Laura. You never have to be afraid again."

"Señora Easely, is everything all right?"

Cora turned away from the window and faced Manuela. No, everything wasn't all right. Sawyer was gone. And it was her fault. He promised he'd come back, but she wouldn't blame him if he didn't. Perhaps sometime in the future she would return to Middlefield and try to reestablish their relationship.

Or maybe she wouldn't. Right now she was too exhausted to think about it. Her gaze went past Manuela's shoulder to the stack of letters on the table.

Manuela glanced at them, then at Cora. "I'm sorry, Señora Easley. I know I shouldn't have interfered. But the letters . . . I thought someday you might want them."

Cora crossed her arms over her thin chest. She'd turned the thermostat up, and the fireplace was on full power. Still, she was chilled. "So you gave them to my grandson instead?"

Manuela nodded and stared at her feet. "I will pack my things." She turned to go.

"Manuela," Cora said. "Wait."

The maid looked up. "Yes, Señora Easley?"

Cora took a breath. "Thank you."

Manuela's eyes went wide. *"Perdóneme?"*

"I said, thank you."

"For what?"

Cora considered the question. Despite her disobedience, perhaps even outright deception, Manuela's heart was in the right place. She had acted in Cora's best interests. Where on earth would Cora could find anyone of equal character to replace her?

"For . . . caring," she said.

"Then I am not fired?"

Cora felt a brief flare of warmth at her core. "No, Manuela. You are not fired."

Manuela smiled. "I will get you some hot tea, *sí?*"

"That would be nice."

When Manuela left, Cora sat back down in front of the fire and picked up one of Kerry's letters. Her chest tightened, as if her heart were being squeezed into a small ball by an invisible force. She blinked back the tears, tears she'd refused to shed for a long time.

It was better that Sawyer found out this way. Through his mother's words. Kerry was honest.

Cora wouldn't have trusted herself to be the same.

Manuela appeared, carrying a silver tray with a white china teapot and matching teacup. She set the tray on the coffee table and poured the tea, then reached into her pocket and pulled out Cora's cell phone. "It rang while I was in the kitchen."

Cora took the phone. As Manuela walked away, Cora looked at the display. Dr. Henry's office. She hadn't expected to hear from him so soon. It had only been two days since her appointment. Two days since Sawyer left.

She redialed the number and requested to speak to the nurse.

"Mrs. Easley, thank you for calling us back. Dr. Henry would like to schedule a follow-up appointment with you as soon as possible."

Cora's hand shook so much that she almost dropped the phone. "Why?"

"I'm afraid I'm not allowed to give specifics over the phone—"

"I will not ask you again. And if you value your job, you will tell me why Dr. Henry is in such a hurry to see me."

There was a pause, and the nurse drew a deep breath. "Mrs. Easley, I do value my job. And I want to keep it. But as I said, I am not allowed to give you that information. If you'll wait a moment, I'll try to get Dr. Henry on the line."

Before Cora could object, there was a click, and a bland Muzak rendition of "My Cherie Amour" filled the earpiece. She sighed, picked up her cup, and sipped at the now-tepid tea.

The nerve of that nurse! Everyone in her employ knew that she hated to be kept waiting, including Dr. Henry and his staff.

The elevator music segued into "Can't Smile without You." Halfway through the second verse, a voice jolted Cora back to the present. "Mrs. Easely. Dr. Henry here. How can I help you?"

"You can tell me what the blazes is going on," Cora snapped. "That rude and uncooperative nurse of yours—"

"Is just doing her job," Dr. Henry interrupted.

"Fine," Cora said. "So you tell me. What's the big rush that I need to come in immediately?"

Dr. Henry cleared his throat. "It's best not to do this over the phone. We need to run a few more tests, and—"

"You've already taken more blood from me than a vampire," Cora said. "I refuse to submit to anything else until I know the diagnosis."

There was a long pause on the other end of the line. "Very well, Mrs. Easley," he said. "You have Parkinson's disease."

CHAPTER 29

Sawyer pulled the rental car into the driveway of the modest Amish house. Laura looked at him and tried to muster a smile. Her eyes were still swollen from crying last night. Even after he'd left to stay in his own room, she'd continued to cry. Not just for her losses, but for his. For the way she'd rejected him. Then, finally, she made her way to happy tears, that she'd found a man who was truly faithful, one she could love and who loved her.

"Are you ready?" Sawyer asked.

Laura nodded. "I want to get this over with."

He smiled and squeezed her hand. "Let's do it."

With each step toward the house, her palms dampened, despite the freezing air. The detective had told her that Mark King was staying with the Yoders, the family that owned this home and the farmland surrounding it. The Yoders had a daughter named Miriam, a year younger than Laura.

Mark's current target. Laura was sure of that.

She felt Sawyer's presence close behind her, bolstering her confidence. She took a deep breath and knocked on the door.

A young girl of about four or five answered "Hello?"

Laura bent down a little. "I'm looking for a man named Mark King. Is he here?"

She shook her head, the strings of her *kapp* swaying against her shoulders. Red fruit juice stained her upper lip. *"Nee."*

"Are you sure?" Laura frowned. She was positive this was the address the detective gave her. "Does Miriam Yoder live here?"

"Who is it, Martha Anne?" A young woman appeared behind the little girl. She looked at Laura, then at Sawyer. "Can I help you?"

Sawyer stepped forward. "Do you know a man named Mark King?"

The young woman frowned. "Martha Anne, go help *Mammi* in the kitchen." She touched the girl's shoulders and gently pushed her farther into the house, then turned back to Laura. "I don't know who you're talking about," she said, crossing her arms.

"Are you Miriam?" Laura asked.

"It's none of your business. I think you should *geh* now." The woman moved to close the door, but Sawyer stopped her.

"It's very important we find Mark King," he said, holding the door so that she couldn't shut it in his face. "He's a dangerous man."

"I already said, I don't know him."

A thought occurred to Laura. "There's a man staying with you. He's a little shorter than him." She gestured to Sawyer. "He has light brown hair and a chipped tooth."

The woman's face went pale. "Matt?"

"He changed his name," Laura said to Sawyer.

"Makes sense," Sawyer said. He looked at Miriam again. "His name isn't Matt. It's Mark King, and we need to see him right away. You and your family could be in danger."

Miriam came out on the front porch, shutting the door behind her. "I don't appreciate you saying such lies about my fiancé."

Laura shook her head. "They aren't lies." She pointed to her face. "See these? Mark did this."

"*Mei mann's* name is Matt. Matt Kingston." She frowned again, then shook her head. "You need to leave now."

Laura looked at Sawyer.

What were they supposed to do now?

"Thank you for your time." Sawyer took Laura by the arm. "Sorry to bother you."

Miriam turned and hurried into the house. The door slammed behind her.

Sawyer led Laura down the steps of the front porch. "What are you doing? We can't just leave."

"We don't have a choice. She's protecting him. We can't force her to tell us where he is."

"Then what are we going to do?"

"Right now, we're going to the car." He escorted her to the rental and opened the passenger door for her. Then he got inside. When he looked at her, he saw her body shaking.

"Cold?"

"Not cold. Mad." She looked at him, fury lighting her eyes. "He wins *again*."

"This isn't about winning, Laura. And I didn't say we were leaving. Not yet, anyway. Just give me a chance to think." He gripped the steering wheel but didn't turn on the car. After a moment he said, "I think we're going to have to call the police."

Laura handed him the cell phone Cora had given her and stared out the window while he dialed. "I guess we don't have a choice. I guess——" She hesitated as a movement caught her eye. Someone was running into the field behind the house. "Wait a minute." She leaned forward. "Look, Sawyer. Is that——?"

"I'm gonna find out." He tossed the phone into her lap and shot out the door.

"Sawyer, wait!"

But he was already running toward the field.

Sawyer's lungs burned. He was gaining on the man, who had to be Mark King, even though his hair was cut in a Yankee haircut. Who else would be running that fast into an empty field?

"Stop!" Sawyer yelled, not really expecting Mark to comply.

But the distraction was enough to slow him down. Mark looked over his shoulder and stumbled. Sawyer picked up speed. He closed in, reached for Mark's shirt, and yanked hard, dragging him to the ground.

Mark scrambled out of his grasp and tried to get to his feet, but Sawyer was too quick for him. He snatched his ankle and pulled the man toward him.

Mark lashed out with a fist and connected with Sawyer's jaw. It was almost enough to shake Sawyer, but he held on, then flipped him over and pinned him to the ground. He straddled his back, holding Mark's arms behind him. "You're not going anywhere."

Mark laughed. A dead, hollow sound. "Are you an undercover cop or something?"

"I'm a friend of Laura's." Despite himself, he tightened his grip on Mark's arms. "A good friend."

Mark laughed again, his cheek pressed to the short grass. "So she's alive, then? Too bad."

Sawyer felt the anger rise in him. The man was crazy and cruel. Sawyer wanted to snap him in two. Black dots swam before his eyes as he fought the urge to pummel Mark.

Then he remembered Laura. *Justice, not revenge*. The promise to his parents about joining the church. If he was Amish, he would be expected to forgive. To let Mark go and trust that God would bring His own justice.

But he wasn't Amish yet. And who was to say this wasn't part of God's plan?

Laura scrambled out of the car and ran to the Yoders' backyard. She could hear a woman screaming. When she rounded the corner of the house, she saw Miriam where the field met the yard, yelling at Sawyer to leave Mark alone.

Laura looked out into the field. She could see Sawyer had Mark against the ground. Neither man moved, but she could hear the faint sound of cold laughter that chilled her heart.

"You have to stop him!" Miriam ran to her and clutched her arm. "He's going to kill him."

"*Nee*. He's not." An unexpected calmness came over her. Sawyer had Mark under control. He would finally get the justice he deserved. She turned to Miriam. "You can't protect Mark anymore."

"His name isn't Mark! And I'm not protecting him." She cast a worried look at the men in the field. "I love him."

"So did I. This is how he repaid me." When Miriam wouldn't turn around, Laura moved to stand in front of her. "Look at *mei* face, Miriam. Mark did this. He tried to kill me. Before that he stole money from *mei familye*."

"You're lying."

"He was so kind at first. So sweet. When I first met him, he gave me all his attention. Said everything I wanted to hear."

Miriam looked away.

"He told me he loved me. Wanted to marry me. Wanted to be a part of *mei familye* and part of our bakery business. And once I said yes, he started asking questions. Lots of them. If I didn't answer them right away, or he thought I might not be telling him everything, he would get agitated." She swallowed, but the memories didn't hurt as much anymore. Neither did they bring up the well of anger that filled her for so many months. "Aren't there times when things seem wrong? When you have a strange feeling inside, and it's not a *gut* one?"

In the distance she could hear the sound of sirens. Laura's shoulders relaxed. It was almost over. "Miriam, hear what I'm telling you. Let him *geh*. He doesn't love you. I don't think he's capable of love." She pointed to her face again. "This is all he's capable of. Pain. Destruction. Regret."

Miriam looked at her, tears in her eyes. "He really did that to you?"

Laura nodded. The sirens grew closer. She looked at Sawyer and Mark in the field. They were now on their feet, with Sawyer holding Mark's arms behind his back. As they neared, she could see the smirk on Mark's face. It changed to pleading when he saw Miriam.

"You have to help me," he said to her.

She backed away from him.

"Miriam? Don't tell me you believe what she said. She's crazy. Look at her. She cut herself with a razor blade. She hates herself that much, just like she hates me."

Laura heard footsteps behind her. She didn't have to turn around to know it was the police.

"I don't hate you, Mark," she said. "I forgive you."

She looked at Sawyer and smiled. "I can finally forgive."

CHAPTER 30

Norman's palms dampened as he fastened his vest. Today's church service would change everything. His relationship with his wife, his son, and hopefully with God.

He had already talked to Bishop Esh yesterday. The man had been shocked, but ultimately agreed with Norman's decision. "It's not only the right thing to do," the bishop had said. "It's the only thing to do."

But while Norman exuded the confidence of a man sure of himself, his heart threatened to burst out of his chest. Was this how Adam felt, when he'd made his confession in front of the church? Norman should have supported his son more that day. He should have done so many things differently. Today was the first step in putting the past permanently behind him.

He put on his black hat. Carol walked into the room.

"You look nice."

He turned and faced her. She had a sad smile on her face. Since their talk last week, not much had changed between them.

The distance was still there. His sin had permeated so much of their lives. He hadn't known. Or perhaps he had, and chose to ignore it.

He walked toward Carol. His wife. His helpmate. His memories traveled back to when they first met. She'd been the prettiest *maedel* at the singing that night. Shy, soft-spoken. But soon he found out underneath the shyness was a strong, faithful woman. She had dealt with three miscarriages after Adam was born. God's decision for them to have only one child hadn't put a wedge in their marriage. It had drawn them closer.

Norman had driven in the wedge that now existed. Today he would yank it out. "Ready?"

She nodded. "Let me just get my shawl. It's downstairs."

"I'll get the buggy."

Carol turned. Norman touched her shoulder. *"Lieb?"*

She froze. "You haven't called me that in a long time."

"I know." He kissed her cheek. "And I'm sorry. For so many things."

She looked away. "I can't do this. Not now." She pulled away from him, leaving him surrounded with silent loneliness.

Hopefully that would change after today. He prayed it would.

Adam entered Aaron Detweiler's barn, filing in after several men to their side of the building for the start of the service. As usual he had driven Emma and Leona to church. They were seated on the other side of the barn with the rest of the women. He couldn't see Emma from where he was at the far end of the bench.

He blew out a breath, a puff of white steam hovering in the air. It wouldn't be long before they would have to move services into family homes. He'd rather be cold in the barn than cooped up inside a house, elbow to elbow with everyone else.

He searched for his parents. Didn't see a sign of them. They had been quiet this week. Distant. He'd given up trying to figure them out. He had his own relationship to focus on. His future with Emma. He loved his parents, but he couldn't forgo his own happiness for them. He had to lay their burdens at God's feet. Only God could fix what was broken.

The singing started. He stood, still looking for his father. As a deacon, his *daed* usually sat near or at the front. But he wasn't there this morning. He must have decided to sit somewhere else. The rise and fall of the worship chant filled the church, and he added his voice to everyone else's and tried to focus on the service.

After the singing the bishop stood. He then called Adam's father to the front of the church.

What was this about?

Norman faced the congregation. "Two months ago, *mei sohn*, Adam, stood here and asked you for forgiveness." He swallowed. "Today I ask you for the same."

Adam's mouth dropped open as his father confessed his sin. He'd kissed Emma's mother? Adam felt the gazes of some of the men around him. Did Emma know about this? Worse, did she think *he* knew and had kept another secret? He had to fight not to look for her. Instead, he kept his eyes straight ahead. He wouldn't embarrass his father by making a scene. Having been in the same position, albeit for a different reason, he knew how hard this had to be for his father.

No. It had to be harder. His *daed* was a deacon. Held up to a different standard. And he was admitting not only to sinning with another woman but to abusing his position.

When his father finished, he sat down. Not in the front, but two rows back, at the end. Like Adam, he kept his gaze straight ahead. Chin lifted. Strong. Yet Adam could see his father's shoulders shaking.

Adam held his breath as he waited to see if the congregation forgave his father. As expected, they did. And they would say they forgot.

But how did someone forget this?

The service continued, but Adam's mind wandered. His heart ached for his *mamm*. Did she know about this? It would certainly explain her strange behavior.

At last the service ended, but even then Adam couldn't move. He didn't know who to seek out. His father? His mother? Emma? He sat there, unable to decide, as everyone left the barn for the midday meal at the Detweilers'.

"Adam?"

He looked up to see Emma standing there. He jumped from the bench, wishing he could pull her into his arms. Yet he couldn't, not here. Her gaze mirrored what he felt. She embraced him with her eyes. That would have to be enough.

"Emma . . . I didn't know."

"I know." She lowered her voice. "I didn't either, until *Grossmammi* told me."

"Why didn't you say anything?"

"I didn't feel it was my place."

"So you let this blindside me?"

Emma sighed. She took a step toward him. "Adam, I understand you're upset."

"I'm not upset. I'm—" He turned from her. He didn't know what he was.

"I thought about telling you. But I realized you needed to find out from your father."

His shoulders slumped. He pushed his black hat back and looked at Emma. "I'm not mad at you."

"Are you mad at your *daed*?"

Adam shook his head. "That would make me a hypocrite, don't you think?" He looked at Emma. "I don't think anything worse of your *mamm*."

Emma let out a puff of frosty air. "*Gut*. I don't either. She made a mistake."

"They both did." He looked at the front of the church. "I know how he felt up there. That had to be the hardest thing he's ever done."

"Are you going to talk to him about it?"

Adam turned to Emma. He paused. "I think we both need to talk to him. And *mei mamm*. It's time for this to be over."

Carol looked out the window as they drove home from church. Norman had attached the winter shield to the front of the buggy this morning and had put the softest lap robe they owned on her side of the seat. On their way to church this morning, she had thought his desire to make her comfortable was a ploy. But she hadn't been prepared for his public confession.

Now, sitting next to him, snuggled in the sea-blue lap robe and protected from the chilly wind by the winter shield, she couldn't speak. All she could do was stare out into the countryside as they slowly made their way back home. The clop of the horse's hooves echoed in her ears.

Why had he done it? She hadn't pressured him to repent in front of everyone. She truly thought they would both take the secret to their graves.

"Warm enough?" Norman asked. He tapped the back of the horse's flank with the reins. The horse didn't have a name. Norman didn't believe in getting attached to the animals.

"*Ya.*" She glanced at his profile, expecting to see the tension that had creased his face for so many months. But he looked almost youthful. Like the man she had loved and married so many years ago, rather than the one she'd lived with for the past few years.

"*Gut.*"

She waited to see if he'd say anything more. Ask her questions. Seek her approval for what he'd done. He remained silent.

But she couldn't, not for much longer. "Why?"

"Why what?"

"Why did you make a public confession?"

"Because I had to." He looked at her for a moment before

turning his attention to the road. "I should have done so a long time ago."

He didn't say anything else the rest of the ride home. She didn't know what to think.

He pulled into the driveway. Adam hadn't followed, and she hadn't sought her son out after church. When Norman had asked if they could leave right after the service, she had quickly agreed. She already felt the curious and, in some cases, pitying gazes of her friends and extended family. She didn't want to stick around and answer their questions.

Norman dropped her off in front of the house. She went inside to prepare Sunday lunch—cold cuts sandwiches, pickles, cold tea. She had set the table by the time he walked into the kitchen. He nodded and they both sat down. Bowed their heads. Said their silent prayer of thanks.

Carol looked up. Norman took a big bite of his sandwich. She couldn't touch hers. "Norman?"

"*Ya?*"

"Will things ever be the same between us?"

Norman paused. Put down his sandwich. He rose from his chair and sat in the seat next to her. He took her hand into his rough one. "*Nee*," he said softly. "I don't think they will."

Her heart lurched. "I see."

"I'm hoping we can make it better." Norman took her other hand and gripped both of them in a tight yet gentle hold. "I'm hoping today is a step toward that. I know now that I had to ask God's forgiveness, publicly and with true repentance, before I could ask for yours."

His image blurred in front of her. "That had to be difficult."

"It was. But now I feel . . . free." He released her hands. "Still, I won't feel complete until you've forgiven me. And I don't expect that to happen right away."

She gazed into the eyes of her husband. Remembered when she first fell in love with him. The qualities she'd been attracted to then—his quiet strength, seriousness of purpose, and unrelenting work ethic—paled in comparison to what he was showing her now. A complete absence of pride. A stripping down of his soul. A courage she didn't know he possessed.

Tears flowed freely down her cheeks. She touched his face. "I forgive you, Norman. How can I not?"

His eyes swam with tears. *"Danki."* He choked on the word and buried his head in her hands. *"Danki, mei lieb."* He lifted his head and gazed at her. Moved his mouth closer to hers.

A thrill she hadn't felt in years drifted down her spine. She expected his kiss. Reveled in anticipation of it. She closed her eyes, ready to accept her husband's demonstration of his love.

The front door slammed. They jerked apart as Adam and Emma came into the room. For the first time since her son had returned to Middlefield, she wished he hadn't come home. Not for the next five minutes, anyway.

"Mamm. Daed." Adam looked at both of them. "Is everything all right?"

Carol wiped her eyes. *"Ya."* She looked at her husband. Her love. "Everything is *perfekt.*"

CHAPTER 31

During the second week of January, Laura watched as Adam and Emma exchanged vows in the Shetlers' living room. The ceremony was similar to ones she'd been to in Tennessee. The room was packed, and everyone was smiling. Especially the bride and groom. She was glad for Emma and Adam. They deserved their happiness.

Adam's hair had grown out enough to be visible underneath the edge of his hat. He looked handsome in his dark suit, his smile nearly as wide as his face. But Emma was the stunner. Her rosy cheeks bloomed as she stood next to Adam, and there was a glow to her complexion Laura had never seen before.

She glanced at Sawyer, sitting next to her. He was in full Amish dress today and looked more handsome than she'd ever seen him. After Mark had been taken into custody, she and Sawyer had gone to the police station together to press charges. She would have to testify to make sure Mark served time for what he did to her, her family, Adam, and the Yoders. But at last she felt free.

The ceremony ended and everyone dispersed.

"I'll be right back," Sawyer said. He gave Laura a grin that warmed her to her toes. He left to join a few of the other men as they stood around Adam, congratulating him. Even though he had yet to join the church, he looked like he belonged. She felt like she belonged here too.

"Hi, Laura."

She turned. It was Katherine Yoder.

After Mark's arrest, Laura had written to her parents saying that she would be staying in Middlefield awhile longer. And during that time, Katherine had been patiently teaching her how to quilt.

"I've been working on those squares," she said. "I still can't get the stitches straight."

"It takes practice." Katherine sighed and looked around the room.

"Are you all right?" Laura asked.

"I'm fine. Just tired of all the weddings."

Laura lifted her brows. "How many have you been to?"

"More than my share." She smiled, but her eyes remained filled with regret. "I wonder when it will be my turn."

Laura couldn't imagine why someone as pretty and sweet as Katherine was still unmarried. "It will, Katherine." She smiled. "I know you'll be married soon."

"That's what everyone tells me." Katherine looked away. Her auburn hair peeked from beneath her white *kapp*. "Like you, they're just being nice."

"Actually, I was being honest."

Katherine smiled. *"Danki."* Her gaze went past Laura's shoulder.

Laura turned, following Katherine's line of sight. Johnny Mullet stood across the room, talking to a young woman. Katherine's eyes held a mix of pain and longing that was all too familiar. "We should see if they need some help in the kitchen."

Katherine hesitated. "*Gut* idea," she finally said.

Late into the evening, the last guest went home. Laura was in the kitchen cleaning the remaining dishes when Leona walked in.

"*Danki* for all your help." The old woman plopped into the chair.

Laura turned around, her hands covered in soapy bubbles. "Washing dishes isn't much."

"It is when the rest of us are exhausted." Leona smiled. "It was a *gut* wedding, *ya?*"

"*Ya.*" She went back to the dishes. She didn't ask where Adam and Emma were. They had already moved their things into Emma's parents' old room the day before. It would feel strange having Adam here in the house. But that wouldn't matter to Laura. She didn't plan to be here much longer.

She dried the last dish, lost in her thoughts. When she finished wiping down the counter, she turned and saw Leona still sitting there. "Sit," Leona said, patting the chair next to her. "I'd like to talk with you."

Laura sat down. "I've wanted to talk to you too."

Leona nodded. "I thought so. Would it have to do with your future plans?"

"*Ya.* It would."

"Before you say anything, I want you to know that you're welcome here. As long as you want."

"I appreciate that."

"But I also have to ask—aren't you missing home?"

Laura rubbed her thumb against her opposite forefinger. "I am. But I promised someone I would stay here a little while longer." She couldn't help but smile.

Leona grinned back. "He's a *gut mann.* I hear he's been talking with the bishop about joining the church."

"*Ya.* But before he makes it official, he wants to visit his grandmother one more time."

"I heard she's an interesting *fraa.*"

"That's putting it nicely."

Leona leaned on her cane and hoisted herself from the chair. "Time to get these old bones to bed. *Guten nacht.*"

"*Guten nacht.*"

Laura straightened up the rest of the kitchen. When she finished, she went to the living room and sat on the couch, tired but not quite ready for bed. She and Sawyer had said good-bye earlier in the evening, but she missed him. She wouldn't see him until Sunday at church. Then not again until work on Monday . . .

Laura chuckled out loud. She sounded like a silly schoolgirl. One who was in love.

As she rose from the couch, she noticed the Bible sitting on the coffee table, where it always rested. Leona read from it often, and she'd seen Emma pick it up a few times, even though both of them had their personal Bibles in their rooms upstairs.

Laura hadn't touched the scriptures since Mark had abandoned her in Tennessee. Before then, she'd been a regular Bible reader. Unlike other Amish families she knew, her parents had encouraged scripture reading.

Laura stared at the book. It had been too long. She opened it to a random page and started to read from Psalms.

> I will be glad and rejoice in thy mercy: for thou hast considered my trouble; thou hast known my soul in adversities . . .

The sound of a knock on the door made her jump. Who would be here this time at night? Maybe it was a wedding guest who forgot something. She closed the Bible, walked to the window, and pulled back the curtain.

A lone figure stood on the front porch. Definitely not a woman. But he wasn't wearing an Amish hat.

Laura opened the door, and an irresistible smile spread over her face. "What are you doing here?"

Sawyer grinned. "Thanks for the warm greeting." His grin faded a bit. "Mind if I come in?"

"Sure." She let him inside. "It's a little late, though. Is something wrong?"

"No. We didn't get much time to talk today." He looked at her. Still wearing his black dress pants, she noticed. Plus a dark jacket. He'd already started letting his hair grow out. He was serious about joining the church, and she had promised she'd stay here until he did.

"Do you want to sit down?" Laura asked. "I can make some coffee."

"Tempting." He grinned again. "Very tempting. But I can't stay long. I wanted to let you know I'm going to New York on Monday."

"Oh." She knew he had planned to visit Cora again, but

hearing him say the words disappointed her. "I hope you have a safe trip."

"I won't be gone long. You'll be here when I get back?"

"*Ya*. I promised I would."

He nodded, then drew closer to her. "Then I wonder if you could make another promise to me?"

She angled her head to one side. "Depends on what it is."

"Promise me you'll marry me."

"Sawyer . . . are you sure?"

He took her face in his hands and kissed her, then let his lips graze against one of the scars on her cheek. He pulled back. "Believe me now?"

She ducked her head and laughed. *"Ya."*

"When I get back from New York, I'm going to join the church. Then we can get married, here or in Tennessee. Wherever you like."

"I think we can talk about that later. When you get back. I have to let *mei* parents know first. I'm sure they'll want to meet you."

"Does that mean you're saying yes?"

She nodded. "Yes, Sawyer. I will marry you."

She leaned against him, feeling his heart beat against hers. A heart of love. A heart of loyalty. The answer to a prayer she never had the courage to pray.

She had come to Middlefield filled with anger and looking for revenge.

Instead, she found acceptance.

And faithfulness.

And love.

DISCUSSION QUESTIONS

1. Sawyer is in an unusual situation—he's a Yankee raised during his teen years in an Amish world. He struggles to find his place and purpose in life. Have you found yourself in a similar situation? How did you resolve it?

2. Laura wants justice for how Mark treated her, yet what she really wants is vengeance. What is the difference between the two?

3. Both Laura and Emma are insecure about their looks (for different reasons). Can you identify with their insecurities? How can we see past the surface to others' hearts the way God does?

4. Cora has an extremely negative reaction to Amish country. What do you think it will take for her to accept Sawyer's desire to become Amish?

5. Do you think Sawyer's decision to become Amish stems from a true belief that the Amish faith and way of life is

what he wants, or is he influenced by his love for Laura? Explain your answer.

6. Do you think Mark has the capacity to change? Why or why not?

7. Laura and Sawyer were able to find healing and forgiveness, not just through each other, but because of God's mercy. Think of a time when you felt bruised and broken. How did God comfort you?

8. Was Norman's public confession necessary? Why do you think admitting his indiscretion in front of the church was the only way for him to find peace?

9. What do you think Sawyer will do when he discovers Cora's illness? How will that affect his relationship with Laura and the rest of the Amish community?

10. Despite Laura pushing Sawyer away, he remained faithful to her. How does God remain faithful to us during the times we feel distant from Him?

ACKNOWLEDGMENTS

My deepest thanks to my editors, Natalie Hanemann and Penelope Stokes for their encouragement, support, and skillful editing of *Faithful to Laura*. Thank you to my agent, Tamela Hancock Murray, who has always been in my corner throughout my writing career. My love to my family. I'm grateful for their patience and understanding, not just of my writing, but me as a person. I'm not always easy to live with!

A special note of thanks to Karla Hanns. Soon after writing *Treasuring Emma*, the first book in this series, I was diagnosed with thyroid cancer. As I went through treatment, Karla made me a prayer quilt. I was fortunate enough to have the actual quilt included on the cover of this book, and it is the model for the quilt Katherine made for Laura. Karla, along with so many family members, friends, and readers prayed for me during my treatment, which as of this writing was successful. For that, there aren't enough thanks in the world. God bless you all!

Enjoy an excerpt from the final book in
Kathleen Fuller's Middlefield Family series,

LETTERS TO KATIE . . .

CHAPTER 1

"Oh, Katherine. This is so *schee*."

Katherine Yoder smiled at her best friend, Mary Beth
Shetler. She'd spent hours working on the baby quilt, making
sure the tiny stitches were as perfect as possible for Mary Beth's
new baby. "I'm glad you like it."

"Of course I do." Mary Beth touched the soft flannel
quilt, running her fingers over the pale yellow, blue, and peach
blocks. Each block had a ragged edge, a new pattern she hadn't
attempted before. The simple style was well suited for a baby,
and Mary Beth's was due in a few weeks.

"I love it." Mary Beth folded the quilt and placed it on her
knees, her expanded belly barely allowing the space. "*Danki* for
such a beautiful gift. Although I don't see how you have the
time, working so many hours at the restaurant."

All I have is time. She pushed the self-pity aside and managed a smile. She didn't want to ruin the moment between them
with jealousy. Unlike Mary Beth Shetler, Katherine didn't have a

husband—and soon a child—to take care of. Outside of working at Mary Yoder's and helping her parents at home, her only other pursuits were her sewing and needlework. She was always busy yet longed for something different. Something more.

Apparently God had other plans.

Mary Beth managed to rise from the chair in her tiny kitchen. Her husband, Chris, had built the four-room home behind Mary Beth's parents' property. The dwelling resembled a *dawdi haus*, and likely would be used as such once the rest of Mary Beth's siblings—Johnny, Caleb, Micah, and Eli—married and left home. But for now, the tidy, cozy home was enough.

And more than Katherine had.

Mary Beth placed the quilt on the table. "I'm glad you came over. Since I've gotten so big, I haven't gotten out much." Her light blue dress draped over her bulging belly.

Katherine's eyes widened. "Are you sure you're not having twins?"

"*Nee.*" Her friend laughed. "But I look like I am." With a waddling gait she moved to the cabinet. "Do you want anything to drink?"

Katherine shook her head. "I can't stay too long. I wanted to make sure you got the quilt before the *boppli* arrived. I have to work later today."

"Maybe just a few minutes?" Mary Beth went back to the table and sat down. She reached for Katherine's hand. "It's been so long since we talked."

"We've both been busy." She squeezed her friend's hand. "And you'll be even busier in a few weeks."

"*Ya.*" A radiant glow appeared on Mary Beth's cheeks. "But I don't want us to drift apart. You're *mei* best friend."

Katherine released her hand. "And I promise I'll be the best *aenti* to your *boppli.*"

"The baby has plenty of *onkels*, that's for sure." Her smile dimmed a little.

Katherine frowned. "What's wrong? It's not the *boppli*, is it?"

"*Nee.*"

"Chris?"

"Chris is fine too. We're happier than we've ever been."

"Then what is it?"

Mary Beth sighed, but she didn't reply.

"You know you can tell me anything. If something's troubling you, I want to help."

Her friend looked at Katherine. "It's Johnny."

Katherine's heart twisted itself into a knot. She glanced away before steeling her emotions. "What about Johnny?"

"Are you sure you want to talk about him?"

"I've accepted that there's no future for us. What I felt for Johnny was a childhood crush."

A crush. The truth was, Katherine had loved Mary Beth's twin brother, Johnny, for as long as she could remember. For years she held out hope for a chance, however small, however remote. She had clung to that dream as if she were drowning and it was her only lifeline.

But not anymore.

She sat straight in the chair, brightened her smile, and said, "What's going on with him?"

"He's been acting . . . different."

"What do you mean?"

"Distant. Partly because he's been working so many hours at the buggy shop. *Mamm* said she barely sees him except for church service. He leaves early in the morning and comes home late. But when he is around, he's quiet."

"That doesn't sound like him," Katherine said. "Do you think he's keeping something from your *familye*?"

Something . . . or *someone*?

Despite Katherine's vow not to care, her heart constricted again at the thought.

"I don't know." Mary Beth's brown eyes had lost the warmth they'd held moments ago. "He's becoming like a stranger to me. To all of us. We've drifted apart." Her smile faded. "Like you and I have."

Katherine shook her head in protest. "You know I'm always here for you."

Tears welled in Mary Beth's eyes.

Katherine drew back. "I'm so sorry. I didn't mean to make you cry."

"I'm always crying." Mary Beth wiped her eyes. "It makes Chris *ab im kopp*. Hormones, I'm sure." She sniffed, wiping her eyes. "I'm glad we're still best friends."

Katherine hugged Mary Beth. "We always will be."

The story continues in Kathleen Fuller's Letters to Katie . . .

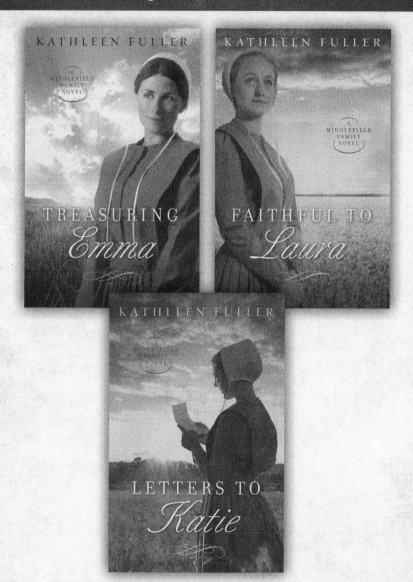

Enjoy
Kathleen Fuller's
Amish of Birch
Creek series!

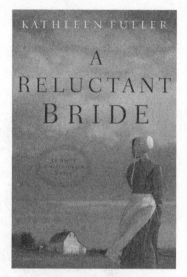

Available in print and e-book.

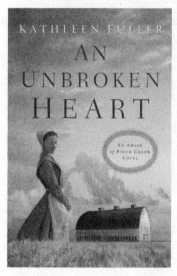

Available in print and e-book.

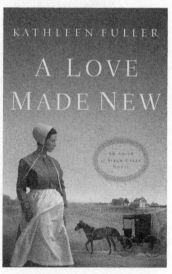

Available in print and e-book
September 2016.

Can Anna Mae heed God's call on her life,
even if it means leaving behind everything
she knows . . . and everyone she loves?

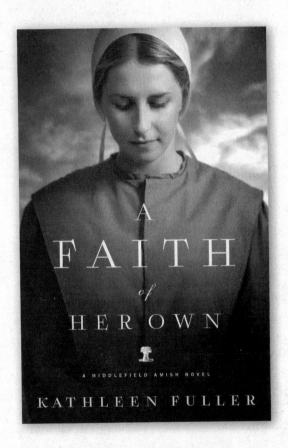

AVAILABLE IN PRINT AND E-BOOK

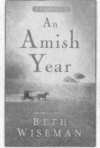

ABOUT THE AUTHOR

Kathleen Fuller is the author of several bestselling novels, including *A Man of His Word* and *Treasuring Emma*, as well as a middle-grade Amish series, the Mysteries of Middlefield.

Visit her online at www.kathleenfuller.com
Twitter: @TheKatJam
Facebook: Kathleen Fuller